BRIGH

THE BRIGHTENING DAY

MICHAEL McLAVERTY

POOLBEG

First published 1965 by
The Macmillan Company, New York

This paperback edition published 1987 by
Poolbeg Press Ltd.,
Knocksedan House,
Swords, Co. Dublin, Ireland.

ISBN 0 905169 87 5

Cover painting by Jane Proctor
Cover design by Steven Hope
Printed by the Guernsey Press Co. Ltd.,
Vale, Guernsey, Channel Islands.

TO

Sean and Mary McKeown

1

COMING BACK along the forsaken shore, his feet crunching in the limpet shells, the stones still damp from the outgoing tide, and the gulls gone inland to forage in the reaped fields, he thought once again of his father and mother and resolved to write to them before the evening light had withdrawn from the sky. In front of him was his bungalow, crouched at the road's edge and staring out to sea. He hastened toward it, climbed up the grassy bank from the beach, and turned the key in the door. It was quiet and welcome, and the fire he had banked up with damp slack filled the room with a warm glow.

He took a pad of notepaper, and sitting at a corner of the table in the light from the window he began a letter that had troubled his conscience for the past four weeks.

MY DEAR FATHER AND MOTHER,

It was cruel and inconsiderate of me not to write to you before this, for I know that my long silence and my unknown whereabouts must have added another burden to your load of worries. I meant to write to you before this, but for some perverse reason or other I kept putting it off.

Please don't worry about me. I am in good health and I am now trying to settle down in this out-of-the-way place and, in time, hope to begin a new life. After the court case I couldn't face home to tell you about it. I was glad, though, that you stayed away on that occasion, for the strain would have been too much for you. God knows you suffered enough on my behalf weeks before the case came off and you didn't deserve to suffer any more. I suppose the local newspaper covered the case in detail and with photographs, not sparing you or me in their thirst for truth.

But the truth you have already heard, time and again, from my own lips, and no matter what was said, directly or indirectly, at the trial my version was the true one. I did strike—*assault* was the word used in court—Marion's husband. I admitted that. The untrue things he said that evening provoked me and I lost control of myself. Schoolteachers, of course, are not permitted to lose their tempers either in school or out of it! Looking back upon it I do believe there was some other motive for his bringing me into court and exposing me and his own wife to the firing squad. Perhaps he wanted to get rid of me from the town and if that were his true motive he has achieved it, and I hope that he and Marion will get along happily now that her friend is away God-knows-where.

I had no friends in that court, not a damned one. And the vulgar cross-examination I was subjected to was loathsome and insulting. There were moments when I was almost driven to say *yes* to many of the things fired at me, but someone must have been praying for me and I held firm.

The hundred pounds damages awarded to him was too much. You'll pay that for me, and someday I'll repay you back in full; yes, I want to pay every single penny of it. But that's not one of the reasons I left home. I left for your sakes mainly. Now that I am no longer seen about the town and out of range of the gossips you'll soon be left in peace, and something more important than a black and bruised bank clerk's eye will attract their attention.

I am convinced that I did the right thing by resigning from the school before the case came off. Anyway I would have been asked to resign and I *won't* grumble at that. In a small town like ours it would have been the proper thing to do with me, no matter how truly innocent I was.

Schoolchildren, unconscious of deep cruelty, would have shouted after me in the street about stealing another man's wife, and anonymous letters would have come to the school or outraged parents would have staged a strike in order to get rid of the scandalgiver from their midst. How my mind runs on! The whole affair is like an act in a play. But, before God, I must say again and again, no matter how I may be disbelieved, that there was nothing but a long and true friendship between me and Marion. You, Mother, believe me—don't you? And, Father, in time you'll believe me too. Who would have thought that Marion's husband was such a fool! But it's strange the sudden and unaccountable twists that suddenly besiege some people as they sense their own inadequacies. I'll try not to dwell on it any more; it's all over and done with, and time and distance, let us hope, will smother it.

You'll forgive me for having disappeared without telling you where I was going. The plain truth is I didn't know where I was headed for. I just wanted to get away, and when I left the courthouse I got into the car and drove blindly northward, and as I sped along I had deep feelings of relief and feelings of remorse—remorse for leaving you in the mean way I did. I sent you a post card from some village I passed through and I hope you got it. I drove for hours and when I stopped for a meal I picked up a newspaper lying on the table and I read in the advertisements of a small seaside bungalow To Let and I decided to head for it.

The bungalow wasn't all it was puffed up to be, but I had already anticipated that and was able to stall my disappointment.

To begin with: it's three miles and more from the nearest bus and nearest village. It has old-world sanitation and I have to go down to the sea in the early mornings with my bucket or if I am too shy to do that I dig a hole at the foot of the garden and empty the contents into the good purging clay and cover it over like a domestic cat.

It's a furnished cottage. By that I mean it has a bed, a jug and basin in each room, and clean floorboards and bare walls. And it is so close to the sea that, during a storm, sand is blown onto the window ledges and spray falls on the roof. The roof was leaking in spots but I managed to climb up and spread tar on the lead flashings and that did the trick. My landlady expects me to keep the place in good trim and advised me to buy a half-dozen mousetraps for since the fields were reaped tiny mice that could hide in a thimble have squirmed their way through the ventilators and have taken up winter quarters in every room, and at night they come out in battalions to eat up the newspapers and gnaw the corners off the doors. But I hope to make short work of them before the long dark nights set in. At present the casualty list stands at five.

The neighbors around are quite friendly. They are curious about me, as you'd expect, but are too polite to ask personal questions as to where I have come from or why I am here. That will come in due course and I'll be prepared for it. I am using my confirmation name John instead of my baptismal name Andrew, and I hope when you write to me you'll address the envelope *Mr. John A. Wade*. I still smart under the unjustified sting of the court case and if I really could have changed my entire name I would have done so. The slight inversion of Andrew and John is as far as I'll go in that direction. Perhaps I'm being overcautious in this matter, for I don't suppose a whimper of what people will call my "past" will ever reach here.

A short while ago I put an advertisement in a local paper announcing that a university graduate with eight years' teaching experience undertakes to coach by correspondence a limited number of pupils for all university entrance exams. Applications are still dribbling in, but if I fail to gather a respectable clientele I'll cross to England or Scotland and get a teaching job like poor old Dan Travers. You remember Dan and how he boozed himself out of every damned job in the country. He's now in Liverpool, I believe, and doing well for himself by all accounts. He got a school over there on the strength of three great testimonials: one from his parish priest, one from his doctor, and a four-star one from the principal of the training college. He wrote them all himself, and I trust he is living up to his high reputation. I don't suppose, if the worst came to the worst, that anyone would give me a recommendation after what has taken place. Forgive me for mentioning that again; I'll try to rid my mind of it.

How is Mark? He'll miss his daily walk and his daily swim in the sea. Come to think of it there's nothing more faithful than a soulless old dog: if you beat him he doesn't hold it against you or lie in wait for revenge. I wish I had him with me. He'd enjoy this place: the sea is only a stick's throw from the front door, and at the back of the house are flat and windy fields alive with hares in the early morning. They even venture into my patch of grass and I can see them feeding there when I'm at my breakfast.

Someday I'll send you a photograph of this retreat; it's a lonely spot no doubt, but for me in my present predicament it's homely, uncomplaining, and uncritical. Please don't give anyone my address or tell anyone where I am. I only want to write to you. A pat on the head to Mark.

Your son,
ANDREW

P.S. Please send all my books that are on the three shelves in my room—just those and no more. You could put them in boxes and drive out in the car and send them from some place where I am unknown. Don't come to see me until the spring, and if you do bring Mark.

When he had finished the letter he addressed the envelope and left it on the window ledge for the postman in the morning. Dusk had settled in the room and the firelight staggered on the walls. He rubbed his eyes, filled up his pipe, and sat in the armchair by the fire. Mist gathered at the windows and spiders came out to patch up their webs. He smoked slowly, listening to the flutter of the fire and watching the flashing light of a buoy appear and disappear like the scratch of a match on one of the windows. A homegoing tractor rumbled past the house and swept its lights along one wall. It was dark now and he lit his two pressure lamps, drew the yellow curtains, and began to prepare his last meal of the day.

He laid everything on a tray and as he sat at the table he missed his mother's small talk and the feel of Mark's cold muzzle resting on his knee. His father seldom spoke to him except to give orders or to complain about the soggy state of the golf course, a game he had taken up after his retirement from the bank two years ago. It was a relief, he was sorry to admit, to be away from his father, away from those sudden spurts of volubility that had seized him prior to the court case when he would wave his knife and fork in the air like a frenzied conductor and threaten to pitch him out of the house for bringing disgrace on their name and ruining his well-earned retirement. At those times he hadn't dared declare his innocence, for it only increased his father's fury, and if his mother intervened and begged him to lower his voice lest the next-door neighbors hear him he would continue to shout: "I don't care who hears me! It'll not be long till it's in the papers for the whole world to hear!" *The whole world*—that was typical of his father's exaggeration.

Recalling those scenes disquieted him and he rose from

his chair, put on his heavy coat, and set off along the sea road for a walk before bedtime. The air was chilly, stars shone in the sky like a bank of primroses, and across the fields a mist had settled, muffling every sound and cough from the unseen cattle. In a short while, he reflected, they would be taken to the byres before the arrival of the heavy frosts and nothing would remain but flocks of lapwings sheltering in the ruts and lamenting with thin cries all the night long. When that time came it would be his testing time, the time of bleak loneliness.

No one passed him on the road, and in the scattered houses that faced the sea the doors were closed and in the squares of light in the curtained windows he could see the shadow of a head or the sturdy glow of a hanging lamp or hear children laughing from an unlighted bedroom. If he were a country curate, he thought, such familiar scenes would surely bruise the heart with loneliness.

He usually walked to the end of a twisted road that opened onto a wide bay where a small house was tucked into a hollow that sheltered it from the sea winds. On his first arrival four weeks ago he had made friends with Pat Quinn, a consumptive who occupied an airy hut outside the house, but with the coming of the hard weather Pat had gone off to a sanatorium in the city and wouldn't be back, he told him, until the spring of the year. Pat's wife and three children lived in the house but he seldom saw them except on their way to Mass on a Sunday or going to school in the mornings. And now as he passed by on the road the house was in darkness as if unoccupied, and for some reason he moved to the grassy edge of the road to silence the noise of his footsteps.

He turned back and saw the lights in the scattered homes being plucked out, one by one, and by the time he reached his own bungalow there was no light anywhere except from the stars and the light from his window extending to the thin mist on the shore.

He went to bed early, for he discovered it saved fuel and lamp oil, and rising early gave him time in the healthy light of morning to prepare tests in English, history, mathematics, and French for his correspondence pupils.

A week after he had sent off the letter to his mother he was always on the lookout for the postman, who called on him each morning with a daily newspaper. Andrew always had a cup of tea and a biscuit ready for him and some corrected work to post to his unseen students. The postman usually had Andrew's newspaper and letters tied with string, but they were never opened or scrutinized till the tea was drunk and he had set off again on his bicycle. Andrew would then pick them up and search for one with his mother's handwriting, but after three weeks of disappointment he felt he was cut out of their lives by his father's decision, and he strove then, but with scant success, to smother all daily expectation of a letter.

And then one morning an envelope bearing handwriting similar to his mother's did arrive, but when he eagerly slit it open with a pencil he discovered a letter with an embossed address requesting him to call any forenoon and discuss the possibility of daily tuition for a crippled boy. The letter was from a Mrs. Newman and the handwriting was thin and evenly spaced, and the stiff expensive notepaper smelled of lavender as if it had lain for some time in her handbag.

The following day he inquired from the postman if he knew Mrs. Newman, and he learned from him that their house—Rock Lodge it was called—stood in its own grounds, was only five miles from his bungalow and that the father of the crippled lad, a lad with braces strapped to his legs, had been a high-ranking officer in the Navy during the war and had been lost at sea, that there was an elder son somewhere in the Far East and a younger daughter in Scotland studying at some university, and that Mrs. Newman with the help of her old mother and a gardener managed the place—and managed it badly, for they had to let most of the land each year and only kept a few cows for their own use. It was a fine place when the boss was alive but it was going downhill badly and the postman thought it would be sold after the old woman's day. The job of teaching the lad, however, would be a good one and he advised Andrew to have a crack at it.

There and then Andrew decided to call at Mrs. Newman's and he went out to the garage to pump up the tires of the car and to jog up the engine, for he hadn't used it since taking over the bungalow, not even to drive to Mass on a Sunday. He was surprised that the car started easily, and after backing it out of the garage he warmed up the engine and went in to shave before setting off.

Just as he had finished shaving and was wiping the soap off the razor he heard a car halt on the road outside and, hurrying into the sitting room and standing well back from the window, he saw his mother and father come out of the car and stare at the house, wondering if they had struck the right spot. Before they had time to knock at the door he scooped up the spent matches from around the hearth and stuffed the old newspapers under the cushion on the armchair.

He began to sing loudly, and hearing the polite tap on the knocker he pretended to come from the back kitchen, still singing as he opened the door.

"So this is where you are!" his mother exclaimed, stepping into the sitting room and embracing him. His father followed, stamping on the springy floorboards, aware of dry rot.

"So this is the Godforsaken place you've condemned yourself to! We had the divil's own job tracking you down," and he rubbed his hands together and blew out his breath in the cold room.

Andrew put a match to the already prepared fire that was covered with dead matches and stained pipe cleaners and advised them to keep on their coats till the place warmed up a bit.

"I don't usually light it till the evening," he said, and turning to his mother he asked where on earth they had dropped from so early in the morning. His father sat on the edge of the table, filled his pipe, stared at the struggling fire, and allowed his wife to do the talking.

They had motored northward yesterday, stayed the night in Newcastle, and all morning had been searching for him, and only for their good fortune in meeting a postman they would still be wandering around the twisty roads of the countryside.

"The place isn't any twistier than our own son and he must come home out of it," his father broke in.

"I'm not going home," the son said quietly.

"An innocent man has no call to bolt."

"Do you still doubt my word?"

"Now, now, in God's name, we don't want to go over all that again. We've had enough of it already," the mother wrung out. "That's not the point or the purpose of our visit, Andrew." And with prepared detail she recounted what would happen if he suddenly took ill and hadn't a friend to hand him a hot drink or make a meal for him or go for the doctor.

"I'm healthy, I'm happy, and I'm working hard," and he pointed to built-in shelves in a corner of the room where his correspondence stood like an array of Christmas cards.

"I'm sure you'll grow fat on conducting a correspondence course," his father said. "Payment by advance or payment by results? It's all as stupid as changing your name to John. I often heard of a young girl changing her name from Maggie to Peg but never, since the good God made me, did I ever hear of a grown man changing his name from Andy to Johnny. That change will lead you into a nice pickle."

"I was thinking of you as much as myself when I decided on that change."

"But you're our son. We'll never disown you," his mother said. "We didn't want you to run away."

"I had no other option. I would have lost my job. I'd have had to clear out sooner or later."

"Ireland's a small place and you can't go very far without meeting some old acquaintance," his father put in.

"Since I've done no harm to anyone it'll not matter much one way or the other."

"And what excuse will you give your new neighbors when they begin to ask awkward questions? They're not damned fools altogether. A stranger out of nowhere suddenly takes up his abode among them!"

"I intend to do some historical research on the decay of the small seaports around here or on the old Charter Schools that were mainly centered in this county. That will occupy me as much as the correspondence courses."

The father gave a scornful laugh and tapped his feet on the floorboards. "I declare to God you've more sense than I thought. I think you could outwit Scotland Yard."

"Listen, Frank, you should go for a walk and leave me to have a good look round the house," the mother suggested. "A walk in the sea air will do you good."

"I suppose I should. Maybe you'll be able to drum sense into his stubborn head. If you could persuade him to come back I might get him a job with Jimmy Dunne the architect," and he put that edge on his voice that always drove his son to defy him. But this time Andrew recoiled in silence, and when his father had gone out and he was alone with his mother she burst into tears.

"All my life I've tried to get the two of you to understand one another and I've failed. He's good and he's kind, but it's the harsh words that always come to his lips, the words he doesn't mean or feel. Don't misjudge him and don't return hardness for hardness. It's that that keeps the two of you apart. Oh, I know him, and I know he's now regretting it, but he'll never show it."

He let her talk without interruption, for he could read the long siege of strain upon her face.

"Come," he said, taking her hand like a lover, "and let me know what you think of this place."

They went into each bedroom in turn. His own bed was unmade and she sent him out to the back of the car for a pair of new blankets and an eiderdown she had brought with her.

And spread out on the back seat along with them he saw shirts and socks, a suit on its hanger, a pullover, and in the trunk of the car boxes filled with his books and a pair of old trousers and heavy boots. As he lifted the blankets he saw his father walking along the shore, hands thrust into his coat pockets and the smoke from his pipe blown by the wind. He stood looking down at him for a moment and then hurried into the house in case he'd turn round and see him.

Together they shook out the blankets and made the bed and she plumped up the pillow as of old and spread the top of the coverlet over it. She lifted the basin of soapy water he had used for shaving and emptied the contents down the sink, and in a short while the room and the bed looked different and the cobwebs were gone from the window corners.

She examined the stove, shoved the kettle onto the hot-plate, and lifted cups and saucers from the shelves and laid them on a tray, and while waiting for the kettle to boil she took the sweeping brush and began to tidy up the dark scullery, opening the back door to give her more light. Her brush knocked against a whisky bottle under the sink and she called out to him in a shocked voice and asked what did this mean.

"Lift it and you'll see for yourself there's precious little taken out of it," he said. "It's only there as a protection, for when the temptation is near at hand I'll be able to keep it at bay."

"All the same it frightens me to see it. Many a lonely man is driven to drink and that's the end of him."

"I'll not be lonely, never fear. The work I do keeps me on the go all day long."

"Promise me one thing, Andrew: If you find yourself drawn toward it you'll let me know. You'll do that for me, in God's name? You may not know it, but the fondness for it is in your blood. Your grandfather would be alive today only for his love for it."

"Don't worry, Mother. If I find myself going under the sink I'll let you know." He patted her playfully on the shoulder and to divert her mind he thanked her for remembering to bring the books.

"It was your father who thought of them and went to the trouble of packing them. It's him you'll have to thank and I hope you'll do it nicely."

"I'll try, though he'll ignore what I say or say something sarcastic in return."

"You're an ungrateful boy to stand there and be so cynical about your own father. Only for the sacrifices he made in giving you a university education you'd be in a fine hobble."

"Surely he shouldn't expect praise for doing his parental duty."

"Andrew, you're growing hard." She closed her eyes and shook her head. "May God forgive you for what you're saying. Your decent father gave you everything you asked for."

"Everything but affection. He has scarcely spoken a civil word to me these past few years. I was always afraid of him and he never tried to understand me."

"If you go on talking like this your stupid old mother won't understand you either."

At that moment the kettle spluttered on the stove and he pushed it to the side. A knock came at the door and as he opened it his father stepped in, muffled to the ears, his face red with cold.

"There's a frosty snap about this place that would skin you. You should have gone to the Arctic while you were at it. Surely to God you don't intend to coop yourself up here for the winter?"

"I'm quite content here. I have no complaints."

"I'm mightly glad to hear it," his father answered in dry mockery. "But I may tell you we're not content! Your poor mother has hardly put her nose outside the door since your departure. That's something you can think about in your hours of exile!"

Hearing his raised voice, she hurried into the sitting room with the tray and begged him to talk of something else for a change, and he threw up his hands and said he'd be mighty pleased to know what else there was to talk about.

In silence she handed him a cup of tea and he drank it in loud sups and in the intervals between each sup he kept saying *Aye* and *No* to himself and nodding his head with a hopeless gesture. He drank a second cup and then filled his pipe while Andrew filled his own and handed him a lighted spill. The father pulled his chair nearer the fire, held out his hands to the heat, and puffed rapidly at his pipe. Andrew smoked leisurely, as he always did, and soon the room was hazed with smoke like a ship's cabin.

The mother was the first to break the silence and besought her son to send her his soiled shirts and socks every week. There was no need to do that, he explained, for there was always a clean breeze from the sea that would whiten any shirt no matter how badly it was washed. She mustn't bother about him in that respect.

"Indeed and I'll bother, for it's galling to think of any son having to wash his own linen."

"He has washed some dirty linen in public already and it'll be nothing new to him," his father said, not looking at him. Mother and son said nothing and he went on: "Did you tell him that Marion's husband has been changed to that God-forsaken bank in the wilds of Kerry and that Marion hasn't gone with him?"

"We promised coming up in the car not to talk about those things. I've kept my promise but you haven't. Anyway

Marion is only staying on at her mother's for a rest and will join her husband when their new house is fixed up."

"You'd think she'd be the one to fix it up. I'm afraid she's not as complacent about the court case as our son here."

"I'm far from being complacent about it, Father, and I'm sorry to hear this about Marion."

"I'm glad something can ruffle you," the father said, sending a contemptuous exhalation of smoke toward the fire. He glanced at the cheap clock on the mantelpiece and then at his watch.

"If we want to get home before dark, Mary, we should start right now. There's little or no twilight at this time of year."

"It was good of you to come so far, Father, and kind of you to bring my books," Andrew said. "It's a pity you didn't bring Mark."

"Mark will stay where he belongs. . . . Well, Mary, I suppose we'd better be on our way. There's nothing more to say."

"No, Frank, there's nothing more to say. You've said everything." She sighed, pulled on one black glove and then the other, not looking at Andrew or his father. She rose to her feet. "I'm sorry, Andrew, to be leaving you with these soiled dishes."

"You've done enough cleaning, Mother, for one day."

The father stamped impatiently on the floorboards in case she'd take off her gloves again and wash up. "You should get your landlady to see about that floor; there's a joist gone somewhere," and he went out and left the door ajar.

"Andrew, son, don't think ill of him in any way. No matter what he says he still thinks the world of you."

"He has a strange way of showing it."

"His years in the bank have undermined his patience and given him an abrupt manner. It was a nerve-racking old job and you'll have to excuse him. Come out to the car and say something, something kind to shorten our journey," and as she squeezed his hands a chill of sorrow shook him.

The horn of the car sounded and he hurried out with her to the road.

"I think, Father, you should break your journey and not try to do it all in one day."

"I hate having to do it all," he said, wiping the inside of the windshield with a chamois. "But I've courage, a word you don't know the meaning of."

"Little did I know that my long and innocent friendship with Marion would lead to this."

"Aye, and to the breakup of two homes, don't forget!"

"Please, please, Frank, we've had enough of this for one day. Let us set off, in God's name, before something worse befalls us. . . . We'll come again to see you, Andrew. And you'll write often, won't you?"

He nodded and smiled, a one-sided smile that hid his true feelings. Above the noise of the engine he shouted "Good-by, Mother; good-by, Father, and Godspeed."

His father smiled: "Good-by, Andrew Wade John—is that the name or have I got it back to front? Take care of yourself."

Andrew stood to the side as the car moved forward. The smoke from the exhaust burled white in the cold air, and from the side window his mother's gloved hand waved like a crow's wing.

He stood on the road till the burr of the car was swallowed up in the distance and the sound of the waves took its place. "There'll be another time," he said to himself, and a patch of oil at his foot stared up at him with its rainbow-colored eye. He turned toward the house, but the sound of a car's horn startled him and he stood at the door and waited. It was his father's car back again; he ran to the road and asked if they had forgotten something.

"No, we haven't," his mother said. "We were just wondering if you have enough money to tide you over the next few months."

"I have, thanks," he lied to them.

"Didn't I know he'd have enough," his father said crossly. "We've lost valuable time by your silly worrying."

"Turn the car at that farmhouse gate, Father. The road's too narrow here," he directed, and went around to his mother's side of the car; noticing that she had been crying he told her not to worry as he was content here.

"You don't look it," she said. "And why haven't you your jacket on? Go into the house and put it on right now."

He watched the car move forward to the farmhouse and before it had turned he had rushed into the house and pulled on his jacket. And this time as the car sped past and the horn was sounded in farewell he knew they were firmly set for the journey, a journey that would be long and unpleasant, a journey that he could have eased by saying yes to their offer of money. This time he had wronged both of them and sent them off, mother and father, sundered by his pride. "God forgive me," he said, and kicking a loose stone from the side of the road he lifted it and threw it into the sea. Then the brown sheen of a plank coming in on the tide caught his eye and he ran down to the shore and retrieved it and carried it dripping wet to the house and placed it upright to dry at the side of the range.

He went into the scullery, and without pausing he took the whisky bottle and poured himself a small drink and quickly swallowed it, not savoring the taste of it. It would do him good on a cold morning and help to scatter the depression that was creeping in upon him. He leaned against the drying-bar in front of the stove and watched a puddle of water gather at the base of the upright plank and spread across the floor. No one would believe that a plank could absorb so much water, he thought, and getting the floor-cloth to wipe up the mess he heard a knock at the front door.

Certain that they had returned once more, he rushed through the sitting room and with joy flung the door wide only to encounter his landlady, Miss Reid, a tall stout woman arriving for her month's rent; a visit, she said, that would save him the trouble of writing to her. She pushed past him into the room and plumped herself down in the armchair, pleased to see a blazing fire in the grate for there was nothing, she said, like a good fire to keep out the damp mists from the sea and prevent mildew growing like moss on the walls and the roof. She spoke loudly as if addressing a political meeting and Andrew feared that some neighbor passing on the road might hear her and think they were quarreling. Her eyes roved from the fire to the tray on the table, and he sensed that she was counting the cups and wondering who had been visiting him. But she made no comment and her eyes now settled on a damp spot on the wall behind him and she announced, like one granting a rare privilege, that if he wished to paint the walls she would raise no objection to any color he wished to select. She herself preferred yellow, for it was a warm summery color and it had found favor with most of her previous tenants, all of whom used a superior brand of paint which in the long run proved more economical than even two coats of inferior quality. As she paused for breath he assured her in a quiet voice that if an opportunity arose to repaint the walls he would follow her instructions to the letter.

She opened her handbag on her lap and picked out a stiff card covered with colored rectangles of glossy paint and told him he could keep that for future reference as she had another one at home. He took it, glanced at the squares of color with an air of dull comprehension, and placed it behind the clock on the mantelpiece.

"I haven't yet decided about giving you a one-year lease," she said suddenly, fingering her earrings that were as heavy as military medals. "We usually give our new tenants a three-months' or six-months' lease to start with."

"That will be all right with me," he said, and in order to

get rid of her he took out his wallet and handed her a month's rent. She got up from the armchair, and the springs released from her weight gave out an audible whinge. Everything about her was on a large scale: her wrists, her ankles, her huge bosom, and as she unscrewed the top of her pen and rested her receipt book on the table she wheezed heavily. She tore off the receipt, blew her breath on it to dry the ink, and ran her finger over the top of the table.

"A little furniture polish applied to that once a week would ward off woodworm and help it to retain its natural shine." Then, expressing a hope that the bedrooms were to his satisfaction, she went into each in turn and sensing the chilly air she advised him to take care of his health and light a little fire in them now and again. She went to the back of the house and gazed up at the roof for signs of a loose slate. All was in good order and as she passed the ashpit she perceived with satisfaction that he had burned all his tins before dumping them out. He told her he had learned that bit of domestic cleanliness from his mother.

"She must be an excellent housekeeper."

"She is, and you just missed seeing her by about ten minutes."

"I guessed you had visitors for I noticed a tray laid for three."

"Father was here with her on a short visit."

"He's retired from business I remember you telling me on our first meeting?"

"Yes, and his health and spirits were never in better shape."

"They motored far, I suppose?"

"About one hundred fifty miles as the crow flies or two hundred and more on the winding roads of our beloved country."

"I see," she said, aware of his reserve. "I must hurry; I've still a few more calls to make."

Before getting into her car she pulled on her gloves and

gazed down the sloping bank to the shore where deep tractor ruts could be seen in the loose shingle. "Keep a strict eye on that foreshore, Mister Wade, and don't allow the country boys to cart away loads of gravel. It's forbidden by law, but these laws are never enforced unless the offenders are caught in the act and their names handed to the police."

He would do his best to be vigilant, he told her, though he imagined that it would be stronger if the complaint came from her and not from a stranger like himself, for fault-finding visitors were never welcome guests.

"But, Mister Wade, you'd be working in the best interests of the community. In time this road could be undermined if the foreshore is deepened by this pilfering of gravel."

"It would be difficult to make the offenders see it in that way."

"But you must make them see it."

"I'll do my best to impress this danger on these simple country people."

"Simple country people! Well, you're a simple man if you think they're simple people."

She got into the car, switched on the ignition, but the engine failed to start. She tried again and again and then asked him politely if he would mind giving her a push down the hill. He didn't mind in the least, for there was nothing like a bit of exercise on a cold day, he told her, and getting to the back of the car he set it in motion and as the car gained momentum the engine started easily, and the smell from its exhaust had scarcely vanished from the air when a tractor appeared from the opposite direction and made its way on to the shore. Two red-faced youths jumped off with long-handled shovels; like grave-diggers they spat on their hands and began to heap the tractor with gravel.

"Is it good?" Andrew shouted down to them.

"Is what good?"

"The gravel, I mean. Is it of the right quality for building?"

"It's the best in the country, the best that money can't buy."

"You haven't to travel far for it. You're damned fortunate."

"Has Miss Isobel Rent been around yet?"

"You mean Miss Reid. You just missed her by a few lengths."

"That's a pity. Give her our best respects next time you see her."

"What name will I give?"

One took off his cap, scratched his head, and put the cap on again. "Tell her Fitzsimons. Nearly everybody in these parts is called Fitzsimons!" He laughed and rested on the handle of the shovel.

Andrew stepped down the slope and took a shovel for a spell, and when the load was complete and battered smooth they threw the shovels on top, pulled on their coats, and asked him how he was off for eggs and potatoes and promised to leave him a few next time they came to his friendly shore for a load of gravel.

"Like decent chaps, don't bother," he said, aware of a polite bribe.

"It'll be no bother to us. We're very grateful to you for the hand you gave us," and they turned the tractor into the deep ruts and moved slowly from the shore.

They waved to him from the road and he waved back and in a few minutes the road and the shore were empty of all sound except the breathing of the sea.

"Well that's enough going and coming for one day," he said, and deciding to postpone his visit to Rock Lodge until tomorrow, he put his own car back into the garage and entering the house began to unpack his books and arrange them on the shelves of the sitting room.

2

THE ARRIVAL of his books enabled him to prepare more varied courses for his correspondence pupils; and all that afternoon he worked steadily, breaking off occasionally to snatch a hurriedly prepared meal or to take a quick walk along the shore. By evening he was so fagged out that, as he sat relaxed in the firelight, the news of Marion's break with her husband, news that he had purposely avoided to dwell on, suddenly struck his tired mind with such unyielding force that his conscience bade him examine the part he had played in it. He sat quite still and stared unflinchingly into the red heart of the fire. Yes, he resolved to face the facts boldly and to accuse himself at every turn if it were necessary.

It was their last meeting that had mattered most, the unfortunate evening of the uncalled-for quarrel. It was easy to recall it and re-enact it in detail. To begin with: there were Marion and himself seated, as they often sat, on separate stools at the piano playing duets; a Beethoven piece that had afforded them much difficulty the whole evening they had at last succeeded in playing without a hitch, and to acclaim the occasion he had sat back and patted her shoulder: "Well done, Marion; that was our best effort."

A voice behind startled both of them: "And it will be your last effort in this house if I'm any judge."

Both of them had swung around. Her husband was standing within the room, his hat in his hand and his raincoat unbuttoned.

"Henry, what's wrong with you? Have you been drinking?" Marion had said, rising to her feet.

"You can go to bed, Marion. I want to have a confidential chat with your friend here."

"What on earth do you mean?" she went on. "Sure you know that Andrew is the best friend we've ever had."

"He may be yours but he's no longer a friend of mine. Do as I say. Go out of the room, please."

"I'll go when you tell me what's the matter with you, and when you cut out this play-acting."

"Go out before I lose my temper."

"I'll go as you say, but I'll return in a minute when you've come to your senses."

When she had gone Andrew took his pipe from his pocket and blew through the shank prior to filling it.

"You needn't smoke in this house, Mister Wade, and you needn't come back here again. I want nothing more to do with you or your like."

"Listen, Henry, you're carrying the joke too far. For God's sake be yourself."

"It's no joke! I'm the laughingstock of this town if you want to know."

"What are you getting at?"

"I should ask what are you getting at? I trusted you as a friend. I've been in this room for over five minutes without your knowing."

"And you heard us playing a duet and I hope you enjoyed it."

"I saw you making love to my wife."

"If you did you should consult an optician about your eyes."

"I saw you putting your arm around her and I'm sure it wasn't the first time you did it. So get out of this house at once!" He threw his hat on a chair.

Marion came back to the room and besought him to lower his voice and have an ounce of sense.

"Don't heed him, Andrew," she had said, "he has taken too much drink. He doesn't know what he's saying."

Henry pushed her aside and told her he was as sober as a judge.

"Well, you're not acting like one," she had said, and at that moment the child, awakened by the noise, had cried out and Marion ran to attend him.

"I'll go, Henry, and leave you in peace," Andrew had said, and as he was going toward the door to fetch his coat Henry caught him roughly by the shoulder and told him he had something more to say to him. His eyes narrowed. He had gone pale with anger. And as he asked Andrew if he had ever heard of the Ninth Commandment, Andrew stepped back from the spittle of rage that fell upon his face.

"Poor fella, you're drunk," Andrew had answered. "I'll come back when you're sober," and at that moment Henry swung at him with his clenched fist, Andrew swerved to the side, struck out at him with his right hand, and fled in panic from the room.

Near home, fear forced him to turn back, and on approaching the house he saw that the light was still on in the sitting room. He rang the bell and it was Marion who opened the door and told him that Henry had gone to bed and had sent for the doctor.

"I'm sorry, Marion, and I want to apologize."

Henry, hearing their voices, had shouted from the bedroom: "Who's there, Marion? Do you hear me?"

"Oh, go, go! You shouldn't have struck him. Why did you do that?"

He hadn't time to explain, for the voice came again from upstairs and she closed the door.

He went home and, without mentioning the incident to his father and mother, wrote an apology, walked all the way back to Marion's house, and—though there was still a light in an upstairs window—quietly dropped the letter into the letter box and turned away.

Two days later he received a letter from Henry's solicitor, and that evening he again called at the house, and it was Henry this time who had come to the door, his eye swollen and his cheek patched with sticking plaster.

"I've come to apologize, Henry."

"It'll take more than an apology to mend this, I may tell you!"

"Do you realize I'll lose my job if this gets around?"

"If you'd a score of jobs to lose I'd see you'd lose every damned one," Henry had replied with cool hatred.

"For Marion's sake, don't let it go any further. And if it's money you need I'll give it to you. I'll do anything you ask."

"You came here as a friend and I trusted you."

"And you can still trust me. You've been listening to gossip, to people who are out to make trouble between us. Call Marion and we can discuss it before her. Will you do that, please?"

"Never while I'm alive will I have any more truck with you."

"For the love of God, Henry, will you listen to reason? Never have I wished for anything but happiness for you and Marion. If I have ever done anything to mar that, I've done it unconsciously. And as for what happened the other night, I regret it with all my heart." He had stretched out his hand in a gesture of friendship but Henry ignored it.

"You can go and face up to what's coming to you. It'll pay your father back for the unkindness he showed to me in the bank before he retired. He persecuted me, but I thought you were different."

"My father has nothing to do with this. Listen, Henry, this will break me."

"I've listened to you long enough," and he had slammed the door and left him standing in the dark.

Things he had wanted to say he didn't get an opportunity of saying. He had wanted to tell him that he had never deceived him in any way, that there was no secrecy in his meetings with Marion, that they were just good friends, friends from their years together in college and with a mutual interest in music. All these things Henry had already known, but somehow he had wanted him to hear them again, and that night he had repeated them over and over again to himself as he wandered along the roads outside the town, and at intervals halted at a field gate and prayed to God to intervene and save him from disgrace, from public exposure in a court that would put an ugly twist on what was as straight and polished as a new blade.

He was forced to reveal his dilemma to his parents; and his father on hearing it had jumped to his feet in anger and had declared, with his usual proud vehemence, that he wouldn't go hat in hand to that popinjay; that, before God, he'd face a year's solitary confinement on bread and water rather than crawl before that upstart. His father was also certain that Henry wouldn't be fool enough to bring it as far as the court, that he was just taking perverse delight in a slow and suspended persecution.

But as day succeeded day and Henry had shown no sign of relenting his father had rounded on Andrew, convinced that there was some unwholesome element in the whole affair that was driving the young husband to the point of insanity. And when the day of the trial did arrive Andrew had set out alone for the courthouse, having persuaded his parents to stay at home.

Over two months had gone by since that day and here he was away from his own home, sundered from his own people, and alone.

"I'll try not to think of it any more," he said aloud to himself. "I'll put it past me. I've survived it, thank God, and for that I should be grateful. But what I will do, and do now, is write to Marion. I'll plead with her to return to Henry."

The fire had burned low, the curtains were not drawn, and the windows were misted over. He got up and drew the curtains, feeling a cave-cold air in that part of the room and hearing the snuffle of the wind under the worn threshold. He lit his two pressure lamps, spread an old coat at the drafty threshold, and in a short while had scattered the chilly air from all corners of the room.

Putting no address on the notepaper, he wrote a long letter to Marion, urging her to look at the affair from Henry's side and to blame some malicious troublemaker for sowing discord between them. The longer they remained apart the stronger would grow the difficulties of an easy reconciliation. Now was the acceptable time. She must think of her child and of her future. By living away from Henry she was only nourishing an injured pride and satisfying the crooked delight of those who were jealous of her. Some day she and Henry and himself would meet again, how he did not know, but willing it and wishing it would surely make it happen. The quarrel, like most quarrels, was useless and stupid, was beyond all reason and only reason could mend it.

Having finished the letter he put it unsealed on the mantelpiece, had a long smoke from his pipe, and before going to bed unfolded the letter and reread it. It now seemed to him flat and stale and interfering, a letter that was too critical of her husband, a letter that would hurt and not heal.

Slowly he tore it into shreds and burned it piece by piece in the fire. No, it would have done no good to send it. He'd wait. He must have patience. When in doubt do nothing, his father used to say. He smiled ironically, staring at the carbon ashes of the letter, pursuing his father's negative admonition.

3

NEXT MORNING he awoke while it was still dark. The dull thunder of rockets from the lightship shook the house and he knew that a fog had settled on the sea and that the noise had wakened him. He groped under his pillow for his pocket flash and shone it on his watch. It was just four o'clock and he turned to sleep again, refusing to consider the day's plan or to recall yesterday's upheaval.

When he woke again the fog had lifted and a weak sun was shining through the yellow curtains of the room. He lifted his folded clothes from the chair and dressed in front of the cookstove that was still warm from the night's fire. Outside in the garden the grass was crusted with frost and a mist lounged around the hedges, but by the time he had finished breakfast the mist had vanished and drops of water dangled on the bare twigs.

He backed the car out over the frozen ground and as he set off for Rock Lodge nothing was visible on the frosty road but an irregular line left by the postman's bicycle. Not wishing to arrive too early he drove leisurely, cutting through the scaffoldings of sunlight that seemed to prop up the hedges that turned their humped backs to the sea.

He drew near the village, passed the church, saw the blue slates of the houses shedding their vests of frost, took the wrong turning, and found himself at a deserted quayside among boats that rested on trestles against the quay wall. There was a smell of tar and the sound of dull hammering from an open doorway of a boathouse. He got out of the car, and from the gloom of the boathouse a little man with shavings on his jersey and a mallet in his hand came forward to meet him.

Andrew inquired the way to Rock Lodge; the little man strode out to the middle of the road and pointing with the handle of the mallet said: "Do you see that road fornenst you there? Well, drive out that road for five or six perches till you see on your right two big gateposts with a bare lion perched on each, but no gate. Turn in there under the trees and before you'd have time to lace your boots you'll see a big house with a lawn in front of it as big as a football ground, and that's Rock Lodge for you. And if you happen to be speaking to Missus Newman herself tell her the bit of teak has arrived to mend *Razorbill* and I'll have her in the water before she hears the cuckoo. You'll not forget?"

"I'll not forget. Thank you very much."

"You're welcome. And by the way, are you the gentleman that's living in Miss Reid's bungalow? You are. Take it from me she's a right oul' hairpin."

"I'll tell her you were asking for her."

"You'll tell her no such thing. I wouldn't drive in a nail for her except it was to make her coffin."

"I'll tell her that too."

"Indeed and you wouldn't. I know by the looks of you you wouldn't. Good day to you, sir, I'll not be keeping you back."

Through the mirror Andrew saw him standing in the road, scratching his head with the mallet and staring after the car to see if he'd take the right road.

In about five minutes he was driving through the gateway, under tall trees and over potholes covered with ice that splintered under the wheels. Presently the gloom gave way to brightness and he was out from the tunnel of trees and into a wide space where the house stood, its geometric shadow stretched on the frosted lawn.

He got out of the car and ascended three stone steps to a wide open doorway where his shoe clinked on a door-scraper as he pressed the bell. A dog barked inside, and through the glass panels of an inner doorway Andrew could see a little woman in a white overall polishing a gong on a mahogany table. She brought him into a long drawing room and told him to take a seat till she would fetch Mrs. Newman for him.

The room was chilly, and in the white marble fireplace a freshly lit fire of logs was giving out less heat than the sun that was shining in the windows. A piano with an open sheet of music was in one corner, and at the far end of the room a dark painting, meshed with cracks, stretched from the ceiling to the floor. Overhead feet rumbled, sending a tinkle from the chandelier.

From where he sat Andrew could see two dogs scampering round a tree in the middle of the frosted parkland. A boy was following them, his legs stiff in steel supports, his arms waving mechanically, his pathetic figure cutting two parallel tracks on the frosted grass. The boy halted for breath, his arms still outstretched, lifeless and dejected as a forsaken scarecrow. He blew a whistle that hung from his neck and the dogs raced back, jumped up on each side of him, the vapors from their bodies enveloping him like an autumn fire. Suddenly the dogs raced off again and disappeared among the trees. The boy, not heeding them, turned toward the house, endeavoring to keep to the dark tracks he had already dredged through the grass.

A cheep in the room made Andrew turn from the window. A canary cage he had not noticed rested on a small table, and in the stillness of the large room he heard the click of the seed and the rattle of the swing as the canary hopped upon it. He went over to it. The bird was molting and a few curled-up feathers lay on the floor of the cage. He cheeped at it and the bird went thin with alertness and cheeped backed at him. Beside the cage was a photograph of a naval officer, Mrs. Newman's husband, he thought, and was about to lift it when Mrs. Newman entered, apologizing for keeping him so long.

She was in black, tall and thin with short black hair and brown eyes. She moved quickly, pushing an armchair nearer the fire for him to sit on. She herself sat opposite him, her back to the window. She took a silver cigarette box from the mantelpiece and offered him a cigarette. She placed her own in a small holder and as he lighted it for her he noticed the rings upon her fingers and the long thin hands.

"And now, Mister Wade, before I ask if you'll teach my son I must give you his history. But before that I must tell you why I wrote to you. I saw you at Mass on Sundays and I inquired who you were and later saw your advertisement in the local paper. Do you intend to stay long in these parts?"

"At least a year," he said, and mentioned that he would like to do some historical research on the decay of the small seaports and on the old Charter Schools.

"If my husband had been alive he could have been of some help to you on the small seaports," she said, and in a quiet voice related his long attachment to the sea and his loss in a destroyer during the war. She spoke also of her only daughter Anne who was at present in Edinburgh studying science at the University. They had an aunt living there and they had reckoned that it was less expensive and more wise to have her living in comfort with her aunt than living in some dreary digs in Belfast or traveling daily to that city in all kinds of weather. Her eldest son was married and was attached to a shipping company in the Far East. Her youngest son Philip, who was fifteen, was her sorest problem. He had been crippled since birth and his schooling on that account was somewhat erratic. He had always attended the village school, but as he grew older his deformity made him quarrelsome, and from the day that Anne left for Scotland he had stubbornly refused to go to school and they had to bring in a Miss Reid to coach him.

"Miss Reid is a sister of your landlady, and if you agree to come here—and I trust you will, for it takes a man to teach a boy—Philip and herself will part company with mutual satisfaction. He doesn't care a great deal for her." She smiled and put the cigarette holder to her lips.

"He may not like me either."

"I have a feeling that he will, Mister Wade. He gets on well with men. I offered the job to Mister O'Brien, the teacher in the village school, but he was unable to fit it in. At any rate he's too old and wouldn't have much relish for it. Another man, a Mister Meighan, lives in the village and teaches outside of it, but he suffers from a lack of energy, and I wouldn't care for him."

"There'll be no likelihood of my making enemies from that quarter if I take the job."

"Are you always afraid of making enemies, Mister Wade?" She laughed, a musical laugh that reminded him of Marion.

"We don't always know when we're making them. If we do it would be better to take steps to avoid them."

"Even if our actions are just?"

"In that case, Mrs. Newman, we'd have to consider who would benefit. If it would be the receiver then I'd say yes."

"Philip will be the receiver in this case, I'm sure of that," she said, recalling Andrew's stillness and concentration at Mass on Sundays when she had often knelt in the seat behind him. "Nothing would give me more joy if you could get him through his matriculation. He could make his own way in the world if he had a university degree. But perhaps I'm saying things that are impossible."

"Nothing's impossible if the boy has the will to do it."

"Anne thinks he has much ability," she said, and extracting the stub of her cigarette from the holder she threw it in the fire. "But you'll soon find that out for yourself. . . . And now about terms? Shall we discuss that now or leave it till you have sampled the goods?"

"Whatever you gave Miss Reid will satisfy me."

"We'll see." Dusting the ash from her frock, she rose to

her feet. "Come, Mister Wade, and I'll show you what we call the schoolroom."

It was close to the drawing room and in it were two desks, a table, and a blackboard on an easel. On one wall was a crucifix and below it shelves with books in disarray. There were two rectangular windows, and on the wall between them was a blue picture of the earth and her satellites, photographs in *passe partout,* and in one corner a brass telescope on a tripod, a rocking horse, two tennis rackets with broken strings, and a model yacht with spots of rust on its sails.

"I must apologize for the state of it. It's a hold-all, really."

"It's very bright and airy, and you have a fine view of the lough."

"Yes, it's pleasant in the summer evenings when the small boats are racing. I often follow the races through that telescope—it belonged to my husband, but Philip has now taken control of it. Often he'll sneak down here out of bed to have a look at the stars. But it's not so good for that kind of viewing. Excuse me, Mister Wade, till I get him for you."

Left alone, he looked at the photographs on the wall: one large one of a destroyer, some of gulls in flight, one of a heron with its sticklike legs about to alight on its lofty nest, one of Philip on a pony, one of an old woman leaning on a stick, and one of a young girl in front of a tennis net—the daughter, he thought; and going closer saw the name *Anne* printed in ink below it.

A shuffling along the corridor made him turn from the photographs and walk to the table at the head of the room. The door was knocked upon and a fair-haired boy came in, his mother behind him. He wore a black jacket and gray flannels, and the steel braces strapped to his boots had grass sticking to them.

"This is Mister Wade, your new teacher, Philip. Shake hands with the gentleman."

"My hands are too grubby," he said, out of breath.

Andrew placed a hand on his shoulder: "I saw you having great sport with the dogs outside."

"They chased a hare and left me. None of them could catch it even if it had only three legs. They're too fat to run."

"I'll leave the two of you till I see Mary about a cup of tea," Mrs. Newman said, and left the room.

"You sit in the desk, Philip, and we'll rehearse our first lesson."

"Could I not wash my hands first?"

"I don't intend to start business today. This is only a bit of make-believe."

"Well, in that case. . . ." As he struggled toward the desk Andrew stepped forward to assist him but Philip shrugged him off with a dexterous air of independence and slid into the desk. "You mustn't take my arm at any time. I used to walk with sticks but now I don't need them."

He rested his chin on his hands and stared up at Andrew with eyes bright and brown as his mother's. He looked more like twelve than fifteen.

"Tell me, Philip, what subjects do you like best?"

"I don't like any best. I dislike them all."

"That's a good start anyway."

"It is not."

"Well, let us say it's an honest start. What has Miss Reid been teaching you?"

"Nothing much. Bits of French, bits of history, bits of English, and sticking colored bits of paper on bits of cardboard. She said I wasn't much of a student and I suppose she's right." He licked the back of his thumb and rubbed off the dirt on his sleeve.

"And what about the bits of mathematics?"

"Oh, we never could get the same answers and she told me I couldn't do them. I told her it was she who couldn't do them and she sulked for a whole hour after that, and said she'd give in her notice to Mother. But she didn't and now she'll have to, and I'll be glad. Tell me this: Do you like *Tom Sawyer* and *Huckleberry Finn*?"

"I do, very much."

"Miss Reid doesn't. She says *Huckleberry* is full of bad grammar."

"Ladies have queer tastes, I'm thinking."

"Do you like photography?"

"Yes, but I'm not much good at it."

Philip slid out of the desk without a word, went to a corner cabinet and carried a photographic album up to the table. He leaned over Andrew, resting a hand upon his shoulder, and eagerly turned the pages of the album with his other hand.

"There's a good one of my sister except for the feet."

The girl was leaning back on a deck chair, her hands under her head.

"Yes, your sister has very large feet indeed."

"Oh, she hasn't really," Philip laughed, his warm moist breath close to Andrew's ear. "Her feet were too near the camera and were out of focus."

"Your mother told me she's now in Edinburgh. Do you miss her very much?"

"I do—sometimes. But she'll be home soon for Christmas."

"Do you write to her often?"

"I'd like to, but I can't write long letters."

"But you can talk—and if you talk in a letter it will be a good one."

"Would it do to tell her she had big feet?"

"It would if she laughs at it."

"Would it do for instance to describe you in a letter?"

"It would if it would interest her. And how would you describe me?"

Philip stood out from the table and looked steadily at him, smiling with closed lips.

"I'd say you were tall and thin; that your fair hair was uncombed like my own, that your collar and shirt did not match, that there was a loose button on your jacket, that your eyes were blue and that there was a scar on your cheek about two inches long and a quarter of an inch broad. Would that do?"

"For an outside finish it wouldn't need another coat."

"Do you mind telling me how you got that scar?"

"When I was four a little girl scratched my cheek with a bit of glass."

"I thought a cat did it. She was a real cat anyway," and he described how his cousins from Scotland, all little girls, used to visit them and break his toys and how he used to get Mary to hide them when he knew they were coming. They broke the rocking horse and he was still there in the corner with one eye missing, his tail pulled out, and his red tongue chipped white.

"They were meddlesome little girls, Philip."

"I hate little girls."

"We'll say we dislike them."

"You may dislike them but I hate them."

Philip turned another page of the album: "That's one of my grandmother sitting in the garden. You haven't met her yet, but you will. She stays in bed most of the time and plays cards. She has an idea that the Jews are persecuting her."

Andrew laughed.

"You mustn't laugh, Mister Wade. She believes it, and neither the priest nor the doctor can cure her."

"Poor woman, I'm sorry for her."

"She isn't poor. She's told me often that she'll leave her money to Anne for Anne is kind to her and I'm not."

Aware that he was listening to conversation that was not meant for him, Andrew asked suddenly what other things he liked besides photography.

"Oh, lots of things. I like to fish and sail *Razorbill.*"

"*Razorbill!* That reminds me: A boatman in the village told me the teak has arrived to mend her."

Philip closed the album and laughed: "The teak has arrived. Oh, that means nothing! James will let it lie till the woodworm bore holes in it like an air gun. We'll have to nag him into mending it. Mother's no good at nagging, but if Anne were here she could get round him without nagging."

"Surely he'd mend it for you?"

"He would not. He's always making fun of me and telling lies to no end. I don't like people who tell lies. When I was small I used to go round to his shed at lunchtime from the school and he told me that the moon was made of cheese, and I believed him."

"And when the moon is only half a moon the cat has taken a bite out of it. I heard that one myself."

"And I suppose he bites away at it till there's nothing left but the rind."

They were both laughing when Mrs. Newman came back; ordering Philip to go and tidy himself she ushered Andrew into the drawing room where a tray with china rested on a hassock on the hearthrug.

"I think he's an intelligent and lively little fellow," Andrew said, sitting in an armchair while Mrs. Newman poured tea from a silver teapot.

"You can depend on him to tell you the truth. I have always insisted on that since he was no size."

Andrew turned sideways to the fire, staring at the frill of flame around the logs. He stirred his tea, and the spoon tinkling against the fine china brought an answering chirp from the canary at the back of the room.

Mrs. Newman gazed steadily at him.

There was something in his presence, in his melancholic smile that appealed to her; she yearned to ask him questions,

questions about himself, his family, his past school, but interested as she was she suppressed her curiosity and asked none of them. In due course all would be revealed, she thought, without the mutual embarrassment of constant questioning. And, she was sure, she'd find it easier to discuss Philip with him than with a Miss Reid who was continually complaining and in a mild rage. And the fact of his being in the house would give her an undefined feeling of confidence, of joy. Why?—she did not know. Perhaps it was her husband's long absences at sea and then her years of widowhood that made her feel this attraction. At her age she was certain that there was no other element in it. And what with Mary and herself and her old mother and Miss Reid and Anne, such a feminine atmosphere was not good for any boy.

"As I have still to inform Miss Reid of the new arrangements we'll not expect you until the day after tomorrow, say, at half nine. That wouldn't be too early for you, Mister Wade?"

"That will do fine," he said, setting his cup down on the tray. "I'll do my very best for your son, you can depend on that."

Philip came into the room, his face washed and his hair showing the tracks of a wet comb.

"You'll have a cup of tea, son?"

"No, thank you, Mother. I'd rather you'd drive me into the village to see *Razorbill*. James told Mister Wade the teak's arrived."

"I was just going to ask Mister Wade to drop Mary in the village on his way through. If he doesn't mind, you may go with her and I'll collect the two of you later."

"They'll be more than welcome, Mrs. Newman," Andrew said. Standing up, he shook her hand warmly and thanked her for her kindness.

He turned the car on the loose gravel in front of the

house and Mary, the housekeeper, got into the back, and when the three dogs jumped in she shooshed them out again.

"Could we not bring the dogs?" Philip pleaded.

"You can't have them destroying the gentleman's car," Mary said. "Sit and behave yourself like a good boy."

"It's an old wreck and they can't do it much harm," Philip said.

"Don't be rude, Philip. You mustn't say things like that," his mother called through the window of the car.

"Even when I'm telling the truth?"

"You mustn't say hurtful things."

"Well, I'll not say them. But your car is an old one—isn't she, Mister Wade?"

"She is indeed, Philip. You'll hear her old joints creaking with rheumatism in a minute. And mind you keep your feet off the floor in case you fall through it."

With a jolt and a burst of dirty smoke the car set off into the low sun. The dogs raced after it, and Mrs. Newman called them back and stood smiling at the slow jiggle of the car and at the dark tracks it unwound on the wet-shining road.

She stood until it disappeared into the nave of trees, and shuddering from the cold she ran up the steps to the door, and entering the drawing room she pushed an armchair close to the fire, stretched out her legs to the heat, and lit a cigarette.

4

Well, she thought, taking a long pull at the cigarette, that interview went off happily. But tomorrow she'd have to face Miss Reid, a meeting that wouldn't be half so pleasing. It was comforting to think, though, that Miss Reid's daily complaints about Philip were about to end. No longer would she have to listen in silence as Philip's litany of faults was unrolled to her: faults of rudeness, of lack of application, of even downright cruelty—a position that no teacher could tolerate, a position no lady could be expected to endure in spite of friendship.

"Am I the teacher or are you, Master Philip?" was a querulous question that often issued from the schoolroom and could be heard even in the drawing room with the door closed. Sounds traveled easily in this large and almost empty house.

But tomorrow would see the end of this impasse. She put the cigarette holder to her lips, inhaled richly, and blew out the smoke in a long condensed column. The interview would be an uncomfortable one: the words of dismissal, of parting, difficult to utter. Oh, if only her husband were alive, she could have left the task to him. A man would know how best to approach it, would leave no loopholes for emotional scenes.

"I'll try not to think about it or let it disturb me," she said aloud to herself. "I've still a whole day left to muster my thoughts. And anyway it's up to Miss Reid to receive it graciously, for she was never done lamenting about her frayed nerves and how the teaching of a spoiled boy was really getting her down." Perhaps that would be the best way to approach her tomorrow.

"Oh Miss Reid," she rehearsed, "how grateful I am for all your help and your saintly patience with Philip. But today I have good news for you. At long last I've succeeded in getting the services of another tutor. The young man who is living in your sister's bungalow is willing to undertake the burdensome task for a while, and I trust you'll give him a few useful hints before he takes charge. . . . But never, never will I forget your kindness, Miss Reid, in helping me out. It's good to know you'll be able to relax now and enjoy your own retirement."

Yes, that's how she would tackle it. But perhaps she shouldn't say that last sentence—it sounded too much like an after-dinner speech.

She finished her cigarette, pushed back the armchair, and crossed to the window. The sun was shining on that part of the house, the grass below was wet, but under the trees unmelted frost still lingered. She could see through the bare trees the blue slates of the outbuildings and Thomas, their yardman, cleaning out a cow-byre and the heap of manure smoking like a fire of damp leaves. Hmm, I suppose it's cold and he's doing some work to warm himself, she thought. He's another of my headaches, a pleasant and plausible fraud. Hibernating Thomas was her mother's name for him, and a good seasonable one it was too.

She straightened the curtain edge, turned from the window, and went over to the canary cage. "I don't think your mistress is in good form this morning," she said to it, and sliding out the floor of the cage she carried it carefully to the fireplace and, blowing away the tiny feathers, she cleaned the tray, dusted it with fresh grit, replaced it in the cage, and unclasping the white porcelain stoup from the wires she went off to fill it with fresh water.

The following morning Miss Reid arrived half an hour earlier than usual, and after Mary had escorted her to the drawing room she went upstairs for Mrs. Newman, who had just washed her hair and was lying on the hearthrug drying it at an electric heater.

"Miss Reid's here, Ma'am. And she's right and early this morning."

"But I didn't hear the car, Mary."

"Her sister drove her as far as the gate and she walked the rest on her own steam."

"Do you think she'll be hurt, Mary, when I tell her of the new arrangements?"

"She'll let on to be. But what odds, she'll get over it in a day or two. We must think of Master Philip's future. Sure what could that child learn from the likes of Miss Reid? And forby she had no control over him. He done what he liked and said what he liked."

"Something tells me she'll take affront, feel slighted in some way."

"Don't upset yourself, Ma'am. She gave it out to all and sundry in the village that it was only on your account that she took on the job at all. To hear her gabbling you'd think she was doing her bit of teaching out of charity."

Mrs. Newman wound a scarf about her head, and with her face red and the powder uneven upon it she descended the stairs, blessed herself outside the drawing room door, and entered.

Miss Reid had draped her coat over the back of an arm-chair and was standing at the canary's cage, cheeping at the bird and wagging her forefinger at the bars.

"He's not in good form this morning, Mrs. Newman. He's beginning to molt."

"I had hoped to have my hair dry before you arrived. You must excuse me."

"I'm a little earlier than usual. But of course Philip is never early when I'm early though I've told him repeatedly he should always be waiting for me. He's incorrigible in that respect."

"He's incorrigible in many respects. Please do sit down, Miss Reid, till we have a private little chat." Lifting her cigarette box from the mantelpiece she offered a cigarette to Miss Reid, and on lighting it for her she marveled that her hand did not shake. Miss Reid crossed her legs, glad of an opportunity to postpone her morning's work.

"For a long time now, Miss Reid"—she could never force herself to call her Dympna—"Philip has worried me, worried me sorely because of his constant worry to you, to you who have been so good and kind to him." She paused, put the cigarette to her lips and blew out the smoke audibly. A strand of hair escaped from under the scarf, and with her fingers she tapped it back into its place.

"And now you'll be pleased to hear that he'll no longer be a perfect nuisance to either of us."

She saw Miss Reid's neck reddening and she glanced away, fumbling for words that would mitigate the words of dismissal, the words that would end the unhappy partnership.

"The little rascal has never realized the shattering he has given your tender nerves. Time and again I've told him that you come here at great inconvenience to yourself and to oblige me. Isn't that so, Miss Reid?"

"In a way it is, I suppose," Miss Reid said, her cigarette having gone out on her.

The canary rattled the swing in his cage and gave out a sharp chirp. Neither of them heard it.

And then slowly, and with refined politeness, Mrs. Newman explained the new arrangements, emphasizing her gratitude for all she had done for Philip, and striving all the while to draw from Miss Reid a meek expression of relief, of applause. But Miss Reid threw her cigarette in the fire, locked her fingers upon her lap, and listened in grim silence. And then, suddenly, her false complaints exposed, she took refuge in anger. She sprang to her feet, lifted her coat and struggled into it, and in a thin rising voice that appalled Mrs. Newman she shouted:

"This is a sudden and unexpected blow to my poor health, Mrs. Newman, one that I didn't think a lady of your standing was capable of administering. You have exploited me in a disgraceful manner—a mean and low and loathsome manner!"

"Hush, please, in case you bring my mother in upon us. I'm sorry, Miss Reid, but wasn't it always understood. . . ?"

"What will people think of me in the village!"

"What they've always thought of you: that you were a highly capable schoolmistress and that it was inconsiderate of me to drag you here from a well-earned retirement. And don't they know that the schoolmaster himself rejected the job when I offered it to him."

"You don't know them as well as I do. Never will I be able to look them straight in the face again."

"What doesn't concern them needs no explanation, Miss Reid."

"They'll concern themselves with my affairs because they have so little of their own to think about."

"The fact that a young man, a university graduate, is willing to take over will muzzle all criticism."

"A university graduate! He advertises himself as such! You're very trusting, Mrs. Newman, I must say. You should ask my sister about him. He's not all that he professes to be."

"You mean he's an impostor!"

Miss Reid, aware that she had shaken Mrs. Newman's confidence, buttoned her coat slowly, arranged a silk scarf around her neck, and lifted her handbag. "Go warily, Mrs. Newman, is my advice to you," and she moved toward the door.

Mrs. Newman hastened in front of her and stood with her back to the door: "Please wait for a cup of tea and I'll take you home in the car."

"The day is fresh and I'll enjoy the walk, thank you."

"I've seen Mister Wade at Mass and Communion every Sunday since he came."

"That proves nothing."

"He's to be here for a year to study history."

"He'll not be a year in our bungalow if my sister is any judge of character."

"Tell me, for the love of God, what you really know."

"I'll hold my peace at this stage. Let me pass, please." Mrs. Newman opened the door and walked with her as far as the main avenue, beseeching her to stay for tea and not to part in a spirit of unfriendliness.

"I'm still your friend and it's a friend's advice I'm giving: Keep a watchful eye on the comings and goings of this stranger."

Mrs. Newman watched her till she had disappeared into the dark archway of the trees. She shook her head. Miss Reid knows more about him than she let fall. Oh, if only Anne were at home, or someone in whom she could confide. An impostor she was inviting to her house to teach her son. Why had she been so impetuous! She should have made more inquiries before engaging him. For one thing she should have consulted Father Lavelle; he might know something about him and could advise her. Yes, that's what she'd do. She'd bring her troubles to him. It wasn't too late to do that and she'd try to see him this very day.

At that moment, sneaking among the trees, she perceived Thomas, the yardman, arriving for his day's work, and all her anger rose up against him, and hurrying into the house she ordered Mary to pull on a coat and tell Thomas she wanted him this instant.

"Yes, Ma'am," Mary said, sensing her mistress' distress.

In a few minutes Thomas arrived and was brought into the chilly office where there was a rolltop desk and pigeon-hole shelves against one wall. Mrs. Newman sat by the desk with her back to the window, and with a pencil in her hand frowned at Thomas as he stood near the door and miserably clutched his cap against his chest. She asked him what he meant by arriving at this time to do a day's work. She trusted him, and he awarded her trust by laziness and deceit. She was tired speaking to him of his sloth and the bad example he was giving the lad she had recently employed to help him.

"I was at the doctor's, Ma'am. I took a pain in my chest and he's going to send me to the hospital for an X ray."

"You didn't get the pain from overwork, I must say. Week after week I have asked you to keep the place neat and tidy —to take some pride in it. It's a disgrace and an eyesore. There are potholes in that avenue that'd break a person's neck on a dark night. Surely, without my telling you, you see that they need a few shovelfuls of gravel; and isn't there as much gravel on our shore that would patch all the roads in the country. And as for the outbuildings, I'd be ashamed to bring a visitor near them. Clots of manure lying all over the place. I suppose you'll be telling me we need a few new yard rakes. I suppose, too, you have the seed potatoes riddled and sacked?"

"They'll be done this very day, Ma'am."

"They should have been done three weeks ago. The boat is due in the harbor any day now."

"The riddler broke a spring. And then, Ma'am, I had these terrible pains."

"If you'd work more you'd have less time to think about pains."

"Yes, Ma'am."

"Oh, you'll say *yes* to everything but you'll not change. Do you know what St. Paul said about work: if a man will not work do not let him eat."

"I'm glad I never wrought for him, Ma'am. He was a hard man."

"Now listen, Thomas. If you don't improve I'll have to look out for someone to fill your place."

"Yes, Ma'am," he said politely.

"You may go now."

"Thank you, Ma'am," and he bowed and backed toward the door till his heel struck against it. "Thank you once again, Ma'am," he said, and slipped away.

Thank God that's over, she sighed, and joined her long hands on the open desk in front of her. If only he had quarreled with her she'd have got some satisfaction from her tirade. But no. He's always polite, always agrees to everything, but goes his own way and does not change. There were times she wished from her heart that her mother would sell the place and buy some little house in the city where they'd be free from this constant worry. But her mother would never do that, never sell out while the Jewish problem was rampant in her poor weak mind. This was no place for a woman to manage on her own. And that Thomas fellow was good for nothing. He had no appetite for work. And she was certain he deceived her when he sold cattle and sheep. How did she know what price he got for anything? She had only his word for it and she had to accept that.

She rubbed her forehead, closed up the desk, and went into the drawing room. Miss Reid's familiar perfume still lingered about the armchair where her coat had lain and it brought back to her mind the real reason for her sudden burst of impatience, impatience that never mended anything. At that moment she saw Miss Reid's cigarette on the hearth and she swept it up and put it in the fire, and the canary, hearing the tinkle of the brass shovel, gave out a few answering notes.

She turned from the fire, but it was the piano and not the canary that caught her attention. On the stand was an open sheet of music, a Bach chorale; pulling out the piano stool, she began to play. She played badly, her long fingers hesitant and stiff on the running notes, her mind not on the music. She lifted the sheet, put it in the piano stool, and hurried from the room.

She'd discuss everything with Mother, she decided, and walked along the landing to the old lady's room.

Her mother was sitting up in bed, knitting, the curtains pulled back and the weak sunlight shining in upon the worn carpet. Her daughter drew a chair to the bedside, and the old lady folded away her knitting, preparing for a morning's chat. The window was open at the bottom to the cold air, and before sitting down the daughter closed it, scaring away the blackbirds and finches that were feeding on the crumbs her mother had strewn on the sill after her breakfast.

"A finch came into the room a while back, Helena, and found its way out again. I thought it would injure itself against the pane, but it didn't. It alighted on the back of that chair you're sitting on. And do you know it had a little metal ring on its leg. Do you think would it be carrying messages?"

"Miss Reid's gone, gone for good. She took her departure very tartly. And now it's possible I've made a mistake—a mistake in employing a complete stranger."

"From your description of him yesterday he seemed to me what you were looking for."

"Miss Reid doesn't think so. She dropped a few hints that have troubled me greatly."

"And what, pray, would Miss Reid know about a young man? Weren't you always praising him when you came home from Mass each Sunday? And isn't he young and tall and vigorous, and a university graduate into the bargain? Isn't that sufficient to dispel all doubts?"

"I don't know what to think, Mother. Perhaps I should call on Father Lavelle and talk things over with him," she said. Getting up, she opened the window to a slit and began tidying the room.

"Before you do anything rash, just send the same Mister Wade up to me and I'll size him up in two jiffs. If you're not expert in asking questions, I am. And what's more, I keep on asking them till I'm answered satisfactorily."

"But you can't be rude, Mother. He seemed shy and unwilling to speak about himself. I let him have his way."

"Well, I'll have my way for a change. Our boy's future is at stake and that's not a matter to be treated lightly."

"I'll go and write to Anne. And I really must see Father Lavelle. He could ease my mind one way or another."

"So you have no trust in my judgment?"

"No, no, that's not what I mean. You know the interest Father Lavelle has always had in us. And look at the sound advice he gave us about Anne and sending her to Edinburgh."

"He never offers sound advice to me. When I mention the Jews he smiles and wags his head as if my mind were deranged and I was talking utter nonsense. And you know and I know and Mary knows that my old mind is as clear and cool as the water in a deep well."

Lest her mother would flaunt forth her tedious stories of how the Jews had persecuted her and had hounded her one summer over various seaside resorts in the South of England her daughter did not answer her. She folded her mother's clothes that were lying in an untidy heap on two chairs, propped another pillow at her back, and—quietly admonishing her to stay in bed the whole day—she suddenly moved toward the door and went out. Behind her she heard her mother call out that she wished the window opened wider, but knowing that this was only an excuse to detain her she continued on her way along the corridor and downstairs to the kitchen to see Mary.

Mary had gone out and on the table under the tall barred window were grated carrots and a knife, and on the raffia mat in front of the cooking range lay a dog and a cat. The dog wagged its tail on hearing Mrs. Newman enter but did not get up, and Mrs. Newman sat down on the rocking chair by the fire and waited, her nerves quietened by the stillness of the room in which nothing stirred except the tick-tock of the pendulum clock on the wall, the hum of the fire, and an occasional hiss from a saucepan of soup on the range. The large table was scrubbed white, the red tiles freshly washed, and the polished dish covers on the walls reflected a curved image of the barred window. Nothing had changed in the room since Mrs. Newman was a young child, nothing except the grocer's calendar that was replaced each New Year's day and shared a place of honor in a corner wall close to a picture of the Sacred Heart where a red lamp burned all day and all night without fail. In winter this room was the warmest in the house and in summer the coolest, for the sun shone into the top half of the window and that only in the early morning. The electric light was usually switched on for most of the day, but this morning there was light enough from the icy blue of the winter sky to prepare the meals, meals that Mary controlled with selfless independence, perturbed only when the old lady descended to the kitchen to order Mary to boil the milk and so destroy all poisonous germs that Jews might have placed there.

Mrs. Newman sighed; and joining her hands on her lap she gazed at the rough dry paws of the dog and at the rise and fall of the cat's and dog's contented breathing. A shadow darkened the room and she turned and saw Mary descending the steps to the outside door. She got up and opened the door for her.

"Oh, Ma'am, I didn't know you were here or I'd have hurried. I went to the garden for a bit of parsley and celery. My goodness but the soil's cold at this time of the year."

"Mary, I came to ask you one thing. Tell me truly what you think of this Mister Wade?"

"I think, Ma'am, he's a gentleman. All the way to the village yesterday in the car Master Philip plastered and pestered him with questions and I couldn't stop him. And what's more Mister Wade answered all of them."

"You don't think he's an impostor?"

"And what in God's good name is that, Ma'am?"

Mrs. Newman smiled. "That he's not what he says he is."

"You mean, Ma'am, that he's not a teacher at all, at all?"

"I don't know really what I mean." Leaning forward, she picked a tiny leaf off the sweet-smelling celery and put it in her mouth. She glanced away from Mary's bemused look and stared at the crumbs of soil clinging to the white roots of the celery.

"It's that Reid wan that's upset you, Ma'am, and I wouldn't pay heed to what a jealous woman would say and she about to lose a pleasant job." She scraped the soil off the vegetables with vigor and crushed the life out of a grub that was crawling over the newspaper spread on the table. "Miss Reid, Miss Reid! No, Ma'am, I'll not stain my soul by saying what I think. You're too soft and too forgiving. Give this new man a chance would be my advice and make the best of him while he's here. I'll say a prayer that you'll do the right thing."

That afternoon Mrs. Newman rang up Father Lavelle, and at four o'clock she was driving through the village and up the hill to the church, and as her car turned through the gates that led to the priest's house the tires squashed over heaps of leaves that his gardener had piled on the path.

Father Lavelle received her in his parlor. He was a thin little man with white hair, and he lowered his head on one elbow and cupped a hand to his ear, an unnecessary gesture that had remained with him after a bout of flu had left him deaf for a short while. He listened without interruption to her story, observing her agitation, her gloved hands clutching the gilt clasp of her handbag upright on her lap. He had known the Newmans since his arrival in the parish twenty years ago and had known that Mrs. Newman had had more than her share of sorrow: her husband lost at sea, a crippled son, and her mother with her comic but pathetic delusions about the Jews. In spite of these misfortunes Rock Lodge was a happy place, a place he enjoyed visiting.

He was sorry now to see her so distressed and he prepared himself to dispel her anxiety. "Well now, Mrs. Newman," he said quietly, "impatience and suspicion are twin enemies of real peace, and if you yourself are fussed and fidgety you'll very soon infect your household with the same mood. You must try to avoid that. If this stranger were in any way an unsavory character the same Miss Reids wouldn't have him long in their neat little place, I'm thinking. I've noticed Mister Wade at Mass on Sundays but from what I have gathered round about, no one, not even the postman, knows much about him. But it will all come out in due course. In the meantime I'd let the arrangements stand as they are until I get an opportunity to drop into the bungalow some evening soon. I did hear from a lady in another parish that her nephew had joined this Mister Wade's correspondence course and is well pleased with the work so far. So now, Mrs. Newman, don't upset yourself any more. To change the subject: How's your mother getting along with the Jewish problem?"

"It's still there, Father, I regret to say. Sometimes it goes underground and then suddenly erupts. I've still to bring her her hot milk at bedtime and I've still, in her presence, to sip some of it before she'll take it."

"She doesn't mind if you're poisoned along with her. Is that it?"

She laughed. "I suppose she has to take all necessary precautions."

They stood at the door looking down at the tide flowing fast like a river and a motorboat making its way across the narrow sleeve of the lough. There was a smell of burning leaves in the air, and at the side of the house the priest's gardener was leaning on a rake near the smoking pile.

"It's well he has that rake to support him or he'd fall

from exhaustion," the priest said. "I've been at him for the past fortnight to sweep up those leaves and for the life of me I can't make him budge. He told me it'd be wiser to wait till they'd all fall and then he'd make one clean sweep. I told him he should climb the trees and snip off the leaves with the scissors for it was exasperating for an energetic man to have to wait on Nature."

"I've a similar problem with my man," Mrs. Newman said. "It's either the sea air or the racing columns in the newspapers that we'll have to blame."

The gardener, hearing their voices, awoke from his contemplation of the sacrificial pile, and resting his rake against the garage he stooped below the leaves and levered them up with a stick.

"That's the way, William," the priest said. "Feed them well with air and burn the lot before dark. There's a load of rain to fall from that sky and it would only double your work."

5

THE PRIEST was right. That night it rained heavily, and in the morning though the sky was a clean blue the edges of the road were flooded and Andrew drove slowly to avoid a slosh of water that might impair the brakes of his old car. He arrived at Rock Lodge before half nine, and after banging the door of the car he heard the dogs barking. No need to ring the doorbell.

Mary was on her knees polishing the hallway, and after bidding him welcome she told him to go right up to the schoolroom, where Philip was waiting for him. The door was ajar and he went in and saw Philip sitting on a hassock, his legs outstretched, one eye to the telescope that rested on a tripod.

"You're very early, Mister Wade. We don't begin till half nine. Do you want to have a peep? Everything's as clear this morning as if it were beside you. At the other side of the lough I can see three pigeons on a roof and I can see their dung like dribbles of paint on the slates." He took his eye from the telescope and smiled. "If Anne were here she'd have made me say droppings instead of dung. Isn't that silly?"

"It is," Andrew said, putting his attaché case on the table and taking out a few books. The room was warm from a three-element electric heater close to the table.

"So you don't want to have a peep? You don't want to see a seagull and the red speck on its yellow beak?"

"I'll just have one look before we start to work. We'll have plenty of time later on to enjoy the sights."

Philip, suppressing a smile, gave the adjustment screw a quick turn and rose to his feet while Andrew knelt on one knee and put his eye to the telescope.

"Well?" said Philip. "What do you think of her?"

"No, I'm afraid I can't handle it."

"Maybe your sight's bad, Mister Wade." He laughed. "Kneel down again and I'll show you the trick. Just turn the screw a tiny weeny bit, and across the lough you'll see the wonders of that cluster of houses that they call a town."

Andrew focused it gently and as he did so each house rose sharp and clear, and he could read the names above the shop-fronts and see a girl rest a bicycle against a wall and take a straw bag from the basket strapped to the handlebars. He looked at the sea; it was calm and the rubbery reflection of a moored boat revealed the movement of the tide. He could make out the uneven stones on the slipway, the pools of water left behind by the outgoing tide, and a wet fishbox lying beside a rusty mooring ring. He had never been across to the other side, but he would some day,—probably in the spring when the days were brighter.

"I must say it's a real good one, Philip."

"If I swing it down toward the outbuildings I could see Thomas reading the newspaper. He has Mother's heart broke. Come on and we'll spy on him."

"No, Philip, it's better not to," and he patted the boy on the shoulder and went back to the table, and following the custom of his old school he began with a prayer:

> Direct, we beseech Thee, O Lord, all our actions by Thy holy Inspiration and carry them on by Thy gracious assistance, that every prayer, word, and work of ours may always begin from Thee and by Thee be happily ended through Christ, Our Lord, Amen.

"Miss Reid never said that prayer," Philip said, sitting down at the desk and lifting the lid to get an exercise book.

"You haven't Miss Reid now so forget about her," Andrew said, and turning to the blackboard he printed in chalk a timetable of the week's work. When Philip had made a copy of it and pinned it underneath the lid of the desk Andrew began oral work in mathematics. The boy revealed some knowledge of arithmetic, but of geometry and algebra he had little or no inkling and because those would be new and fresh subjects Andrew decided to introduce them right away.

They worked hard, and after two hours Mary arrived with tea on a tray.

"And now after we drink this," Philip explained, "we open the windows wide and you go for a walk and a smoke. There's a pond down among the trees to the left and there's a walled garden and the door to it is never locked. I'll blow my whistle when the room is aired."

"But why don't you come and show me them?"

"No, find them for yourself. I'd only keep you back."

Andrew didn't coax him. He'd try to respect the boy's strong independence of spirit and in that way learn to know him, for in knowing him well he could be of more use to him.

Leaving him in the room fingering through the books on the table Andrew made his way out by the front of the house and down by a path at the back which led under the black soaked trees to a lily pond that was covered so thickly with brown leaves a bird could have hopped across it without wetting its feet. He stood by a green garden seat, too damp to sit upon, and heard the water trickle through a clogged iron grille and disappear underground on its way to the sea which could be seen through the trees. There was a slight click from the leaves and a wet whisper from the soaked soil, and as he stood quite still, holding his breath, he sensed that something was watching him. He coughed and spat into the pond, and suddenly from the shaggy bank a waterhen burst out with a shriek, cut a black channel through the leaves and disappeared with a plout below the water. The leaves curved on the waves like a buckled floor, and a sound like a breeze lisped from all parts of the pond, and water lapped against the bank. He was sure that the bird had surfaced and was watching him from under a hood of leaves, but though he stooped and scanned the level of the water he failed to see it, and walking to the farther end of the pond he made his way under the drenched trees till he reached the sea and saw the long narrow lough with its many islands stretched out before him. The air was strong and clean and he breathed it in deeply and watched the tide recede from the wet stones of the beach. And then as he was making his way toward a boathouse with its small concrete slip he heard three blasts from Philip's whistle and, smiling to himself, he knocked out his pipe on the heel of his boot and returned refreshed to the house.

He read to Philip a Chekhov story about a circus dog and when he had finished it and questioned him about the parts that had appealed to him he took from his wallet a short poem, "The Child on the Swing" by Alexander Henderson, which he had clipped out from a recent number of *The Listener*.

He read it slowly, trying to capture the magic, the grace, the beauty of it:

"They have all gone home from the park;
twilight has come;
the child is alone and swings,
watching the dark,

watching the eyes, the furred slow pace;
sits on the swing
alone and rocks with a dream
to a far place

halfway to joy and back to fear,
alone, alone
in the still park where the soft
gray paws creep near."

"Read it again, please," Philip said, his eyes wide with comprehension. "Read it again. That's me he's writing about."

Andrew read it again, twice, and gave it to him to copy into a notebook, and while he was transcribing it Andrew wandered to the back of the room and touching the rocking horse on the head he listened to its rhythmic knocking on the bare floor. He touched it again with greater pressure, but this time the horse slewed around on its rockers like a live thing and faced him. He smiled, set it in gentle motion, and returned to the head of the room. He then read aloud a short letter of Katherine Mansfield's in which she had noted the morning sounds in a French village and told Philip he was to write a letter like that to his sister.

"And make her homesick?"

"No, it'll probably make her happy."

"And have I to show you the letter?"

"Not exactly. I'll expect you to read a bit of it to me."

"Not the bit that will describe you?"

"No, not that," he smiled and put the books into his attaché case.

"You're not going yet. Mother expects you to stay for lunch and you'll have to stay. Wait here till I fetch her," and he got out from behind the desk and dragged his feet in a painful fashion to the door. "Now don't stir, Mister Wade, till I come back. Mother will be vexed if you do. See, you're my prisoner," and taking a key from his pocket he went out and locked the door.

In a few minutes he returned with his mother. She was in black, her hair neatly set, a gold chain with a Celtic cross on her neck.

"I came to release you, Mister Wade," she said with a smile, "and to celebrate your release you must have lunch with us."

"Yes, the judge and jury have decided on that," Philip interjected. "And while you're getting ready I'll give the dogs a run."

"I suppose I must obey the ruling of the court," Andrew

said. "I'll do it this time, but I wouldn't like to impose on you every day."

"It's as easy to make lunch for four as it is for three. And I want you to meet my mother," Mrs. Newman said and switched off the electric heater with her foot. "I suppose it's too soon to ask you what you think of Philip?"

"He'll do well, I believe, and I'll do my best for him."

As she led him along the corridor to the drawing room she warned him not to take too seriously some of the things her mother might say; there were times when she spoke and acted queerly and she hoped he'd understand.

On entering the drawing room they could not see the old lady; she was hidden behind a folding screen that sheltered her from the drafts of the door. But at the other side of it, deep within the shoulders of an armchair, she sat, a tartan shawl around her head and a hot-water bottle resting on her knees. The round table holding the canary cage had been brought beside her.

"Don't stir, Mother. I've brought you Mister Wade, Philip's new teacher. I'll leave the two of you for a while till I see about the lunch."

Andrew stretched out his hand and shook hers gently but with feeling, a gesture that induced friendliness.

"Sit down, young man, and make yourself comfortable," she said in a dry, aged voice. "It's a nice fresh day outside for those who have the health to enjoy it. Always thank God for your bit of health, and thank Him for your senses while you have them. I suppose you never think of doing that?"

"On rare occasions I do."

"Let them be frequent occasions," she said and began to cough, a thin dry cough with no body in it. "Look at me. I was handsome at one time and rode with the hounds. Every word I say is true. I had good health till the Jews laid me low. And now I'm only a shell. I'll tell you this: that canary has more life in its body than I have. It's sad to see a tree lose its leaves and it's sad to see a bird molting. What do you think of them? The Jews, I mean."

He glanced across at her, and her frailty and her age dulled all desire to disquieten her.

"What do I think of the Jews?" he said, allowing himself time to choose words that would conceal any suspicion that he had been forewarned of her delusions. "I'll say this for them: they keep the world of music alive. Our best performers in that line are nearly all Jews."

"I never gave much thought to that branch of their activities. But I don't doubt your word, young man, I do not." She pressed closer into the armchair and the rubber bottle fell on to the hearthrug. He lifted it and placed it on her lap.

"Would you believe it, Mister Wade, if I told you these same Jews tried to poison me on a few occasions?"

"Oh, I could well believe it if you say it."

"Well, that's something I'm relieved to hear. You're the first person who has believed me. And your belief gladdens me. Pull your chair closer. That's better. And now put that bottle under my feet, for there's no warmth in them at this time of year."

She joined her hands on her lap and he could see the rings shine on her thin fingers. Slowly she launched into a world of her own making and told how the Jews had tried to waylay her in Edinburgh, and how when she had gone on a holiday to the South of England they had followed her to Brighton, to Torquay, and to smaller places like Looe and Polperro. Many a time she was violently sick after a meal and it was the sickness that purged her system of the poisons that would have destroyed her. She had often seen the poisons on the tip of her spoon, little crescent-shaped creatures that wriggled like eels.

"Do you believe that, Mister Wade?"

"I wouldn't doubt it for one moment," and he glanced at the canary swinging in its cage.

"Have you seen any Jews peddling their wares round the country since you came?"

He told her that a car drove up recently and that a man stepped out of it and tried to sell him a roll of linoleum.

"But I don't suppose he was a Jew for he didn't look like one and didn't speak like one."

"Well, I suppose he was one. Some day they'll track me down or maybe they'll try to get in league with you or with Mary," she said, giving him a hunted and distracted look that drew his sympathy.

"They'll never track you down while I'm around. From now on I'll be your protector. They have no wiles and whims that can escape me. Be at rest now and don't give them any more of your thought."

"Come here to me," she said, raising her hand.

Reluctantly he rose and stood beside her. She took his hand and stroked it, and the feeling of suppressed amusement that had pursued him gave place to guilt. He had gone too far to turn back and he bore her confidence in silence.

"How good and kind you are," she went on, pressing his hand to her cheek. "When my daughter told me about you I knew I would like you. I had full faith in my intuition. It's the only faculty left in me that needs no outside assurance. I hope you'll find Philip keen to learn. And you'll meet Anne when she's at home for Christmas. She's in Edinburgh. I don't write to her for fear my letters would fall into their hands and they'd seek me out here."

"They'll never seek you out again. I'll see to that."

Mrs. Newman entered, and noticing his constraint and embarrassment she gave him a glance of sympathy and complete understanding.

"Mister Wade and I are going to be great friends, Helena," the old lady said. "Yes, we are going to be great friends. And now we shall have lunch together. It seems a long time since we've had a man with us for lunch—a very long time indeed."

She rested her hands on the arms of the chair in an attempt to rise, and he stooped over her, and with his arm round her waist he gently helped her to her feet. She took his arm, and her daughter handed her her walking stick and in that way they shuffled along the corridor to the dining room. Mrs. Newman noticed with amusement that her mother's frailty had deteriorated, an affected frailty that would have suited an accomplished actress.

When the meal was over and Andrew had driven off and they were alone and smoking a cigarette she asked her mother if she had questioned Mr. Wade about his family. The old lady looked startled for a moment and then smiled: "Upon my word, Helena, I clean forgot to ask him. Isn't that strange? Now how did I forget that? I think it was he who did the talking and whatever he talked about he put all questions with regard to himself clean out of my mind. I must say I like him. His voice attracts me, and he has a quiet way with him."

"What were the two of you talking about when I came into the room and you were holding his hand?"

"We were just sharing little secrets between us."

"You don't know him and I don't know him, and yet you talk about sharing secrets. Now listen, Mother, I'll make it my business to find out more about him before we welcome him to the house as if he were a nephew or a son-in-law. When I left you alone with him I thought you'd seek some information or other from him."

"Take care, Helena, before you rouse the hare and lose it. Don't probe too far at this stage. We have Philip to think of. If the boy develops under the young man's care we must be grateful and do all in our power to hold him. Yes, to hold him and welcome him and to see he gets good nourishing food. We must take proper care of him for our son's sake.

And if it would be better for the boy's education that he would come every day in the week, then I say, let him come and I'll foot the bill if need be. Make him contented and happy and don't let your eye have one look of suspicion in it. If he wishes to speak about himself let him; if he doesn't, leave him be."

"That's not the advice you gave me before."

"Thank God I know when to change my mind, and I have changed it in this case for the better. I feel it deep in here," she tapped her breast, "we have now in the house a young man, an understanding man, who has the patience and politeness to listen to an old woman. Oh, yes, Helena:

By mutual confidence and mutual aid,
Great deeds are done and great discoveries made."

"I'll leave the discoveries to Father Lavelle. I'll bide my time in patience till I hear what he has to say."

"And you'll find, Helena, that he'll agree with me."

6

A WEEK later Father Lavelle, returning from a sick call, took the opportunity to visit the bungalow. It was an evening of hard dark rain, rain that had fallen all day and was swept by an east wind through the loose-fitting sashes of the windows till it flooded the sills and streamed onto the floor.

Andrew had welcomed the rain, for he was already behind in his work and his forced confinement induced him to set into the unwelcome task of tedious corrections. In a letter from his mother in the morning's post he learned that Marion had rejoined her husband. The unexpectedness of that news gave him an access of energy and purpose.

As darkness fell he lit his two lamps and drew the yellow curtains, dulling the sound of the sea that had noised all day on the shore below. He now sat at the table correcting the last batch of students' work, and when the curtains shook as if the windows were open he raised his head and saw the hems sweep the sill and a dark stain like a shadow spread up the yellow fabric.

"There'll be moles of mildew on the curtains if Miss Reid doesn't see to her windows," he thought, and bending to his work he clipped some scripts together; adding a note of praise along the margins he stowed them in an envelope and left it on top of a completed pile on the table. There were still three more envelopes to fill. His students, mostly girls, were certainly working hard and following his detailed instructions with a grim uniformity that attracted and appalled him. He was aware of the methods that satisfied official examiners and he decided not to deviate from the well-worn paths. But with Philip he would be different; he would allow the boy to develop in his own way, for the boy absorbed knowledge easily and retained it. Each week he would try to introduce him to a poem or piece of prose that would be revelant to his age and surroundings.

He yawned, rubbed his eyes, and rose from the table. A heavy downpour struck the roof and he stood listening to it as it dabbed like a flock of feeding pigeons. Stray drops stumbled down the chimney and onto the fire, and outside the gutters overflowed and the water ran in rills down the path to the gate. The dark avenue to Rock Lodge would be like a river tonight, he thought, and the leaves in the pond would sink under that weight of rain.

He put coal on the fire and after he had filled his pipe and was ready to light it a knock came at the door. He blew out the match and, wondering who could be calling on such a night, waited until the knock came again. The bread man, the grocer, and the butcher had passed in their vans hours ago; it might be Mrs. Quinn or one of her boys calling on some errand.

He opened the door and the light lit up the pale face of the priest and illuminated the diagonal streaks of rain that blew into the verandah. The priest introduced himself and said, "I was passing in the car and I saw the light and I stopped."

"You're welcome, Father," Andrew said, shaking his hand. He pulled the armchair around to the fire, propped a cushion at the back of it, and asked the priest for his coat.

"I'll just keep it on, for I'll not be staying long. I'm only disturbing the good work."

"Not in the least, Father. I've been hard at it all day and I'm glad of a break," Andrew said, and as he tidied up the table he told the priest of his correspondence courses.

"I've heard of it, Mister Wade, and I hope it's prospering."

"It's going along nicely and I've no complaints to make. I also go a few days a week to Rock Lodge to teach the lad there."

"I've heard of that too. You can't step far in this country without someone hearing it and reporting it."

"I hope the reports are good, Father?"

"They're favorable but a bit lopsided—a bit curious, if I may say so," the priest said, taking out a packet of cigarettes.

"Maybe you'd take a spot of whisky. I've a little in the kitchen and it's the only cheerful thing I have to offer."

"If you're taking one yourself I'll take a spoonful."

Andrew went to the kitchen where a little oil lamp gave out a dim glow. He raised the wick and carrying the lamp to the cold scullery he took the bottle from below the sink, a bottle he hadn't touched since the day of his parents' visit. His hands were shaking; he held the bottle firmly and strove to quell his agitation. If he asks me about myself I'll have to tell him everything, he thought, everything—including the court case and my resignation from the school. But since I've done no harm there's no need to be ashamed.

He half-filled two glasses with whisky, arranged them on a tray with a jug of water and shuffled back to the sitting room.

"The rain's eased off," Andrew said.

"Good. That's good; the bad stretches on the road will have drained away by the time I'm leaving."

The priest lifted one of the glasses, and as Andrew dribbled some water into it from the jug the priest signaled with his finger, an action that reminded Andrew of his boyhood when he used to serve Mass in a Midland convent.

"Here's to your good health, Father."

"And to yours and to success."

They took a drink and left the glasses within reach on the table. Andrew stooped to the hearth and jabbed at a large piece of coal till it broke and flared into yellow heartening flames.

"You find this a lonely spot, Mister Wade?"

"It is, but it's quiet and it gives me an opportunity to read and to work."

"Whatever else you do, keep up the reading. A man must read and read with discrimination if he is to enjoy his old age. It's a pleasure that seldom wanes. At my age if you haven't an intellectual interest of one kind or another you'll find the days a bore and a burden. You've long years to travel before you're my age."

Andrew smiled; the priest sat sideways to him, took a pull at his cigarette and, feeling the heat of the fire, unbuttoned his overcoat.

"I think you were going to say something about Philip Newman a few minutes ago," the priest said. "Do you think that boy could ever get his matric?"

"He's an intelligent lad and he's keen to learn and that's half the battle."

"You've had much teaching experience, Mister Wade?"

"About eight years, Father." He took another sip from his glass. A few more questions and he would be cornered. He could sense them taking shape in the priest's mind, filing up for polite release.

"Eight years—that's a good spell."

"It is, Father. It's a good spell, as you say." Noticing the long ash on the priest's cigarette, he placed a seashell that served as an ashtray, on the arm of the chair. Andrew lit his pipe, making loud pouts to ease the silence, hesitant to divert the direction of the conversation.

"Yes, yes," the priest said, as if answering some questions in his own mind. "Yes, yes, a brave little fellow," he went on, and spoke slowly and warmly of the Newmans and of the poor old grandmother and her deep-rooted delusions about the Jews.

"You've met her, I suppose, and have laughed at her sprightly delusions."

"I'm afraid, Father, I've sided with her. Not from conviction, though. I was off guard when I did it and I may let it rest at that. Her notions are harmless, and at her age it's better for her to reveal them than to conceal them."

"Maybe you're right, maybe you're right. From now on you'll be her white-headed boy."

The priest lit another cigarette. "Will you be staying long in these parts, Mister Wade?"

"I hope to do some historical research on the old Charter Schools—that should keep me busy for at least a year."

"And then you'll return to your old school, I suppose?"

"No, Father, I'm sorry to say I'll not."

He paused and felt his face burn, but the gentle look of the priest pushed away his cramped fear and drew forth his confidence. "I may as well be frank with you. I taught in a school in Gilvalley, I resigned from it. I had to resign and I came here——"

"I see," the priest said and, not being cold or indifferent to personal emotion, stretched out his hand and patted Andrew's knee. "You needn't go on; I understand."

"But I want to tell you all, Father. I want to rid myself of it no matter the cost. I'll tell you everything for I know it will not go any farther."

"Not if you wish it," the priest said, threw his cigarette in the fire, and cupped a hand to his ear.

"My father was a bank manager until his retirement two years ago," Andrew began. "Prior to that we had moved up and down the length of Ireland and had moved across it from east to west. Like tinkers we had no settled home; in no place were we allowed to remain for any length of time. As soon as we had made friends in one town we were transferred at a month's notice to another. My father was never a contented man, and the system nourished his discontent. When he was posted as a clerk to a bank in Dublin he complained that the work was too heavy, and when he was installed in a bank in the country he complained that the work was too light and the people so crude it was unwise to make friends with them. And later when he became a manager in the west he declared that the people were too sly and not like the decent, homespun people he had just left. He always compared the new place with the old; and the old place in his memories always shone forth with a radiance it never possessed. He looked forward to his retirement, to the day of liberation, as he called it, when he would be free to build a settled home. He planned a long cruise. But the cruise never came off. His doctor advised him that the bare sea breezes would aggravate his rheumatism, and on hearing that my father gathered together all the glossy brochures he had accumulated from travel agencies and burned them one night at the foot of the garden. I remember that night well, and I remember the blue flames and the green flames and the hard shiny ash that broke like a biscuit when my father poked them. 'There's the bank's parting legacy,' he moaned, 'a laceration of nerves and a broken life.' He bitterly rued the day he ever joined the bank and he thanked God that he had sent me to the University to avoid following in his footsteps."

Andrew cleared his throat, lifted his glass, and drained it.

"A pity, a pity," the priest said, "that your father didn't become reconciled to his vocation. At some time or other in our lives, priests as well as laymen all rue the day we followed our vocation. But, thank God, with most of us that fever, that temptation, soon passes us by, and we grow in acceptance and would live our lives over again in the same way if need be. Life is an eternal seesaw. To seek always for contentment is like seeking for a day without a night, a summer without a winter, an Easter without a Good Friday. Aye, aye, we'll not put up with much discomfort without bemoaning our lot. . . . And your father, he's still living, of course?"

"He is. He is living with Mother in Gilvalley and doing a spot of gardening and a round or two of golf. And I'm living here away from them—all through my own fault."

With long pauses that placed doubts in the priest's mind he told of his college days and his friendship with Marion and of her marriage to a clerk in his father's bank. He related how his friendship had continued after her marriage, and how her husband and he had quarreled one evening—a quarrel that had led to a court case and his resignation from the school.

"And you're sure there was nothing else between you and this married girl?"

"Nothing, Father, nothing except a long friendship—a dangerous one, perhaps."

"And he dragged you through the courts. . . . Well, well," the priest nodded slowly.

"It was in the papers for all to see."

"There are so many things in the papers these days, it's hard to keep track of them. . . . And where are they now, these people?"

"They were apart for a while, but now, thank God, everything's fixed up between them and they're living together in Dunvargan."

The wind had died away, the curtains no longer shook, and the rain had ceased. The heat from the fire was strong and the priest closed his eyes and thought of the countless times he had been brought in to settle disputes and how difficult it was to discover the real truth on those occasions. There were always many sides to the one story. Was this another one of them? Was the young man beside him in love with this young girl and she with him, and however much they had hidden it from themselves and not spoken of it it was there? Were they deluding themselves, deceiving their own hearts?

He yawned gently and opened his eyes. He would probe no further. What was said this evening and with such painful candor he would believe.

"I must go or I'll fall asleep," and he raised himself from the chair, flexed his right knee gently, and buttoned his coat. "Keep yourself warm and avoid rheumatism. I'll tell Mrs. Newman I called to see you. She was a bit troubled in her mind about you. Nothing serious. Just a shade curious, as you'd expect."

"And now?"

"Her mind will be at ease."

"And the court case: Will that not upset her?"

"That's your private affair and it's wiser not to reveal it unless you have to. It may increase doubts and not allay them. Lift yourself up again—in joy. And put the past behind you. If you are at peace with yourself you'll create peace around you."

"Thank you, Father."

Outside it was cold and damp and a smell of salt came from the sea. The waves sloshed loudly and rattled the pebbles on the shore like a sieve. The sky had cleared, stars bloomed, and the buoy at the entrance to the lough was flashing brightly in the cleansed air.

"Go in, young man, and don't catch cold. Good night now, and thanks."

Andrew watched the car move off and the red rear lights shine on the wet road. He shivered and turned in to the warmth of the house.

Relieved of his burden, an intense feeling of happiness flooded his heart. He pumped the lamps to full pressure, and the light increasing shone like summer on the yellow curtains. He lifted a book from the shelves and sat in the armchair vacated by the priest. He opened the book and, seeing Andrew J. Wade written diagonally across the flyleaf, he stared at it and realized, for the first time that evening, that he had not confessed everything, that he had omitted to tell of the transposition of his Christian names.

Doubts once more encroached upon his mind, and joy fled from him. The opportunity to establish his full identity had arisen and he had failed to grasp it. His father had warned him that the inversion of his name would sooner or later trammel him in difficulties. He should have listened to that advice and not followed his own stubborn inexperience.

7

On arriving home from the bungalow Father Lavelle phoned Mrs. Newman and, without referring to the intimacies of his conversation, assured her she need have no worries about having employed the young man to teach Philip. He seemed to him a sincere young man, but since he had doubts about his remaining in this part of the country for long, it would be as well to make the best use of him while he was here.

The message gladdened her and the following morning, a Sunday, after Mass Philip made his way to the car to avoid the women who usually gossiped with his mother. She, however, was on the lookout for Andrew, and seeing him ahead of her she hurried forward and touched his arm.

He turned round with a start: "Oh, good morning, Mrs. Newman," and he smiled at his own nervousness.

For a moment she was silent. The two Miss Reids were almost beside her and as she got ready to greet them they looked away from her and walked past.

"We're nicely and truly snubbed this morning, Mister Wade," she said, putting a hand to her hat to hold it against the breeze.

"If I'm not careful she'll probably give me my notice to quit one of these days."

"Not during the winter months, I can assure you. You're keeping the bungalow warmed and aired for her and she's not liable to order out a good tenant. But this is really what I wish to say," she went on, smiling gaily as the wind bent back the wide brim of her black hat. "We're wondering if you could spend this evening with us?"

"I'll be glad to," Andrew said, and then in case he should

arrive empty-handed he inquired if it was somebody's birthday.

"Oh, no, it's just that Mother and I would like to have you," she added, and her voice alive with friendly urgency quelled the desire to tell him that she was sure his Sunday evenings were long and lonely. "There'll be no one there but ourselves. Come about six. Mother, I may say, is fond of you and there are really few people she takes to nowadays."

"Is she out with you this morning?" he asked, looking at the groups of people standing around the chapel gates.

"No, no, she's not out this morning. Just Philip and Mary are with me and they are probably seated in the car."

To cover up his mistake he said quickly: "A woman of her years is not expected to attend Mass."

"I would like she would, though. However . . ." She gave her usual wide smile, and reminding him to come around six she strode off down the hill to the car.

The absence of her mother from Mass on Sundays always aggravated Mrs. Newman and provoked many a quarrel, Mrs. Newman maintaining that a woman who could move nimbly around the garden when she was in the mood could easily step into the car on a Sunday and attend Mass with the rest of them. For the past year or more she had not ventured out to the Church except at Christmas and Easter Sunday, and even then she was sure she shouldn't have gone for spies would have seen her and would have reported her movements to Jewish headquarters.

And so she stayed in her room on Sunday mornings and turned the key in the lock while the others were at Mass. A fire with logs that did not sparkle was lighted early in the morning and was kept alight all day from a pile in a brass-belted barrel at the side of the hearth. The filling of the barrel was an irksome ritual for Mary, for she had to struggle with the baskets up the steep stairs from the kitchen and wait patiently while the old lady scrutinized each log to ensure that Thomas, the yardman, had scraped off all decayed moss and that there were no cracks or crevices where woodlice could hide. The old lady detested woodlice, for one recent evening as she lifted a log with the tongs and placed it on the fire two woodlice raced out of a smoking slit, scurried to the edge of the log, and before she could save them they had stumbled into the flames and were consumed. It gave her nausea, and all that day the sight of food revolted her and she had rung for Mary and scolded her for fetching a split log in her basket for she was sure it was the Jews who were stuffing the crevices with woodlice to upset her.

"Woman dear, hold your tongue," Mary had said, irritated by her journeyings up and down the stairs. "Why would Jews come here to chop up trees, I ask you? They never do sweaty work, never work with a hatchet or saw as far as I know. Now, please, set your mind at rest like a sensible woman."

"Mary, you don't know them as well as I do."

"Thanks be to the good God for that."

"Did you ever speak to one for instance?"

"Why would a Jewman speak to the likes of me."

"To get at me—that's why!"

Mary sighed, and inwardly thanking God for her own five senses she bestowed on the old woman a look of deep pity: "Well, I can tell you there's no splits in them blocks, for I examined them as carefully as the district nurse examines a sore finger. And what's more they'll burn so quietly you'll not hear them. Attend to your knitting, in God's good name, and don't be staring at the poor misfortunate blocks."

Despite Mary's assurances, the old lady eyed each log she placed on the fire, and on Sunday mornings when she was alone in the house she sat well back from the hearth, had the canary brought to her for company, and with the window open so as to hear the six strokes from the belltower that was rung in unison with the altar bell at the Consecration, she would join her hands in prayer, aware that in a short while they would all troop home again and the noise of barking dogs and the sound of feet in the passageways would quiet the beating of her heart and dispel the constant fears that cramped her.

"If Mister Wade comes this evening," she said to herself on the Sunday that her daughter was to invite him, "I'll ask him about the woodlice." She closed the rattling window after hearing the comforting strokes from the bell and drawing her chair nearer the fire, she saw dark initials *R H* cut out from the bark of a burning log. The flames curled round it like grasping fingers and she fumbled in her mind for some significant association that would make sense of the initials but nothing came to her except Rabbi and Hebrew, and she clutched her shawl in fear and pushed back her chair. Then the corners of the bark curled back from the flames, the two letters disintegrated, and she remembered with a start that *H* stood for her daughter Helena and *R* for Richard, her son-in-law who had been torpedoed at sea.

"Ah," she sighed, "a more graceful pair you wouldn't have seen in the length and breadth of the county. Helena, tall and slim as a young birch, and Richard, a shade taller, and his lovely Dublin voice that was a joy to listen to. Poor Richard, God have mercy on him. Poor Helena! A curse upon all wars and on all those who make them!"

She poked at the flames with the tip of the poker trying to retrieve a section of the letters but at that moment the bedroom door was knocked and the old lady unlocked it, and into the room stepped Helena and behind her came Philip to do his usual Sunday reading from the gospel and epistle of the day's Mass.

"Well, Mother, I've good news for you," Helena said, not having taken off her hat and coat. "Mister Wade will be here this evening to see you, and in order that you'll look your best I'd advise you to take a nice sleep to yourself in the afternoon."

"I'm glad he's coming," the old lady said, and not wishing

to dampen her daughter's brightness she refrained from mentioning the initials that had now disappeared into the heart of the fire.

"And now, Mother," Helena said as she plumped up the cushions at her mother's back, "I'll leave Philip with you, for I'm sure he's dying to get on with his readings." She slipped out, smiled back at Philip, and shook her long finger at him.

"And now, Master Philip, before I begin to hear the sacred words, tell me what Father Lavelle was preaching about this morning."

"He told us to be patient with the old and the cranky."

"I hope he included himself in that remark. . . . What else?"

"He told us that many a son and many a daughter would reap a heavenly reward if they were patient with the old and the cranky."

"Don't repeat yourself, like a good boy. . . . Continue."

"He told us that many old people were on this earth to irritate us, but if we didn't let them annoy us our reward would be great on this earth and in the world to come. He said a whole lot of other things but I forget them, Grandmother."

"Maybe it's as well you have forgotten them. And now for the readings. Don't sniff, child. Take your handkerchief and give your nose a good blow. . . . That's better. Now begin, and if you read slowly you'll be finished all the quicker."

"At that time when Jesus entered into the boat."

"Stop! Leave the boats out of it for a moment. Read the epistle first."

She seemed to know everything, he thought, and gazing into the fire he saw yeasty bubbles at the end of a log and he remembered a boy in school who used to take fits and lie on the floor and how white froth gathered at the corners of his mouth.

"Continue, Philip, and stop dreaming. I'm waiting patiently for the sacred words."

"Brethren, owe no man anything, but to love one another . . ."

"That's St. Paul writing to the Romans."

"Please, Grandmother, don't interrupt me till I've finished."

"You have little patience."

"For he that loveth his neighbor hath . . ."

"Stop! Begin at the beginning. And do keep your fingers out of your hair. Some fine day I'll snip off that fringe and you'll not be able to twist it."

Outside he could hear the dogs barking and he knew they were waiting for him and he pressed his hand against his pocket and felt the hard shape of his whistle. He sighed, and the old lady, shielding the side of her face with her hand, inclined one ear toward him. He read quickly and without interruption, and when he almost shouted the last line: "Love therefore is the fulfilling of the law," she closed her eyes and shook her head.

"Wretched, deplorable reading. I must speak to Mister Wade about it. Upon my word, when you read the gospel in that tone of voice my faith is in danger. Give me a kiss, and go and play yourself and send Mary up to me for a few minutes."

"Thank you, Grandmother."

"Don't dare to thank me for not asking you to read the Lord's words. Go in peace."

He swayed toward the door, closed it gently, and she knew by the absence of any sound that he was now sliding in a sideways movement down the banisters.

Presently Mary, out of breath, stumbled into the room, and left the door open, a sign that she would not allow her morning to be filched from her. The old lady questioned her about Father Lavelle's sermon.

"I'm not sure if it was a sermon or a scolding. He advised the young to be more thoughtful and less selfish with the old. A day would come when they too would be old and if they weren't kind now with the aged and the helpless they would get it hot and heavy in this life and in the next."

"I'm glad he gave it to them."

"He laid into us too. He said our nerves were in tatters and our tempers in flitters, and many a one could become a saint by living with an old woman and she as cranky and crabbed and cantankerous as a coil of barbed wire and it rough with rust into the bargain."

"He's speaking out of his own tantrums and not from Scripture if he said all that."

"I'll be off now for I have to draw a couple of chickens for Mister Wade's coming."

"Thank you, Mary, and on your way down you could take the canary back to the drawing room. I didn't sleep a wink last night and I now feel drowsy."

"Never postpone a sleep if that's the way you feel. The doctor gave me that advice years ago."

Mary lifted the cage by the brass ring, and the old lady lay down on top of the bed, pulled an eiderdown over her, and slept. By evening she was well refreshed, and having dressed she made her way down to the drawing room where Philip was sitting on the hearthrug with the dogs, his back against a hassock, a copy of *David Copperfield* on his lap. Hearing her approach, he stuffed the book under a cushion, struggled to his feet, and made his way to the back of the room which was in semidarkness. He sat on the piano stool, stroked the white keys of the piano, but didn't play. His grandmother entered the room, stepped over the dogs, and sat in an armchair under the light of a pedestal lamp fringed with beads. He saw her light a cigarette; the smoke from it hung like a thin blue scarf above the fireplace.

She began to talk to herself and had forgotten about his

presence or was unaware that he was in the room. From his position near the window he could see only the back of her head and the slow movement of her hand as she put the cigarette to her lips. She began to talk and gesticulate as if addressing a meeting: "Are we, mothers of families, going to allow our sons to take part in another holocaust? We will not; we must not; now is the acceptable time, the time to rise from sleep, the time to shake off the garments of lethargy and let our voice be heard in the four quarters of the globe. We must not spin one thread that could be used to make a weapon of destruction. We shall refuse to do so. You have all read my letters to the newspapers. They have not printed them all. They dare not. They haven't jailed me yet. But that will come as sure as night follows the day. But I am ready for it, my limbs girt in the habiliments of justice. They know that if we use the pen and let our voice be heard we can end wars. But the Jews don't want that. Like oil they will not mix, and after the whirlpool of chaos they will rise like oil to the top. This evening I am glad to welcome to our meeting the golden-voiced Mrs. Sprigett, that great champion of peace."

She gave a slight clap with her hands, and one of the dogs arose from the rug near her armchair and sat down in a more comfortable position.

Philip, accustomed as he was to these periodic harangues of his grandmother, knew not to distract her. She lived in a world of her own and he had not reached the age where her conduct would embarrass him. She was silent now and he saw a great cloud of smoke from her cigarette float up to the beaded fringe of the lamp and disappear.

He crossed to one of the windows, put his hands to the side of his face, and peered through the cold dark pane out into the night and to the lights at the other side of the lough that were blurred by the rain. Across the lawn he could see a swaying light moving about the yard of the outbuildings as Thomas prepared to bed down the cattle for the night. Because of the rain and the cold Thomas would be cross with the cattle and would say rude words to them—"Make way, you bastards! What are you lying down for? Get up and eat!"—and he would kick them and they would struggle to their feet, their sad eyes turned to the lantern and to the armfuls of hay tossed into the manger. The byre would be warm and snug, the wooden posts polished like brown leather, and the heavy rain falling outside would channel the threshold like a pig's trough. Philip sighed and glanced toward the dark tunnel of trees that hid the road along which Mr. Wade would come in his ramshackle car. There was no sign of him, no hint of light or movement.

He withdrew from the window and approached the lighted end of the room.

"I don't think he'll come, Grandmother. The sea road will be flooded and water will get into the engine of his old car."

"Wish hard for him to come, and he will come. How often have I told you to think of success and not of failure. Mister Wade will not fail us."

"It's his car that will fail us. It's as drafty as a sheep pen and it will fall to bits under him."

She put a hand over her eyes, sat quite still for a few minutes, and then raising her head exclaimed: "He's coming! He's on his way! Look out and you'll see him."

Philip went to the window and as he looked into the rainy darkness he saw the beams of a car sway through the trees and stretch like theater-light over the green grass.

"Yes, he's coming, Grandmother. You're right, you're right," and he went out to the hallway where his mother was rearranging chrysanthemums in a brass jug and placing an envelope beside it on a semicircular table. The grandfather clock chimed six, and at that moment the doorbell rang, and Mrs. Newman after a last look at herself in the hall mirror hastened to the door.

"How good of you to come on such a horrid night," she said, taking Andrew's hat.

"How good of you to ask me," he answered, pulling off his overcoat and smiling at Philip who was peeping round a doorway.

"I thought your old car had broken down," Philip said.

"Not a bit of her. There's no holding her back when she gets a drop or two of rain."

In the drawing room the old lady stretched out both hands to welcome him: "I knew you wouldn't fail us, Mister Wade. I sensed it in here," and she tapped her shrunken breast.

Mrs. Newman shooshed the dogs from the rug, pushed a chair near to the fire, and told him to make himself at home.

The high windows rattled in the wind, rain struck against them like hailstones, and all three were hushed as they listened to the squall.

"If it doesn't clear up you'll have to stay the night, Mister Wade. Anne's room is ready and you could have it. Couldn't he, Helena?" the old lady suggested.

"Yes, of course he could," Mrs. Newman answered as she drew a trolley with sherry glasses from the center of the room.

He thanked them, but he really couldn't stay the night. He had left two lamps lighted, the fire banked up, and a kettle at the side of the cookstove.

"None of those things would take a bit of hurt," the old lady pressed, taking a glass of sherry from her daughter.

"You'll have to stay! You'll have to stay! The rain is here for a night and a day!" Philip chanted.

"Now, Philip, that's enough, please. Allow Mister Wade to make up his own mind," Mrs. Newman chided, holding out the tray to Andrew.

He took a glass and raised it head-high: "Here's to your good health and to Philip's success."

"And to Anne's success too," the old lady said. "We must never forget the absent ones. Anne never forgets us. If a single week passed without a letter from her you would know that something was amiss." She took a sip from her glass and as she began once more to talk of Anne Mrs. Newman bowed herself quietly from the room and went off to help Mary with the table.

Philip began to sketch yachts in his drawing-book and as Andrew leaned forward to look at them a loose button hanging from his jacket caught the old lady's attention and she ordered Philip to get her a needle and thread from the kitchen. Andrew reluctantly handed over his jacket and she draped a shawl about his shoulders. One of his shirtsleeves had no cufflink and he hid it with his hand and eyed the old lady as she plucked off the loose button from his jacket and picked away the broken threads with her fingernails.

Philip returned with the needle; seeing Andrew draped with the shawl he laughed: "Now we have two old women in the house and not one. You're bossing Mister Wade, Grandmother, and he'll not come back."

"Mister Wade doesn't mind—sure you don't?"

Andrew reddened, and to hide his embarrassment and Philip's constant staring he took a sheet from the drawing-book, folded it in four, and to the boy's astonishment began tearing pieces from the corners and throwing them into the fire. In a few minutes he shook out the sheet, held it up by two corners, displaying four similar yachts, their sails and hulls clipped out as if done with scissors.

"Do that again, please, and let me see," Philip said.

"Some other time I'll let you into the secret but not now."

Philip handed him another sheet and pleaded with him to do it again.

"In a minute," he said as he watched the old lady finish her sewing. He thanked her, struggled into his jacket (which now felt cold), and draped the shawl gently around her shoulders. His embarrassment fled, and folding the drawing-sheet to the tune of "Jack and Jill" he once more tore pieces out of the folds and this time made four little Dutch girls with baskets in their hands.

"That's something you must learn, Philip," she said as he spread the sheet out on her lap. Mrs. Newman returned and hoping they were all as peckish as she was she led them to the dining room, where a large fire burned in the grate and the chandelier lights above the table were reflected in the dark windows. Mrs. Newman sat erect at the head of the table, the rings on her long slender fingers catching the light as she handed round the plates. The grandmother and Philip sat at one side of the table, their backs to the window, and Andrew sat opposite them.

"You attend to Philip, Mother, and encourage him to eat," Mrs. Newman teased, her lively voice rising clear above the noise of the wind and the roar of the fire.

"That chimney wouldn't go on fire, Helena," the grandmother said, staring at the leap of the flames.

"Content yourself, Mother. There's no soot in it; it was only last week I got Thomas to give it a thorough cleaning."

Twice during the meal heavy rain squalls struck the window. The reflected lights were blurred by thick streams of rain and a door slammed shut in some part of the house.

"No going out in that, Mister Wade. We couldn't allow it. Isn't that right, Mother?"

"Yes," her mother agreed, "and we'll hold him even if we have to use physical force."

"We'll see," he said, not wishing to be disagreeable and at the same time hoping that the strong wind would have spent itself by the time he was to leave.

He felt no constraint in their company and sensed that his presence, for some reason, gave them pleasure. During the meal the old lady urged him to drink more wine, telling him that it would go to waste if he didn't, he was the only man in the house except Thomas and his palate was geared for rougher material.

After dinner, and when they were all seated in the drawing room the old lady said she was sure Mr. Wade could sing, for his voice reminded her of poor Richard's, one of whose favorite songs was "The Snowy-Breasted Pearl," and if Mr. Wade could sing that it would be a wonderfully joyful evening altogether.

He agreed to give it a try if Mrs. Newman would accompany him on the piano.

"I'll do that with pleasure," she said, springing to her feet. He mumbled the words of the song to himself to refresh his memory while Mrs. Newman switched on the light above the piano, and from a drawer in a tallboy drew out a bundle of tattered music books; she found what she was looking for and, adjusting her pearl earrings, sat down on the piano stool and played the accompaniment over once to accustom herself to the run of notes.

The last time he had sung for anyone was in Marion's drawing room, and the memory of his last evening with her confronted him suddenly like a treacherous lie.

"Ready?" Mrs. Newman whispered, looking up at the strained expression on his face. "You mustn't be nervous with us. I'll give you a few more minutes," and her long thin fingers rippled over the keys. He could see her reflection in the window, the square-cut neck of her black frock, her short black hair, and the light from her rings moving with the rapid movement of her fingers. Her long thin body swayed slightly and then suddenly stopped and she was looking up at him, smiling, her brown eyes darker now because of the light.

"Maybe you'd rather not, Mister Wade?"

"No, no, I'll try. It's just that I might not be good enough." He cleared his throat.

The room was large. It suited his voice, and after the first line he had found the right pitch, and each word rang out, full and clear:

"There's a colleen fair as May,
For a year and for a day
I've sought by every way her heart to gain.
There's no art of tongue or eye,
Fond youths with maiden try
But I've tried with ceaseless sigh, yet tried in vain. . . ."

He put his heart into it as if the song itself, mournful though it was, made articulate the gratitude he felt for all the Newmans had done for him. The words, their sincerity, he enunciated clearly, singing them without affectation, and when he had finished and the old lady was applauding from the far end of the room, Mrs. Newman stretched out her hand and pressed his where it rested on the piano. Then quickly, she inclined her head away from him, hiding the tears in her eyes, leafing through the pages of the book as if searching for another song.

"Come here, young man," the old lady called in her husky voice from the end of the room. "Oh, how well you sang! You sang it from the heart, as if you yourself had been disappointed in love. I hope you haven't. I hope you never will be. It's the one disappointment that leaves an ineffaceable scar."

"No, I haven't had any disappointments of that kind so far."

"God keep you that way."

Helena was playing now, playing Beethoven's *Pathétique,* and they sat still listening to her while Philip folded sheets of drawing paper and tore pieces from the corners in an endeavor to make a pattern.

Outside the wind had fallen, but no one noticed it or heard the last drops of rain fall from the slates.

"How well you play," Andrew said as Mrs. Newman closed the piano and turned round on her stool.

"No, I played it badly. I practice very little nowadays. I've no heart for it, really."

"And now we'll have a game of cards. Whist for small stakes," the old lady announced, and ordered Philip to tidy up the hearthrug and make room for the cardtable.

"Mother will partner me," Mrs. Newman whispered to Andrew, as she unfolded the cardtable. "Let her win. It'll give her great pleasure and something to boast about for days."

As they arranged the chairs Andrew left the room to find Mary. Light came from the open door of the dining room and inside he found her folding up the tablecloth.

"The meal was lovely, Mary," he said, slipping a few shillings into her hand.

"Ah, sir, that's not necessary. But thanks, thanks all the same. I heard you singing, Mister Wade. That song was Mister Newman's favorite—you didn't know that. Ah, how well he sang it, nearly as good as yourself. They'll never forget you for singing it."

"They don't know me, Mary."

"They know you're a gentleman."

"I wouldn't agree to that," he said, bidding her good night.

For an hour they played cards, and he managed without obvious carelessness to allow the old lady to win, and when he was leaving she promised to lend him a book on how to improve his whist.

In the hallway Mrs. Newman helped him into his coat, and firmly pressed out the creases on the shoulders, and gave him the envelope that lay on the hall table.

"We'll pay you fortnightly if you don't mind. It will save you a weekly trip across the ferry to cash it. Our village isn't large enough to require a bank of its own."

She opened the door and Philip stood beside her, her arm round his shoulder. The air was cold, the scoured moon was high above the trees, and the night seemed wide and spacious now that the wind had dropped.

"You'll have a quiet journey home after all," she said brightly. "And thanks for the lovely evening you gave us, Mister Wade."

"The thanks is all on my side, I'm thinking," and he got into the car. Mother and son watched it move off and unwind dark tracks on the wet, moonlit road.

On entering his bungalow he pumped up his lamps, slit open the envelope and saw that the check was made out to John Wade. The name looked strange, as if made out to another person entirely. If only he had told her to make it out to J. A. Wade it would have weakened the import of his deception until the time was ripe for him to make a clean revelation. Some day he would have to tell them, or at least tell Father Lavelle in the hope that he would do it for him.

And what if someone in the bank knew him or knew his father and would recall the court case and spread it abroad with an ugly twist to it? "And supposing someone in the bank did know me or heard of me?" he said aloud to himself. "What of it?" He had done no harm to anyone. His conscience, surely, was clear on that. Why should he be afraid then, or why should he flinch before anyone? Yes, that's the way he should think of it, and that's the way he would think of it. A day would come when he would slough off this burden that weighed upon him, and until that day came he could never walk as a free man.

8

FOR NEARLY a week the check lay in Andrew's wallet, but on Saturday he decided to cross the ferry and cash it. Afterward he would drive to the city and consult some books on the old Charter Schools.

He rose early on a morning that looked good. Frost lay on the road, the sea was calm, and a red sun struggled through the haze on the horizon. He arrived at the village as the shops were opening. He parked his car near a bus that had its windows tissue-papered with frost and made his way to the deserted quayside where waves lipped against the slipway and the ferryboat straining on its mooring ropes creaked against the quay. He stamped his feet to keep warm, and the echoes, like a flock of birds, sped away into the mist. Boats lay on trestles against the quaywall and among them was *Razorbill* covered in green canvas, the unmended hole at her bow gaping like the eye socket of a dead fish. Inside the hole a cat lay on a pile of shavings and it didn't move when Andrew poked his head in to examine the damage. He was still examining it and admiring the strength of her timbers and the weight of iron on her keel when the ferryman arrived, muffled to the ears in a heavy coat.

"*Razorbill* is still on the disabled list, but it'll not be for long. I'll get at her after Christmas and she'll be out showing her heels in the first race of the season. That's something you can tell young Philip. You'll not forget."

"I'll not forget."

"I know you won't. You didn't forget to tell about the teak, and the young lad's tormented me ever since. But she'll be mended all right. She'll be mended in God's slow time," he said, stepping into the ferryboat.

He swept frost off a seat with the sleeve of his coat and invited Andrew to sit. But Andrew preferred to stand, and as the motorboat moved out from the quay the air struck sharply against his face and numbed the lobes of his ears.

"You're early on the go, this morning."

"I'm going to the city for the day but I need to visit the bank first."

"Ten minutes will take us across. Two minutes after that you'll be at the bank, and a few minutes later we'll be on our way back. You couldn't beat that for speed."

Andrew questioned him about the bank and inquired if he knew any of the clerks. No, he didn't know any of them except the manager. The clerks were changed as often as the clothes in a shopwindow and he couldn't remember any of their names. But the manager was a settled sort of man—a man who sailed a boat, fished in season, golfed, and tended a garden that grew many a prize rose. He had been settled here about a dozen years and was likely to remain on after his retirement.

The boat had now reached the other side and Andrew stepped carefully onto the slippery stones and made his way up the short hill that led to the Square. The bank was at the right-hand corner and a charwoman was polishing the brass nameplate at the side of the door. Andrew walked past the entrance and stood at a shopwindow where a shopboy, wiping the moisture from the inside of the pane, paused to wink at him. Andrew moved away. He felt like a schoolboy about to commit a theft. He looked toward the bank again and saw the charwoman throwing handfuls of sand on the frost around the entrance. She went inside and there was no one around now except a man slowly crossing the Square and reading a newspaper. Andrew took the check from his wallet and held it in his hand. If he went in now he would have the business over and done with in a few minutes. If some clerk did happen to know him, what matter? He hadn't harmed anyone and the check he carried was genuine.

His feet crunched over the sand at the entrance; pausing to wipe them on the stiff mat in the vestibule he heard the quick tapping of a typewriter, and as he opened the glass-paneled door that led to the counter the clacking of the typewriter was louder and helped to ease his fear.

Without a word he handed the check to the cashier. The cashier scrutinized it, turned it over, and looked at Andrew.

"You want cash for this?"

"Yes, please."

"Sign your name on the back of it, like a good man."

Andrew lifted the pen from the inkpot on the counter, but the nib was broad and scratchy and he had to put it aside and finish the signature with his own pen. He dried it on the blotting pad in front of him and handed it to the cashier.

"It would be better if you would sign your name without the *A*. The check is made out to *John Wade* and you have signed *John A. Wade*."

"Sorry," Andrew said, his voice unsteady, and he stroked out his first signature and wrote John Wade.

The typewriter had ceased its comforting click and a girl in a blue overall unrolled a sheet of paper from the machine and glanced across at the cashier's desk.

The cashier once more examined the check, spread it flat on the counter, and looked at Andrew.

"If you wish you may ring up Mrs. Newman," Andrew said.

"Oh, not at all. I've no doubt whatsoever that the check is made payable to you." Aware that he had embarrassed a client, he inquired about Mrs. Newman and asked if he was staying at the other side of the lough.

"Only for a short while," Andrew said coldly, suppressing the clerk's desire to be sociable.

The clerk dipped his thumb on a sponge that lay in a small receptacle and counted the notes twice before handing them across the counter.

Andrew thanked him, stowed the notes in his wallet

without counting them, and bidding him good morning he walked out and stumbled over the thick mat in the hallway.

"Thank God that's over for another while," he said to himself, feeling a flush upon his face. "I suppose they're on the phone now to Mrs. Newman and in a short while she'll be telling them that Mr. John Wade is giving tuition to her little boy."

The boatman saw him coming down the hill and started up the engine, and in a few minutes they were moving out freely into the fresh cold air of the sea. Andrew could see part of Rock Lodge through the bare trees; thinking that Philip might be looking at the boat through his telescope he waved a hand with a perfunctory gesture. He paid the boatman a couple of shillings above the usual fare, and before starting for the city made a visit to the church and prayed for his father and mother, for the success of his correspondence courses, and for the old lady in Rock Lodge that her mind would soon shed her delusions about the poor maligned and unfortunate Jews. Finally he made a firm resolution to establish once and for all his real name with the Newmans.

On going out he met Mrs. Quinn on the steps with a basket in her hand and he stopped and asked about her husband.

"I'm just going up to the city to see him," she said. "The bus will be leaving in about ten minutes and I've just time to say a mouthful of prayers."

"If you like you can come with me," Andrew said. "I'll be staying about three hours in the city if that would suit you."

"It wouldn't be too much trouble?" she said, thinking of the busfare she would save if she went with him.

"No trouble at all. You'll be company for me on the thirty miles. I've the car in the Square and I'll be ready to go when you're ready. Take your time."

"Thank you kindly, Mister Wade."

He collected his letters and newspaper at the post office

and had time to read the headlines of the newspaper before he saw her coming slowly down the hill. She looked thin and cold in her blue raincoat, and her high cheekbones and pale face reminded him of her husband and the last time he had seen him lying in his bed with the strong sea air moving freshly through the opened sides of his hut. He missed him on his daily walk along the shore road and he told her so and hoped that they would have an early spring and her husband would be strong enough to come home to enjoy it.

He drove slowly on the frosty roads and, conscious of the drift of air through the ill-fitting doors, he made her take an old plaid rug that covered a dent in the back seat and spread it about her knees. She hid her hands under the rug and smiled her thanks.

"I'll never forgive myself, Mrs. Quinn, if you catch your death of cold in this ramshackle vehicle."

"I mayn't look it, Mister Wade, but I'm as hardy as a seagull and I seldom catch a cold. Don't worry about me. I'm grateful for the convenience and I'll be home earlier than I expected. A neighbor is looking after the three children and she'll be right glad to see me if I get back early."

He closed all the windows to keep out the cold and slowed down occasionally to wipe away the mist that gathered on the inside of the windshield. On the main road he made better speed, for the sun and the moving traffic had cleared away the grains of frost and left a wet, tacky surface.

At a village shop he bought some fruit, and at the entrance gate of the sanatorium he drew up and placed the bag on top of her basket.

"Give him that from me and tell him to hurry up and get better."

"That's far too much, Mister Wade. Half of it would have done. You're far too generous entirely."

"I'll be back for you on the dot of three and you'll be home again before dark. Take care of yourself."

She waved and smiled at him, and her blue eyes shadowed

with worry looked at that moment as bright and feverish as her husband's.

He inquired his way to the principal reference library in the city and there in its atmosphere of purposeful industry he consulted old books on the Charter Schools: government reports on the conditions of the buildings, the misappropriation of funds by the governors of the schools, the undernourished and ill-clad children, their hands hacked with chilblains, their damp straw beds, and the thin gruel served for supper. It was a Dickensian world of cruelty, meanness, and inhumanity, and as he made abstracts of what he read he was impelled to copy out the direct quotations historical theses demanded.

The time passed quickly, and now and again he would pause to glance at other historians burrowing intently into bound volumes of old newspapers, stacks of white cards at their elbows on which they scribbled snippets of information that would help to resurrect the social life of a past century. "We're all gravediggers," he remembered someone saying, "digging up clods of knowledge from one graveyard to inter them in another."

At two o'clock he handed in his books, made his way to a nearby café for something to eat, and at three o'clock arrived on time at the hospital where Mrs. Quinn was waiting for him.

"I didn't keep you waiting too long in the cold?"

"No, Mister Wade, I'm not long here," she said, though she had arrived at the gates half an hour before her time. "We had tea together and a good long chat. He's in great form and well mended. He enjoyed the fruit and hopes you'll call to see him next time you're this way."

"I'll not forget to call. Tell him that when you're writing to him."

They arrived back at the shore while there was still light in the sky, and as he drove up to her house her three children were playing shop in their father's hut, all the shutters thrown back like a booth at a fairground. They stopped in their play and stared at the car without moving. Their mother came out backways, and thinking that their father might also be in the car they stood still, their hands by their sides, their eyes fixed on the open door of the car.

"Would you not come in, Mister Wade, and have a cup of tea? We'd be right and glad to have you."

"Some other day, Mrs. Quinn, but not now. We're in for another night of frost and I'd like to get the fires going. But thanks all the same," and sounding the horn in farewell he returned along the shore road as the first stars pierced the sky.

He put a match to the already laid fire in the sitting room, and held a newspaper across it to increase the draft. The kitchen stove had long since gone out, mist had filmed the windows, and a chilly air had settled in every corner of the house. He kept his coat on, lit his lamps, made his bed, and to scatter the chill from his bones took a drink of whisky from the bottle below the sink. The bottle was more than half full, a fact that would please his mother should she happen to pay another surprise visit before Christmas.

He went to bed early and pulled his heavy coat over the eiderdown. His throat was husky, his head ached, and the fear of catching a cold increased the pulsebeat of his heart.

He got up and searched in a drawer for aspirin. He found the bottle, but the cotton wool had gone from it and the aspirin were soft as wet chalk, and clung to the roof of his mouth. He closed the window against the night air and opened the bedroom door.

He slept for a while, but sweat breaking out on him woke him into restlessness, and turning on his side he could feel the cold pressing on his back like a damp cloth. The room was deep in darkness and he sought the line of light that usually slipped through the curtains onto the opposite wall, but he failed to find it. The starlight was too feeble to penetrate the moisture on the windows and he could distinguish nothing, not even the outline of the mirror on the dressing table, and could hear no cheep from the shore birds or the breathing of the sea. The night was still, muffled in frost, and the honest and unfailing daylight would not steal over the sea until late in the morning.

From somewhere in the scullery a mouse rattled a saucepan, and some minutes later one scrabbled under the bed and fistled in a newspaper that lay in the firegrate in the room. "Shush!" Andrew shouted, and the mouse was silenced for a few minutes and then with slow, exasperating caution began once more to scratch at the paper.

Andrew got up, rattled a shoe at the fireplace and closed the bedroom door. With the hem of the curtain he wiped the mist from the window and peered out at the bright glint of stars in the sky, their thin tails of light in the water, and the sparkle of frost on the road.

With his hand he felt the cold air seep through the sashes of the window and, satisfied that enough air came in to ventilate the room, he got back to bed.

His throat was raw, and an intolerable heat suffused his whole body. "What if you fell ill and no one to go for the doctor," he remembered his mother saying. He shook his head to drive away the thought and told himself he'd be all right and that he mustn't panic. He'd stay in bed the whole day, and in the morning he'd leave the back door on the latch and ask the postman to come in and bring a message to Rock Lodge.

The decision eased his mind and he fell asleep. When he awoke the darkness had gone from the room and a fine rain was blowing in from the sea and tipping against the window like the scratch of a mouse. He pulled on the overcoat that lay on top of the bed, made his way to the kitchen, stoked up the stove, and unlocked the back door. He put on the kettle, made himself a hot drink of whisky, and got back into bed.

The postman tapped at the knocker, and Andrew spoke to

him through the window and asked him to come in by the back door because he was spending the day in bed. The postman stomped around by the side of the house, lifted the latch, and stumbled up the two steps into the kitchen. He came into the room, his face red with cold, his black cape shining like a rock on the shore. He had letters for Andrew in his wet hand and he left them on the dressing table.

"That's a bad throat you have, Mister Wade, and the only thing that will shift it is a shovelful of hot salt. Will you let me make the cure for you, and I'll have you back in harness in no time."

"If you think it will shift it I'm agreeable," and he told him where to get the salt and a shovel.

In a few minutes he returned to the room: "She's heating up now and when the damp's gone out of her she'll be ready with the cure. I'll fill up one of your old socks with the salt and tie it round your neck. It's a bad business when a lone man takes sick—a bad business entirely. But I'll not mention it to anyone for you'd have half the women of the country in to nurse you. You wouldn't want that, Mister Wade, and you such a private person."

"I would not. But, maybe, on your way back to the village you'd drop in at Rock Lodge and tell Mrs. Newman I'll not be able to get in today."

"Nor the next day nor the day after. Don't rise too soon, whatever you do," and he told of three people in the parish who got up too soon from a sickbed and were now lying in the graveyard. "I'll bring up coal for you and stoke up the range. A chilly house puts a chill on the heart and when the heart's chilled the mind chills with it and depression creeps into the body and stays there like an east wind. . . . I hear the salt crackling and eager for the job."

Taking a sock from the line and scooping the salt from the heated shovel with a spoon, he filled up the sock and carried it to the room.

"You haven't a safety pin about the place? Whisht now,

and I'll find a nail. Hold the sock round your throat and I'll be back in a jiff."

He found a nail in a canister, stapled it through the fabric of the sock, and fastened it as tight as a collar round Andrew's neck. "How's that, Mister Wade?"

"It's nice and hot and it's sure to do good. I'm very grateful to you."

"That's all right, Mister Wade. Now put your mind at ease and turn round and sleep. I'll light the fire for you in the sitting room."

"Don't go to any more trouble; you've done enough."

"It's no trouble at all, at all. I only wish I could stay the whole day with you. And that's the truth."

Andrew heard him rake out the old cinders from the grate and shovel them into the kitchen stove. The heavy movements about the house brought him comfort and restored his courage.

There would be no one coming to disturb him. The milkman would drop a bottle of milk on the grass inside the front gate and the bread man wouldn't be due on his rounds until tomorrow. There was nothing to worry about, and snuggling contentedly under the warm clothes he rejoiced in the oven-heat from the salt, and fell asleep.

A gentle knock at the front door wakened him and he lay still and wondered who it might be. He looked at his watch. It was three o'clock and the low sun was filling the room with a subdued glow. The knock came again; hearing the voices of Philip and Mrs. Newman on the verandah he got up, pulled on the overcoat that lay on the foot of the bed, combed his hair with his fingers, and opened the front door.

"We heard from the postman that you were laid up and we came out with a few things Mary cooked for you," Mrs. Newman said.

"Come in, come in. I'm glad to see you." Bidding them sit down, he broke the crust of coals on top of the fire and put new life into it.

Noticing his pallor and the huskiness of his voice, she pleaded with him to get back into bed and she would warm up some soup she had brought with her.

"Don't worry about me, Mrs. Newman. I've broken the back of the cold and I'll be all right by tomorrow."

"You'll get a relapse after leaving a warm bed—that's what will happen. Like a good man, take my advice and get back again. Or if you'd wrap yourself in warm blankets and come home with us it would ease all our minds."

"You're very kind. But I wouldn't think of that."

"If you don't come with us, then I insist on your going back to bed. You must be sensible and do that for me."

Andrew smiled, ran his hand over his unshaven chin, and looked at Philip. "Your mother's a dreadful boss, Philip. She's as strong-willed as my own mother, and that would take some beating."

He got up from the chair, shuffled back to his room, and when he was in bed Philip came in and Mrs. Newman went to the kitchen and stirred up the range fire.

"Although you've fair hair, Mister Wade," Philip said, "your beard would be black if you let it grow. But do you know, there are no hairs on that scar on your cheek."

"I'll not grow a beard then."

"If you did you'd frighten me."

"That's another reason I'll not grow one."

"I'd a letter from Anne this morning and she says my letters are improving. Would you like to see it? She says you must be a nice sort of man."

"It would be better, then, if I didn't see it. I'd become very conceited and that wouldn't be good for me."

"I sent her a photograph I took of you from an open window. It wasn't a very good one, but she liked it and asked for a different one."

"And have you taken another one?"

"No, I didn't get a chance and Mother told me not to unless I got your permission."

"I see."

"You see what?"

"That your mother has great wisdom."

"And I have none. Is that what you mean?" Philip turned to the window, rubbed the moisture off the pane and looked out at their car and the sea beyond it. The boy was hurt, and in the sudden silence that had come between them he pressed his finger on a blob of moisture that was crawling down the pane.

Andrew stretched out a hand and held the boy's sleeve. "You mustn't take things too seriously, Philip. You're my friend."

"But when Anne comes home next week you'll be her friend. I heard Grandmother say to Mother she'd pray for that."

"Prayers are not always answered in the way we want." Andrew laughed. "You'll always be my friend no matter what happens. Isn't that so? And who would have thought of coming out to see me besides you?"

"It was Mother who thought of it. And it was she who asked Mary to cook a chicken for you."

"Philip!" his mother called from the kitchen. "Come here a minute, please." Philip excused himself and left the room.

He was a strange boy, Andrew thought. He was oversensitive, overhonest, and possessed the strong self-will of the very proud. His physical infirmity nourished his determination to be independent and made him stubborn when he needed direction.

The bedroom door opened and Mrs. Newman carried in a tray. "Now, Mister Wade, sit up and take this and put something warm round your shoulders."

She rested the tray on the bed and put a hand to Andrew's forehead: "You haven't a temperature. You're nice and cool. But I'd advise you not to get up today. You'll do that—won't you?"

"I'll do what you say."

She propped the pillows at his back and placed the tray beside him.

"Drink the soup while it's hot. There's nothing like hot chicken soup for killing a cold."

"You're spoiling me. I couldn't get better attention in a posh hospital."

Outside a car door slammed and presently there was the sound of footsteps on the path and a knock at the door.

"I'll open it," Philip said, and as he did so they could hear Miss Isobel Reid exclaimed, "So it's you, is it?"

"Yes, it's me it is," Philip answered as she swept past him into the sitting room.

"Oh, I didn't expect to find you here also!" she said to Mrs. Newman, who hurried from the bedroom on hearing her voice.

"Indeed, I didn't expect to find myself here," Mrs. Newman said cheerfully, ignoring the harsh hostility of Miss Reid's remark. "I came out, I might say, on a mission of mercy. Mister Wade is laid up with a bad cold."

"And I, you might say, am here on a mercenary mission."

Philip, sensing the unfriendly tone of the conversation, slipped off unnoticed to Andrew's bedroom.

Miss Reid took a cigarette from her bag and lit it snappily with a lighter. She exhaled the smoke loudly and frowned at the low fire in the grate.

"It's no wonder our stranger has caught cold. I warned him not to spare the coal."

"The room's quite warm."

"I'm glad someone feels it warm." She twitched her shoulders and pressed back against the cushions in the chair. "And the place! Phew, it's so untidy it makes me want to scream."

"For a lone man he's not doing too badly. It always has been a neat little place."

"And the road outside! You needn't tell me it's neat too. You could break your neck on the spilled gravel. I told him it was his duty as well as mine to protect the shore from these gravel thieves. But, really, he must look the other way when they rumble past. He has no social sense. And then there's this talk about himself and Mrs. Quinn."

"What talk, Miss Reid?"

"Haven't you heard? It has been whispered he is very intimate with her. I don't know if he has yet invited her into this house of mine, but I do know he drove her to Belfast yesterday and drove her back again in the dead of night. That expedition wouldn't help his cold!"

"I don't suppose there was anything in it beyond an act of kindness. Mister Wade had to go to Belfast on some business, I presume, and Mrs. Quinn happened to be going to see her husband."

Miss Reid took the cigarette from her lips and tapped the ash from it into the scalloped shell that lay within reach. She crossed her legs: "I'm glad you brought Master Philip with you on this occasion. The neighbors might add something more to their unkind rumors."

"The neighbors, I hope, will mind their own business. I'm past the age when neighbors, as you call them, are apt to misconstrue my visit."

"I didn't mean any offense, Mrs. Newman. I just wished to put you on your guard. If unpleasant talk began to gather round this little place of mine and it should reach the ears of Father Lavelle I would be mortified."

"You shouldn't let it worry you to that extent," Mrs. Newman said with mock innocence. "When the people get to know Mister Wade they'll take to him as Philip does. Listen to the laughter of the two of them in the room. They understand one another perfectly. And Philip is making great progress in his work."

"My own sister's tuition was not up to the required standard!"

"Don't misunderstand me, please. I meant no affront whatsoever. It takes a man to handle a boy, especially one so difficult as Philip. Your sister—and I am grateful to her—did her best."

"And failed to satisfy you!"

"No, she failed to satisfy herself. And the reason for that lay with Philip."

"She has taken her dismissal very much to heart. Her nerves are unsettled since it."

"I thought her nerves would have improved when she was released from a task she loathed. It was to oblige me that she undertook the job."

"She never said so to me. You used her and then turned her out as soon as this stranger turned up from God knows where!" Miss Isobel Reid threw the stub of her cigarette in the fire, pulled on her gloves, and as she moved toward the door she deliberately drew her hand over the edge of the mahogany table and left the print of her fingers in the dust.

"Tell Mister Wade I shall call again shortly. I have a few things to settle with him."

"Perhaps I could settle them and it would save you another journey."

"It's a private matter I wish to settle with the man himself."

"Forgive me. I thought it was a mercenary matter."

"Really, Mrs. Newman, you speak as if he were your own son! And, indeed, he's old enough to be that!"

"I know him through Philip. And that satisfies me."

"I hope your satisfaction will last."

"I hope it does."

Mrs. Newman opened the door for Miss Reid, and after her car had driven off she came inside and sat in the armchair to still the rapid beating of her heart. She yearned to be alone, but the sounds coming from the adjoining room distracted her and she knew that at any moment Philip would come out to her.

She felt uneasy, and the friendliness and expectation with which she had set out on the visit were swept away by Miss Reid's outburst of ill-humor. Jealousy, and nothing more, was at the source of it. The ugly rumors, she assured herself, emanated from Miss Reid alone and not from the people themselves, people who always had, she knew, respect and friendliness for strangers who came among them. If Mr. Wade was of the kind who held himself aloof from them it would be a different matter. But in him there was no evidence of patronage or uppishness. She had often heard him speak with affection and sympathy for Mrs. Quinn and her invalid husband.

She shook her head to drive away the thought that was alien to her nature. There was nothing, of course, in that journey to Belfast—nothing but an act of friendliness. She was glad she had had the courage to say so to Miss Reid, and was glad she had braced herself against the other insinuations, insinuations that didn't seem to distress Miss Reid's conscience in any way. It was obvious she was bent on harming him, of dragging him down, and of tearing him away from Rock Lodge. But in spite of what she had said they would try to hold him. There was nothing in this rumor; it followed the same pattern as her sister's on the day she gave her her dismissal. She gripped the armrests of the chair, held herself erect, and refused to dwell any more upon it.

Philip came out to her.

"You're very quiet, Mother. What did Miss Reid say to annoy you? We heard her shouting."

"I hope she wasn't shouting. Her voice is naturally loud and she can't alter it to suit us."

"She can speak quietly when she wants to. She always

spoke quietly when she called at our house for Miss Dympna."

"Ask Mister Wade is he ready for some tea."

"He's ready ages ago. He's eating bread and chicken and I'm sure he's as thirsty as a blacksmith."

She got up with a sigh and carried in a pot of tea to the bedroom.

"You'll need a cup yourself, Mrs. Newman, after that harangue with Miss Reid. Once or twice she sounded as if she were going to maim you."

"It's her unfortunate manner that's at fault. If we had offered her a cup of tea it would have calmed or cheered her."

"It would have poisoned her, if we are to judge by the sound of her voice. I suppose she wanted another installment of the rent. I had forgotten it was due. She has demanded payment in advance and takes due care that it's done."

"She did say she had some business with you."

"The exchange of money is the only commerce I have with her and it's all I wish to have. No matter what I do I can't please her, and some fine day she'll give me my marching orders."

"And what would you do then?"

"That I don't know. I have my correspondence pupils. But that could be managed from home."

"But what about me?" Philip put in.

Andrew smiled. "We'll see about that when the time comes. I'll not let you down whatever else I do."

"That's a promise," Mrs. Newman said. "A promise we'll not hold you to if it would inconvenience you in any way."

"Would it inconvenience you, though?"

She stirred the tea in her cup and rested the spoon gently on the saucer.

"If that were to happen we would have to plan anew."

"But you'll not go! You must stay!" Philip said earnestly. "You promised to stay for a year, and you can't go back on your word. Mother wants you to stay. Grandma wants you to stay. We all want you to stay—and you will stay. I know you will! Isn't that so, Mother?"

"I suppose it is, Philip. But we must allow Mister Wade to decide for himself. We mustn't force our will on his."

"My mind is made up. I'll stay. I'll be going home for Christmas for a few days but I'll be back, never fear."

"You'll meet Anne before you go. And you'll be here again before she goes back," Philip said. "And you'll be invited to her twenty-first birthday party. Won't he, Mother?"

"Of course he will if he's here."

"But he will be here. He said so himself. Didn't you, Mister Wade?"

"Yes, I suppose I did," Andrew said, not looking at either of them. He drank the last of the tea in his cup and arranged the dishes on a neat pile on the tray. "I feel much better now and I'll be in tomorrow as usual." Then, aware of the itching sock around his throat, he explained to them how the postman had contrived to cure him and how the cure had succeeded.

"Since I came here everybody wants to do something for me: the postman ties a sock round my throat, buttons are sewn on my coat, Mary cooks a chicken for me, and Miss Reid is dying to give me my notice."

"And now, Philip, it's time we gave Mister Wade peace. Don't come tomorrow if you don't feel up to the mark. We'll not expect you. Be sensible and don't take risks."

9

Each morning of the following week Andrew arrived at Rock Lodge at his usual time and to his surprise discovered Philip in the schoolroom. The room was well heated; Philip had been there for at least half an hour, working unusually hard. He had sensed that Andrew might not return after Christmas, and being determined to prevent that he strove to please and obey him at every turn. Of all his studies geometry came the most naturally to him, and in the evenings he puzzled over problems from textbooks he had discovered in his father's bookcase and from these he often devised problems of his own.

At the end of each schoolday, if a section of work remained incomplete, he acquiesced immediately if Andrew suggested that they remain on to finish what they had begun.

At the end of that week, on the day Anne was due to arrive home, Mrs. Newman declared it a holiday and arranged with Andrew to keep her mother company while she and Philip drove in to Belfast to meet the morning boat from Glasgow. They would be back at noon or shortly after.

It was a still morning with a low sky from which snow had fallen during the night and from which more fell as the heavy car, polished by Thomas the previous day, set out on its thirty-mile journey to the city.

In the drawing room a large fire of logs had burned from early morning and the old lady was now huddled close to it, dressed in a long black frock, three rows of jet beads round her neck, and a black hat on her head as if she had just returned from a funeral. She asked Andrew to read aloud to her from the morning paper, a paper she had already read while taking her breakfast in bed. She liked to hear him read, for the sound of his strong voice gave her courage and eased a nervous unrest that always possessed her when their car was out on the wintry roads and the snow falling.

"Anne is my favorite," she said, interrupting him in the middle of the obituary column. "I hope you like her."

"I am sure I will," he said quietly.

"You don't know how she looks?"

"I've seen photographs of her," and he folded up the paper with controlled haste and tucked it under the cushion of his chair.

"She never looks well in a photograph. At least they never show her at her best. Her hair is black. But not a Jewish black, I'd have you know. And her eyes are not dark brown like her mother's. They are a greenish-gray. They're the color of a thistle before it opens out—do you know the color that is? And she dresses simply. Simplicity in dress is the greatest ornament of any dress. No heavy jewelry such as I wear. It wouldn't look well on a young girl. There are occasions, though, when it could relieve a sad expression." She paused and glanced across at him as he sat relaxed, one side of his face reddened by the fire. "Yes, yes," she went on, answering some question in her own mind. "Sorrows are a necessary discomfort which we must expect. He may scourge us, but He will deliver us; He may lead us down to the depths of suffering, but He will bring us back joy. You should read Tobias, young man, and the Psalms. The harvest grain will not dry and harden unless it faces strong winds. When I was a child I had beads made out of well-seasoned grain. They were painted as red as berries, but the mice ate them on me after I had stowed them away in a drawer. They were wrapped in tissue paper but they ate that too. Nasty things, mice." She gave a little laugh and held out her hands to the heat. "Your own mother, does she wear jewelry?"

Andrew reflected for a moment but couldn't recall anything beyond the customary wedding rings on her finger.

"Not much, as far as I can remember."

"Whatever it is it doesn't draw attention to itself and I am sure it's in good taste. You'll bring her here sometime?"

"I'll do that if she visits me again after the New Year."

"You'll be going home for Christmas and you'll be coming back. You promised that, I believe."

"I'll be back all right. My work here is not complete."

"In the New Year we want you to come every day if you can afford time off. It will benefit Philip to no end." She glanced at the clock on the mantelpiece. "They'll be here before one. Perhaps we should take a stroll round the garden and gather an appetite for lunch. The air will be cleansed of all dross."

Andrew turned his head to the window where large flakes were falling, falling slowly enough for a child to count.

"The snow is still on," he said, "and it may be rather cold, don't you think?"

"It will be quiet and the trees will be deserted. I should like you to see the garden and the garden seats upholstered in snow, and the marks of the birds' feet lying like broken twigs. It's extraordinary the different marks they make at this time of the year. And at night they hustle together in the shrubbery where the weasel or the fox can't find them."

Joining her hands on her lap she closed her eyes and thought of the hushed world outside. The waterfowl would be in their holes out of the snow; their *churruck, churruck*—a call that was fraught with danger—she would not hear. How often on a summer's day that call which seemed to contain its own echo would make her flee from the pond to the garden, and sometimes while she was there the wood pigeons hidden in the trees would call out in their slow misty voices: "Take her now Jew-man! Take her now!" The snow would silence them, and it would silence the impertinent thrush that always perched on top of the wall spying into the garden and shouting hurriedly: "She's here! She's here! Come quick! Come quick!" Winter was merciful: they'd all be sheltering except the robin, the modest wren, the thin chaffinches, and the pauper sparrows—little birds that minded their own business and were grateful for the shakings of a tablecloth. Yes, she must go and enjoy for an hour this white world of silence and security.

She stretched out her hand and pushed the bell at the side of the fireplace.

"Would it not be better to postpone our walk until Mrs. Newman comes back? We could all go together then," Andrew suggested.

"Never procrastinate, young man. What we would see now would be different from what we would see if the sun shone forth. People come out with the sun and insects emerge from underground and we would not be alone. We would be spied upon by many eyes."

The door was knocked and Mary entered.

"Please, Mary, bring me my fur coat. Mister Wade and I are going for a pleasant stroll round the garden."

"You couldn't venture out in that weather, Ma'am! The snow's falling so thick you couldn't get your breath. What would Mrs. Newman say if you were laid up and Christmas on top of us."

"Mister Wade will protect me."

"The poor boy can't protect himself. Look at the throat he gave himself last week. Do you want to kill him outright! A nice wholesome morning you select for strolling, I must say. Let Mister Wade play the piano for you. He's dying to be asked," and she signaled to Andrew with a tilt of her head. "Some Irish airs, like a good man: sad ones that will make us thankful to God that we're alive and have a good fire to sit at."

She draped a plaid rug around the old lady's shoulders, arranged the cushions at her back, and placed a hassock beside her for her feet.

"There now, that's better. We mustn't catch cold and Anne ready to step in on us at any moment and expecting to see you in your usual place."

She put more logs on the fire and brought the canary from the back of the room. "There's your friend yearning for a bit of notice. Be charitable now and talk to him."

The canary cheeped, stretched one wing and then the other, and beat out an arpeggio on the perch as if in time to the music of the piano. The old lady smiled at its antics and poked the temples of her spectacles between the bars of the cage, watching the canary grow thin and cock its head to the side.

Mary slipped away from the room, and the old lady joined her hands; drowsy from the heat and the softly playing piano, she closed her eyes and turned her mind back to the days when she was young and hunted with the hounds across the frosted fields.

She fell asleep and Andrew took up his place at the windowseat, correcting exercise books and glancing now and then at the snow falling on the roof of his car and swirling a white petticoat round the leg of a tree. He signed each of the corrected tasks with the initials *A. J. W.* and looped a little circle round them, hoping by this method to establish, without an open declaration, the correct order of his name, and in time have his tuition checks made out to A. J. Wade without a sudden and embarrassing inquiry. In that way he would free his conscience from its burden of duplicity.

The old lady's breathing turned to a sharp whistle, and lest the canary would respond with similar notes Andrew tiptoed across the carpet, and on carrying the cage back to the far end of the room heard the slamming of car doors. He looked out, and noticing two parallel tracks in the snow he knew they had arrived. He laid a hand gently on the old lady's shoulder and she wakened and stared at him in terror.

"They're here," Andrew said. "Mrs. Newman's back from the city."

He helped her to her feet, and in the pier glass above the mantelpiece she adjusted her hat that had fallen over her brow, pushed into place a few wisps of hair, and gripped her stick. But before she had time to reach the door Anne entered with Mrs. Newman.

She threw her arms round the old lady, kissed her, and stood back. "Oh, Grandma, I'm glad to be home again and to see you looking so well. It was lovely to smell burning wood as I stepped out of the car." And then she turned to Andrew and held out her hand in greeting: "I'm pleased to meet you though I seem to have known you for a long time. You have been very patient with Philip. His letters were full of you, and his descriptions were accurate and complimentary for a change."

"And had you a nice crossing?" the old lady broke in. "I must hear all about it," and while she made her sit down beside her on the hassock Mrs. Newman drew Andrew aside and inquired how he had put in his morning. He told her about the suggested stroll and how Mary had skilfully maneuvered her away from that sudden notion.

"She can be a heavy strain at times, and I'm sure you're exhausted," Mrs. Newman commented.

"Not in the least. We got on well together and when she fell asleep I was able to correct all Philip's homework. He's developing very quickly."

"We feel that, and we are all very pleased. You'll come back after Christmas—won't you?"

"Yes, I promised that, Mrs. Newman. Why do you ask?"

"I don't really know. I feel that you may be lonely here and that your mother may prevail on you not to return."

"I have a thesis to write, I have my correspondence courses, and I have Philip. I haven't much time to be lonely or even to think of it."

Anne was kneeling now beside her grandmother, holding her hands in hers, and talking to her with great liveliness. Then she jumped to her feet, took off her own hat, a gray tweed like a fisherman's, and then carefully took off her grandmother's.

"You'll be staying for lunch, Mister Wade," she called across the room.

"Of course he will," her mother answered. "We can't make use of him and then turn him away. He'll be here till evening, we hope."

"I'll go now and see Mary," Anne smiled and was gone.

At the lunch table Andrew was seated next to her. She talked about Edinburgh, a city she liked in spite of a rampant east wind that blew round every corner of it, a wind that kept one on the alert and was reputed to sharpen to a keen edge the dullest mind. She told him about her studies, and then with guileless naturalness she asked him about his own university and why he had drifted up here of all places. Detecting no premeditated inquisitiveness in her manner, he told her as much about himself as he could: his courses at the university, his teaching school for some years, and resigning because he yearned to write a thesis on the old Charter Schools that had been situated in this part of the country. Of the court case—the real reason for his resignation—he made no mention. Some day he would tell them, but that time was not ripe. To further questioning he told her that he was an only child, that his father was retired and was living in Gilvalley. Whether Father Lavelle had already told them these things he did not know, but the fact of his telling them cleared his mind of a burden that had weighed heavily upon him since his arrival in the bungalow. In some way—how he did not yet know—they would learn of his public exposure and, he hoped, the injustice of it.

Philip, at the other end of the large table, stared across at them and said suddenly:

"Anne, you shouldn't be talking about me in my presence. It's very rude."

"We're not talking about you, Mister Eavesdropper. We're talking about something more interesting."

"If you are you don't want me to hear."

"What do you intend to do after lunch, Philip?" his mother interrupted.

"I'll take out the sleigh if Mister Wade helps me. Won't you come?" he asked Andrew. "Just this once, please. We mightn't have snow again this winter."

"Could you not give Mister Wade a little peace?" the old lady said. "He's not equipped for the snow."

"I know where there's a pair of sea boots that will fit him. He'll come because I've asked him."

"You're a stubborn little boy," Anne said. "You want your own way no matter whom it inconveniences."

"If Mister Wade wishes to go out for a while that will be all right," Mrs. Newman said. "But you may count Anne out of it. She'll be tired after her journey. A rest is what she needs."

"I'm not in the least bit tired, Mother. I'll join them later."

"Yes!" said Philip. "When we've the donkey-work done—the sleigh cleaned and dusted and maybe a new rope fitted to it."

He excused himself, struggled up from his place, and taking Andrew by the sleeve they made off to a store in the basement where they retrieved the sleigh from the rafters, and from a tea chest drew out a pair of Wellingtons that were stiff and cracked, a piece coming off in Andrew's hand as he pressed his feet into them. They hauled the sleigh to the top of the slope near the avenue and the dogs followed, chasing each other through the snow, boxing one another playfully, and coughing hoarsely when the snow jammed their nostrils.

By the time Anne appeared, dressed in tartan trousers and stockings and wearing a tight-fitting yellow jersey and woolen cap, the sleigh had already dredged a smooth surface on top of the snow, and from the windowseat in the drawing room Mrs. Newman with her mother were looking out at them. Philip was lying full length in the sleigh and Anne was pushing him off and sliding down behind him with Andrew close beside her. Then they saw her fall, roll over, and jump to her feet, laughing. Both, then, hauled on the sleigh rope, one at each side, and returned with Philip to the top of the slope, their voices clear in the sharp air.

Anne took her turn, sitting upright and holding the rope like a pair of reins. Andrew pushed her off, and before the sleigh had gathered full speed he hopped lightly onto the back of it, his hands resting on her shoulders.

"I hope they don't catch cold, Mother. It would be too bad if Mister Wade got a relapse."

"The clean air and exercise will be good for him. The snow has ceased."

"I don't think they should stay out too long. They've had enough for one day. Should I call them in?"

"Let them enjoy themselves, Helena. The darkness will fall down quickly enough."

She saw Philip sitting in the snow at the top of the slope, the dogs having fled after the sleigh, and she opened the window and called out to him to get up at once or he'd catch a cold.

He obeyed her immediately and moved toward Andrew's car that was parked close by, and on the layer of snow on the hood he scratched out his initials *P N* and below it *J W*. And then, suddenly conscious of the stillness around him, he saw Anne and Mr. Wade stride away from the sleigh at the foot of the paddock and move off through the trees in the direction of the pond. He cupped his hands to his mouth and called to them. His voice traveled clearly but they did not turn or wave to him. He called again, his voice coarse and compelling, edged with anger.

Andrew halted and waved to him, and Anne called out that they would be back in a minute. The dogs followed them, but Philip blew his whistle and they turned and ran up to him. With one rapid stroke he swept away the initials and set off down the slope, avoiding the polished path made by the sleigh. At the foot of the slope he saw Anne through the bare trees hurling stones at the little islets of snow that lay on the lily pond. For a moment he hesitated, wondering whether he should follow her, but when he saw her scoop the snow from the garden seat and throw it furtively at Andrew he turned and gripped the rope of the sleigh and endeavored to haul it up the slope by himself. Halfway up he stumbled and fell; he rose at once, but one of the dogs jumped up on him, and he fell again, one elbow striking the side of the sleigh and sending a line of pain through his arm. He clawed at the gripless snow and tried to rise but his legs failed him, and through his tears saw Andrew hurrying toward him. But before Andrew could reach him he had managed to wriggle his chest onto the sleigh and by pressing with his full weight, to prevent it slipping, he had with one final heave got to his feet.

"Why didn't you wait for us?" Andrew said out of breath.

"You've no time for me! You've fallen in love with Anne."

"Don't be silly, Philip."

"It's true and you can't deny it."

"I can deny it."

"I wouldn't believe you if you did."

"There's no point in my denying it, then. You say things too old for your years. Now no more of this nonsense, Philip. Sit tight and I'll drag you to the top."

"It's not nonsense. I feel it deep inside me."

Andrew smiled, leaned forward, and pulled on the rope. His feet were wet and cold because of the snow that oozed through the cracked rubber of his boots.

Anne hallooed to them and Andrew turned round and waved to her.

"Don't go!" Philip said.

"Come quickly! A fox," Anne called.

Andrew let the rope go slack and it fell on the snow. Dusk

had gathered among the trees and he could just distinguish her yellow jersey and no more. A light appeared in a doorway of one of the outbuildings and above their snowy roofs a few moist stars were visible.

"Don't go, I tell you!" Philip replied as Andrew was about to leave him. "She wants your company but not mine."

Andrew crouched low till his face was on a level with Philip's.

"What's wrong with you at all? You're behaving strangely."

"I'll tell you something. Anne was engaged!"

"I don't want to hear any more." He gripped the rope, turned his back on the sleigh, and ran with it to the edge of the avenue.

"She was engaged to a married man," the boy went on. "She didn't know he was married. It was all broken off and hushed up. He was an officer in a ship."

"Philip, I'm disappointed in you. You told me something I shouldn't hear." He looked down at him sitting on the sleigh; his hands red with cold, crumbling the snow.

"You must tell your sister you told me this."

"Never!"

"Then I'll forget about it."

"You'll never forget about it, because you're in love with her."

"You're angry, Philip, and you must control it. Do you hear me?" He put his hand under the boy's chin and tried to make him look up.

"I'm not angry!" Philip shrugged him away.

Anne plodded up to them, her figure dark against the snow.

"I saw a fox," she said and stopped to gather breath. "It was at the far side of the pond. It stared at me and I was frightened. But when I called out it fled through the shrubbery."

"A fox! I'm sure it was an old dog from the village," Philip said.

"If you had seen it it would have been a fox. But because I saw it it is only a dog in your estimation."

"We'll go in," Andrew said quietly. "I'm afraid these boots are leaking."

"I should think they are," Anne said, seeing a sole had detached itself from the upper and was lying open like the mouth of a dogfish.

Lights had sprung up in the house, and the framework of the windows was outlined on the snow. Philip sat on the sleigh, and Anne and Andrew, one at each side of the rope, dragged it to the storeroom at the back of the house. They switched on the light and their shadows spreading out through the open door mingled with the shadow of Mrs. Newman as she drew the heavy curtains in the drawing room. The storeroom was cold and their breaths turned white in the light as they propped the wet sleigh against one wall.

They went around to Mary's kitchen and the three dogs slunk in behind them, glancing at Mary, awaiting a curt dismissal. The room was hot and smelled of the damp linen she was ironing at the table. She was listening to the radio at the same time, and she switched it off when they entered and drew chairs near the humming range, glad of their company.

"You must be famished," she said, feeling Philip's jacket and Anne's jersey. Andrew carried his shoes in his hand, but when she saw the broken boots on his feet she ordered him to take them off and hurry to the bathroom and plunge his feet into warm water. From a drawer she fished out a pair of gray stockings and told him to squeeze his feet into them and give her his wet socks and she'd rinse them out and have them dry by the time he'd be ready to go home. She crouched beside him and while he held on to the seat of his chair she pulled off the rubber boots that encased his feet. His trousers were wrinkled and dark with wet, and when he had peeled off his socks his feet were red and ridged by the fabric of the sock, and she handed him a rough towel to put life in them.

"You embarrass me with kindness," he said.

"What would your mother think if you arrived at Christmas with a heavy thumper of a cold on you. Be sensible now and do what you're told," and she threw him an old pair of carpet slippers and made him stand close to the fire till the steam ceased to rise from the wet folds of his trousers.

When he had gone off to the bathroom and the dogs had slunk out from under the table and had nosed their way between the chairs Philip began to say softly: "Mary, I'll tell you a secret. Anne is in love."

"With whom, pray?" Anne said.

"With Mister Wade."

"I'll cuff your ears, Philip, if you ever say that again. It's not in the least bit funny."

"You mustn't anger your sister," Mary said. "And what's more you'll annoy Mister Wade if he hears you, and he mightn't come back here after Christmas and you'd be left without a teacher. Of course Miss Reid is still round the corner if you'd prefer her!"

"And that would be the price of him, Mary."

"Well, I just thought you might be in love," Philip said.

"Think something else for a change, something in keeping with your age. Don't be making remarks about a complete stranger, remarks that make me uncomfortable. And don't ever say those things in Mister Wade's presence."

"I'm sorry," Philip said and he stared through the bars of the grate at the red heart of the fire.

10

"YOU'LL NOT see Anne this morning," Philip greeted him next day. "She went to Mass and rang up to say she was having breakfast with Father Lavelle. You'll be disappointed."

"Come now, Philip, and buckle down to a bit of work."

"Are you vexed with me about what I told you yesterday?"

"I was surprised you hadn't more self-control."

"You're displeased with me."

"I'll be pleased if you get to work," and lifting an exercise book he corrected a few difficulties Philip had encountered in his algebra and geometry. He then gave him some problems to do that had similar difficulties, and when he had these mastered he turned to his French lessons, and later to English, and while Philip was writing a short appreciation of Wordsworth's "Westminster Bridge" Andrew strolled to the back of the room where the rocking horse lay on its side and the telescope stood with a cover over it like an old-fashioned camera.

He took out from his pocket a letter from his mother and reread it. It was in answer to one he had written telling her he would probably spend his Christmas in Dublin, for if he stayed on in the bungalow he would become an object of suspicion as well as sympathy. In her letter she pleaded with him to come home and enclosed a ten-pound note in case he should need it. A visit now would reveal an attachment to his home, she said, and would give new heart to his father, who had been depressed of late. He pondered each sentence, weaving into them the things that were left unsaid.

His conscience urged him to obey her but his oversensitiveness sought an excuse. He envisaged his presence in the town, the meeting with former friends, their recalling of the court case and, perhaps, their uttering a disingenuous remark about injustice. No, he couldn't bear it. And if he did go, and only ventured out at night, he'd still have his father to contend with, a man who thought it virtuous to speak his mind. No, he couldn't face it. His mother didn't understand—if she did she wouldn't press him. And yet he couldn't remain on in the bungalow, the Newmans inviting him to their Christmas dinner and wondering to themselves what had he done to prevent his returning home. He must go away, but where?—he'd decide that later.

He placed the rocking horse upright, and though it rocked a few times Philip didn't turn to look at it. The boy had the grace of stillness about him, a quality nourished by his disablement. The speedy scratch of his pen traveled to the back of the room, and a wintry sun stared through the window and shone on the boy's head. Below the window the snow had already melted from the lawns and the grass lay flat as if a river had poured over it during the night.

Andrew strode up to the head of the room and sat down. Philip, after a quick flourish of his pen, raised his head and said he had finished. Andrew took the loose sheet and stowed it in his attaché case.

"Ah, are you not going to criticize it?"

"Not just now; I'll correct it this evening and bring it back the day after tomorrow. I'm going to Belfast tomorrow."

"And it will be signed *A J W* and not the usual *J A W* for fear I'd nickname you 'Jaw.' Is that the reason for the change?"

"I've two Christian names: Andrew and John."

"Anne would prefer Andrew. Saint Andrew, you see, is the patron saint of Scotland."

"I wouldn't mind the change."

"Would you like to know what they said about you last night?"

"It's not your duty to tell me and it's not my business to know what was said about me in my absence. If you continue like this I'll loathe coming back here. I mean that!"

"Who's losing control now, I'd like to know."

"I've every reason to be annoyed. Come now, be sensible. Let me hear the few scraps from Wordsworth I asked you to learn."

"You're allowed to be angry but I'm not! It's not fair. Anne thinks you're nice and Grandmother says—"

"It's Wordsworth I want to hear! 'As the mute swan . . .' "

"Do you want me to stand or sit?"

"Whichever you prefer."

Philip cleared his throat:

"As the mute swan that floats adown the stream,
Or, on the waters of the unruffled lake,
Anchors her placid beauty.

"*Anchors* is a lovely word, Philip. Go on, another few lines. Lines that have appealed to you."

Philip scratched the back of his head: *"Many a time at evening when the earliest stars began to move along the edges of the hills.* Do you know, Mister Wade, I often say those lines when I'm in bed and can see the stars slink above the trees. And when I waken I often say *While the morning light was yellowing the hilltops* or, if I see Thomas carrying buckets of grain to the byres I repeat *stringed like a poor man's heifer at his feed* or, seeing my mother, I say in my own mind *she who was the heart and hinge of all our learnings and our love."*

"Good work, Philip. And here are a few more lines about a swan that you may make a note of. An Irishman, W. B. Yeats, wrote them:

So arrogantly pure, a child might think
It can be murdered with a spot of ink.

"We'll now read a section Wordsworth wrote about a winter among the hills and about skating in the moonlight. It would be an appropriate time to read them."

"It would not. The snow's gone and there'll be no ice over Christmas,—so the weather reports said over the radio. For your sake I was glad to hear that. I'm always afraid your old car will skid and land you over the hedge. . . . Put old Wordsworth away and let us talk for a while. Please?" He rested his head on his elbows on the desk and smiled up at him. "I nearly forgot to tell you: Anne was right after all about the fox. I saw him myself this morning."

"And you only believe what your own eyes tell you?"

"I really didn't believe Anne yesterday. I thought she only said it in order to take you away from me."

"It would be a sly fox that could do that."

"Mister Wade, you don't keep in bad form for very long!" Lowering his head, he doodled with a pencil on the desk.

"Did you apologize to Anne for contradicting her?"

"I didn't get a chance. But I will if you promise to come back here after Christmas."

"Why must you exact a promise over that? Your own conscience tells you what to do and you must heed that. I've told you already I'm coming back and I will."

"They said last night that you mightn't. They think this place is too lonely for you."

"The days will brighten after Christmas and the dark nights will shorten."

"But before that there'll be my party and you'll not be here for it. Every year Thomas digs up the Christmas tree and when we're finished with it he plants it back again in a corner in the garden. Five years ago I was big as it and now it's taller than Anne. Thomas says this will be its last year, for it's getting too big to cart around. It will be rigged up in the drawing room at the bay window and if you were in the village you could see its lights through the trees if you knew where to stand. It would be great if you were here for the party and tearing up the pieces of paper into designs—the boys would enjoy that. But you'll be here for Anne's birthday party. It'll be a swell affair. You'll be one of the first to be invited, I heard them saying."

"I'll enjoy that."

"And when the good weather comes we'll have *Razorbill* in the water and you'll enjoy that too. We'll enter her for every race in the lough." The brown eyes brightened. "Oh, you'll love it then, Mister Wade, and we could take the punt and go fishing up the lough. And maybe you'll teach me to swim. I read in the papers that boys like me can be taught to swim. They can be carried into the water and it seems—well, that they can swim." He smiled, a broken sort of smile, in anticipation of that accomplishment.

Andrew looked at his watch and put away his books, and as he was driving along the avenue he saw the Newmans' car coming toward him and he slowed down and moved close to the edge. It was Anne, and she drew up beside him and stopped. She lowered the window.

"How did Philip do this morning, Mister Wade?"

"I think he's doing very well."

"You're having a good influence on him." She had no make-up on and the pallor of her face emphasized the blackness of her hair and the thistle-green—or was it gray—of her eyes. Her kid gloves smoothed the steering wheel.

"Father Lavelle called to see you, I believe. It's up to you to call on him. He'd love that. He leads a lonely enough life, lonelier even than your own."

"Mine may seem lonely but it really isn't. My work fills it to the brim." And he told her he would be doing some more historical digging in the Belfast libraries tomorrow and that at the end of the week he might go to Dublin for the same purpose and then set out for home for Christmas.

"You'll write to Philip—won't you? He'll be counting the days until your return."

"He'll have you."

"Yes." She smiled, showing her fine teeth. "Somebody to quarrel with, I'm afraid. He never quarrels with you, I believe."

"Being his teacher I don't allow such liberties."

"Any time I try to teach him he sulks. We get along better at a distance. When I'm in Scotland he writes the most friendly letters, full of affection, an affection that seems to freeze once I appear in person."

"His real self is in the letters. The harmless quarrels are a sign of intimacy."

"I'd prefer less intimacy if that's the case. I hope you get a letter with his real self. He'll be yearning for your return, and so will my grandmother. She's a different person since you came. Good-by now. I'll see you tomorrow."

"No, the day after."

"Oh, I forgot. I'll see you then." She set the engine going, waved her hand, and moved off.

A lovely girl, he said to himself—made finer, he supposed, by her broken engagement. Yes, and he would call to see Father Lavelle, but he'd leave that to the last.

Near the bungalow he met the Quinn boys and told them he'd call for their mother in the morning if she wanted a lift to the hospital; it would be his last trip to the city until after Christmas.

That afternoon and late into the evening he worked hard, correcting the final pre-Christmas papers of his correspondence pupils and hoping that most of them would continue with him next term. They were all conscientious workers and he hoped that some day—in summer if he were still here—he could arrange a picnic for them, have an open day and invite his mother to take charge.

He didn't notice the fire dying out, and it was the sudden

chill in the room and the loss of pressure in the lamps that made him realize the lateness of the hour. He shivered, flexed his arms, and going to the scullery he made himself some hot punch from the whisky that had lain so long untouched.

Next morning he was a bit late arriving at the Quinns' and he apologized to her as she sat down beside him in her blue raincoat with a basket on her lap. And as on the previous occasion he stopped in the village square and gave her the morning's paper to read until he came back from his errand across the ferry.

He had two of Mrs. Newman's checks to cash and he approached the cashier's desk in a hurry. The bank was deserted, the cashier was leafing through a ledger, and as he turned and looked at Andrew his face stiffened in silent surprise. Andrew reddened. The clerk took off his spectacles and stretched out his hand.

"Andy Wade! Where on earth did you drop from! I haven't laid an eye on you since . . . since you left home." He joined his hands and rested them on the desk, in no hurry to transact business. In a low voice, not wishing to be heard by other members of the staff working in their partitioned compartments, Andrew told him he was living at the other side of the lough, was engaged on a thesis for a higher degree, and was doing a bit of private tuition in his spare time.

A typewriter clicked pleasantly. The clerk looked around, then leaned forward and spoke quietly. "If you like this place as much as I do you'll not be long here. I was posted to this dump a fortnight ago and it seems like six months. Give me your address and I'll call some evening for a good yarn. I could call on a Sunday or on a Saturday afternoon."

"I live in a very inconvenient place. You'd have to cross the ferry and walk nearly four miles to get me."

"I'd swim across for one good evening, and I wouldn't mind the walk." Once more he looked around, then spoke in a very low voice about the court case and how mean and vulgar it was of Burns to drag him before the public. He related how everyone in the old bank was disgusted with the action and how there was a clean sweep after it: Burns shifted in quick style to the mountainy breezes of the south and the cashier shifted to some Godforsaken place in north Mayo.

He put a hand to the side of his mouth and winked. "And then the axe fell on me. And this is where I'm exiled. I'll die of boredom or the DTs if they keep me here long."

Andrew, eager to get away and aware that talk would induce more talk, handed over his two checks. "You'll get over it."

As the clerk was putting on his spectacles Andrew told him that the checks were payment for tuition he gave a young Newman boy of Rock Lodge.

"Mrs. Newman was here the other day. A very attractive person in spite of her age. I'd say she was a fine-looking woman in her young days."

"You may give it to me in single notes."

"They're made out to John Wade."

"The clerk who was here before you made no bones about that. My full name is Andrew John but for some reason they call me John. Either name is in order."

"I see." The clerk eyed him with benevolent understanding. "I see. Yes, yes, I see." He counted out the notes and asked how and where he could find him.

Andrew lifted a lodgement form, drew a penciled map on the back of it, and marked the bungalow with an X.

"But you mustn't come over till after Christmas. I'm going home for a few days."

Two men entered the bank and Andrew snapped at the opportunity to get away.

"I'll see you soon again. You'll be acclimated by that time."

"Remember me to all the friends in Gilvalley." He waved a hand and turned to attend the two men.

Andrew never cared much for this Tim Doonan. He was too smooth-voiced and too fond of the drink and the cards for his taste. In a few minutes Tim, he thought, would be seeking out the bank manager and saying "Do you know that chap who has just gone out? Did you ever hear of a manager in our bank by the name of Dan Wade?"

"I heard of him, but I never met him," the bank manager would say.

"Well, that's a son of his."

"But I thought he had only one son. A fellow that was involved in a nasty court case."

"That's the very man that has just gone out. He left Gilvalley after the action and it was rumored he had gone abroad or to England to live it down. I don't suppose Mrs. Newman knows who he is."

"That matter is outside our domain. We are chiefly concerned with private, financial business."

Yes, he said to himself, that would be the drift of their conversation but not the end of it. Each Sunday, if he weren't careful, he would have Doonan on his doorstep. But he would try not to encourage him. Drinking and playing cards and swapping dirty stories wasn't his idea of an enjoyable evening. If he could contrive to be paid in cash and not by check he might manage to keep him at a comfortable distance.

In the car on his way to Belfast he strove to push aside his self-absorption, to concentrate on the road, and to talk to the thin silent woman beside him. He spoke of her husband and the great pity it was that he wouldn't be allowed home for Christmas. Yes, she said, they would all miss him, the boys especially. He inquired what they intended to do when they grew up, but whether she answered him or not he couldn't say, for his mind had once more returned to Tim Doonan and to evenings he had met him at the Burns', where their usual musical program was spoiled by Doonan's pleading for card games at high stakes. Somehow Doonan always got his way, and the evenings became stiff and silent, not a word spoken until each game was ended and laments passed for not having played this or that.

"His loud mocking laugh made me sick."

"Whose laugh?" Mrs. Quinn asked, jolting him back to the present moment.

"Forgive me. I was thinking of a group at home."

He drove badly, shifting the gears roughly on a hill, the car slowing down and then bouncing forward in kangaroo leaps.

"I'm sorry," he said, the woman beside him not knowing what he was being sorry for.

In the library he delved into old parliamentary reports on the state of education in Ireland, opened them at the pages that dealt with the Charter Schools, and strove to make notes while his mind continually turned to the sudden encounter with Doonan. He put down his pen and tried to gain self-control. He can do me no harm because I've done no harm, he assured himself. I'm worrying unnecessarily.

He shrugged his shoulders, and in his pocket diary tabulated some things he must do before leaving the city. He would buy a fountain pen for Philip as a Christmas present and a few clockwork toys for the Quinn boys. He mustn't allow Doonan to paralyze his mind; he must concentrate on the present moment and swerve away from this crippling sensitivity. He must be active and think more of others and less about himself.

He sighed, tore a sheet from his notebook, and with an instinctive rush of filial loyalty wrote to his mother to say he would go home for Christmas.

Before leaving the city he posted the letter, bought his presents, and set out for the hospital. He was early and he drove up the avenue to the hospital and sought out Mr.

Quinn's ward. Mrs. Quinn was getting ready to leave when he entered.

Her husband was half-seated in the bed, his head propped against three pillows. Since leaving his wooden hut that overlooked the sea he had got stouter and his cheeks had no longer the deathlike color that forced Mrs. Quinn to hush the children at their play.

"I'm right and glad to see you, Mister Wade," and he held Andrew's hand firmly as he spoke to him. "You're very kind to give my wife a lift. I may tell you it means much to us."

"It's no trouble to me as I am coming in in any case. And in the New Year I'll be coming oftener and your wife can join me any time she wishes."

"I'm glad you'll be with us for another while. The shore road's a lonely place at night and it's a great comfort to us to see another light shining onto the sea. I wish to the good God I was at home to see it."

"Now, Pat, content yourself; fretting won't help," his wife said, buttoning her coat.

"Ah, if the spring were here they might give me my walking papers." He clenched his fist, opened it slowly, and gazed at the pale palm of his hand. "I'd mend quicker at home. The air is good and strong and when your own are around you the days don't seem long."

With her fingers his wife combed back the hair from his brow and told him she'd be in again on Christmas Eve and bring the boys.

"I'll see them in the spring of the year. You can't put that expense on yourself."

"They could all have come in with me today if I'd thought of it," Andrew said.

"They're bad travelers, the three of them. They'd be sick all over your car," Mrs. Quinn said.

"It would be worse for you if they were sick all over the bus. I'll tell you what we'll do. We'll bring the three of them here tomorrow morning. I'll drive slowly and we'll let them out for a run in the air every now and then. How would that do?"

They protested loudly, then shamefacedly lowered their voices in case the other patients in the ward thought they were quarreling.

"It's all settled," Andrew declared. "Unless the old car breaks down we'll be here in the morning. And, please God, I'll have them back at home again in time for their dinner."

On setting off again he asked Mrs. Quinn to remind him to stop in the village: he'd have to phone the Rock Lodge people and tell them he wouldn't be in until tomorrow afternoon.

"But you shouldn't upset your day because of us, Mister Wade."

"They'll not mind in the least."

"I suppose they won't. Mrs. Newman has been more than good to me since my husband went away. But she wouldn't want anyone to know that. And the poor woman has had more than her share of trouble, as you well know."

Here was his opportunity to find out more about the Newmans than he already knew. He had only to ask a few questions for the woman beside him to give tongue from the warmth of confidence. But having hushed Philip from speaking of Anne's engagement, it would be mean of him to ferret it out from another source, like spying on people through the telescope.

"Yes, her life is hard," was all he said, "and yours is too."

"But I've my three boys, and they're all strong and healthy, thank God. We've all something to be thankful for if we only take the trouble to look round us."

"Health's a great blessing," he said conventionally, and to ward off more talk he began to sing. The time flew past like the hedges, and it was still bright when he made his phone call, and bright enough for the children to play when he left Mrs. Quinn at her house and handed her the parcel with the clockwork toys and told her he'd call in the morning.

11

BEFORE LEAVING for the Christmas holidays Andrew spent his last evening at the Newmans. The large drawing room had all its lights ablaze, and in the bay window the Christmas tree had been installed, each branch abloom with lights, and on the topmost twig an illuminated five-pointed star outshone the rest.

At one side of the fire Mrs. Newman was finishing a scarf, a Christmas present, for her mother, and at the large elliptical table Philip was constructing a cabin cruiser, a squeezed tube of glue beside him and a sheet of brown paper protecting the polished table from the strokes of his knife. Opposite him sat Anne in a green frock, a pile of envelopes and invitation cards in front of her. Andrew moved around the Christmas tree tying crackers to the tips of all the branches and searching now and again for the scissors he was forever mislaying amid the parceled boxes that lay at his side of the table. The old grandmother had already fallen asleep from the heat of the fire, and between her and Mrs. Newman two dogs lay on their sides on the hearthrug.

The room was very bright, bright from the lights of the two chandeliers and the dimmer-colored lights that hung like fruit in the branches of the tree. The canary cage, too, its bars streaked with light, was a thing of polished brightness. Mrs. Newman paused often at her knitting to glance at the activity around the table, and when her eyes were not on it she was still conscious of the sounds that were made: the rattle of the scissors, the click of Philip's braces, or the soft thump of Anne's fist as she pressed down the seals of the envelopes.

Mrs. Newman sighed and gave a tired smile. She should be

filled with joy these days, she said to herself; yet in spite of everything her heart was heavy, for her thoughts swung back to past Christmases when her husband was alive, and her son Frank also home and with no thought of marrying and settling in Hong Kong. There was a similar purposeful activity in those days, her husband helping make the little boat, Anne reading a book or making a doll's frock, and Philip strapped in his chair, his little deformed legs, thin as pencils, devoid of those restless movements that belong to every healthy child. She sighed again, and one of the dogs whined in its sleep and moved a paw convulsively.

This time three years ago, she said to herself, Anne was seated at the same table, an engagement ring on her finger, a ring that flashed as she smoothed back her hair or hung a cracker on the branch of the tree. She was a happy girl then, but when Father Lavelle had discovered that her fiancé was already married she had broken down, and for weeks on end she didn't leave the house or the garden. Except for Father Lavelle they wouldn't have known what to do. It was his firm and encouraging help that saved them. It was he who had persuaded her to lift herself up and to study in another country where by hard work and God's grace she would learn to subdue her sorrow.

Anne was happier now than she had ever seen her this past two years—and Philip was less peevish, less self-willed since Mr. Wade had come among them. But it's a pity he has to go away for a while; somehow he has made himself one of the family and if only he were here for Christmas he'd bring back a sense of the past and a sense of that strength and confidence and security that they all feel when a man they could trust was moving about the place.

Philip dropped his knife on the table and she looked around with a start. He held the boat up in his hands, examined the bow, the stern, and the cabin with its two windows, one of red glass and one of green. He placed it on its keel on the table and pushed it gently along, his head sideways as he scrutinized its lines and its movements. She rested the knitting on her lap and smiled.

When the boat was finished and the rough-glass lamp filled with colza oil and placed in the hull he would be pleading with her to come down to the pond to launch it. And she would have to go in spite of the darkness and the cold, push her feet into musty Wellingtons, and stand in the chilly air that hung around the dead eye of the pond. Since Frank's time it had always been the custom to launch it at night, its red and green reflections in the water affording them great joy. But for her it would bring nothing but sadness, burdened with many bright memories which death and exile had edged with sorrow. But she must strive to hide those memories and bestir herself, however forced it may be, to rid herself of this melancholic mood.

"Let me see the boat for a moment, Philip," she asked, and he brought it over to her and told her to hold it gently as the glue was not quite dry.

"It's beautiful," she exclaimed. "It's even nicer than last year's. And have you decided on its name yet?"

"Yes, *Saint Andrew.*"

"And why, may I ask, did you choose that?"

"In honor of Mister Wade. Andrew is one of his names as well as John. And I also thought of Anne: Saint Andrew, you see, is the patron saint of Scotland."

At that moment Andrew had his back to them as he furtively tied to a branch a narrow box containing a fountain pen for Philip, and on hearing his name he turned round involuntarily, but neither Philip nor Mrs. Newman seemed aware of him and he blushed and hurriedly picked up another box, rustling the paper vigorously to prevent any more of the conversation from reaching him.

Philip returned to the table and Andrew continued to print names on the parcels and score them off from a printed list in front of him. Occasionally he would inquire from Philip who the particular boys were, and he would learn that one was the doctor's son and owned a .22 rifle, that another was a great mimic and could play an accordion, and others were stamp collectors, breeders of white rabbits, or makers of model yachts as good as any that could be bought in a toy shop.

And when all the parcels, decorated with Christmas wrapping, had been affixed to the branches, Andrew moved around to Anne's side of the table to help with the invitations to her party.

"There's your invitation," she said, "and you can't make an excuse it wasn't delivered. Philip's a witness."

"Yes," Philip said, glancing over the hull of his boat. "I see all."

"I'll be here, never fear," Andrew said, looking at his name *John Andrew Wade* printed in ink on a dotted line in the center of the card.

"That's a prompt reply at any rate. If they were all so prompt it would save me many a headache." With a quick lick of her tongue she sealed another envelope and began to print the address upon it.

At the fire the old lady stirred in her armchair, opened her eyes, and rubbed them gently with her finger.

"I must have fallen asleep, Helena. What time is it by that clock? Good gracious, I must have slept for an hour or more!"

"You needed it, Mother."

"I'll pay up for it later on. I'll lie awake for hours once I'm in bed."

"It doesn't matter a great deal when one sleeps or where."

Philip printed ST. ANDREW with indelible ink on each side of the bow and carried the boat over to his grandmother.

"No, no, Grandma, don't take it in your hands. I'll hold it."

"It's the loveliest I've ever seen. You should keep this one."

"And not launch it at all!"

"No, I don't mean that. I mean you shouldn't burn it with the holly and other things."

"But we must burn it. It's the custom. Isn't that so?" he appealed to his mother for corroboration.

"That's for you to decide."

"But I want to sacrifice it, no matter how good it is." He paused and looked from one to the other. "I must do what was done in other years. She's ready for launching now. Come on with us, Mother."

"Couldn't you postpone the launching till tomorrow night?"

"I couldn't. Mister Wade won't be here then."

"Aren't three of you enough to launch it without dragging your mother out into the cold?" the grandmother said.

"But she comes every year. Don't you, Mother?"

"I'll stay here and look at it from the window. There are other nights for me to see it."

"But it'll not be the same then, and the rain might seep in and quench the light."

It was something he looked forward to each year: the launching of the boat, and then on the twelfth day after Christmas retrieving it with a long fishing rod, removing the glass bowl from the hull, soaking a rag with paraffin and setting the boat alight. It would drift across the pond, flare up like a torch, slowly disintegrate, the lighted strips hissing for a minute on the water, proclaiming the end of another Christmas and all its joys.

"All right, I'll go with you," the mother said, rolling up her knitting.

"And you, Grandma. Would you look at it through the telescope? I'll focus it for you?" Philip said.

"I'll stay where I am, thanks. Your cold schoolroom is

no place for an old woman. You can tell me all about it when you come back."

"All ready," he ordered, coming to the table and putting his hand on Anne's shoulder. "Come on. Mother's away to get ready."

"Have patience, please, till I finish another two cards. Don't forget the box of matches like you did last year."

He placed the boat on the table and watched her. Her black hair shone in the light, and the charms on her bracelet jingled on the table as she moved the pen.

"Anne," he said, smiling, "try to write without putting out your tongue. I bet you couldn't."

She raised her head and shrugged her shoulders. Her lips were moist, and her eyes in the lights from the Christmas tree were brighter than he had ever seen them.

"Oh, Anne, you said you'd only do two and now you're doing another. It's not a bit fair and you've told a lie into the bargain."

"I suppose we'll have to go," she sighed and passed two envelopes to Andrew to put stamps on.

And presently with heavy coats on they moved into the darkness of the night. A light shone from an outbuilding where Thomas was bedding down the cattle for the night, and behind them an inclined plane of light shone from Mary's kitchen and from the second story the lights on the Christmas tree shone in a blur through the moisture on the windowpanes.

In the darkness Mrs. Newman linked Andrew's arm, recalling other times when she had come out on the same mission with her husband, Philip in his arms holding a small boat.

Presently they reached the black path that led under the trees to the pond. A chilly breath came from the water and a faint gray like new steel marked out its oval surface. The leaves that lay upon it during the autumn had been submerged by the weight of recent snow and the level of the water had almost reached the edge of the path.

The top of the oil bowl was removed and Andrew struck a match and lit the wick that projected from a metal disc based with cork. The light shone red on his face and on the vapor of his breath as he crouched on a little platform of stones and pushed the boat into the pond. Its bow wrinkled the water, and then as the wick brightened, a red reflection from the porthole dangled below the water like a concertina.

Andrew stood up, Anne beside him; Philip stood with his mother, her hand resting on his head in the darkness. They waited in silence and heard the stirred water lap the sides of the pond and the outlet at the other side stumble through the leaf-choked grid on its journey to the sea. The sound of the waves was there beyond the trees, but they were only conscious of the moving surface of the pond and the dark boat broadening its red reflection. Then the boat stopped and in the silence there was the faint crack of a stick in the shrubbery behind them.

"That'll be the fox," Anne whispered, clutching Andrew's sleeve and looking round at the dark bundled laurels.

"Don't be frightened," he said, holding her hand firmly.

"It's afraid of us," Philip shouted, and for a moment they heard a thumping on the moist earth like the hollow thumps of their own beating hearts.

"We'll move down to the other end and see the green reflection," Philip said.

"No, we'll go back," Anne said. "We've seen enough."

"There's nothing to be afraid of. There's a man with us," and Philip moved ahead in the darkness, the others following him. At the farther end of the pond, in a gap between the trees, they were aware of the cold breath of the sea, the fall of the incoming waves on the stones, and the salt smell of the wrack. The green light shone in the water like a child's ribbon, but no movement came from it until Philip took the squeezed-out tube of glue from his pocket and tossed it into the pond. It splashed loudly, and instantly the surface of the water was alive with black ripples, and from the boat a green reflection twisted and turned like an eel.

"Now you're satisfied!" Anne said, and realizing that Andrew still held her hand she disengaged it politely and put up the collar of her coat.

As they turned back to the house Philip took Andrew's hand, feeling the strength of the thick fingers, a man's fingers, like his own father's, his father who used to carry him in summer down to the green seat at the pond from where they watched the model yacht cut across it like a swan. He must try to bring back those days again and must besiege Thomas to clean out the leaves and the waterlilies of the pond.

Mary handed around tea to them on their return and they all sat around the fire. Philip drank his quickly, stuffed a few cakes in his pocket, and stole off unnoticed to the schoolroom where he sat in front of his telescope and focused it on his boat that floated like a blood-red star upon the water. Later he might be able to spy out the water hen and watch her antics in front of this strange light that gathered strength from the night.

In the drawing room they had rolled back the carpet and Mrs. Newman and Andrew were doing an old-time waltz, Anne sitting on the table attending the record player. Her mother and Andrew were the same height, she noticed. They were tall and elegant and they moved as one, around the edge of the table where the boards were more polished, then up the center toward the fire, the old lady eyeing them keenly and rubbing the backs of her withered hands in time to the music.

A new record was put on, a Highland schottische, and Philip, hearing it, rose and opened the drawing-room door and peered in. Anne was dancing with Andrew and their feet tapped sharply on the floor; holding hands, they glided to the foot of the room, revolved together along one wall, then around the Christmas tree where Anne's hair caught in a branch and she stumbled and would have fallen only Andrew held her firmly, his hand wrinkling the back of her frock. She smiled, showing her teeth, and as the dance ended she rubbed her hands on the handkerchief tucked in her bangle, and out of breath sat once more on the table, swinging her legs.

Philip pulled the door closed, released the knob without clicking it, and then slowly walked along the corridor, past the schoolroom, the dining room, his mother's room, and up the short flight of stairs to his own room.

They played some more records and then sat round the fire talking: Anne on the rug with her hands clasped about her knees, and Andrew on a hassock beside her. When the clock struck eleven he stood up and said he must go as he had a long jaunt ahead of him tomorrow.

"I suppose it would be selfish to hold you any longer," the old lady said. "I'm sorry you must go."

"We're all sorry," Mrs. Newman said.

"Where's Philip?" Anne exclaimed, looking around. "Oh, I know where he'll be!" She jumped to her feet and hurried from the room.

She expected to find him at the telescope, but he wasn't there, and on going quietly to the kitchen she saw Mary on her knees saying the rosary, and not wishing to disturb her she withdrew without being seen and stole up to Philip's room and, switching on the light, found him in bed.

"Are you not feeling well?" she asked, putting a hand on his forehead.

"Leave me alone, please." He shrugged roughly away from her.

"Are you not going to say good-by to Mister Wade?" she entreated.

"You do it for me."

"That wouldn't be the same at all."

"It would be much better—and you know it."

"Know what?"

"That he'd rather speak to you than to me."

"Don't say such stupid things. They only annoy me. In a short while I'll be back in Edinburgh and you'll have him all to yourself."

"It'll never be the same. He'll only use me to reach you."

"Mister Wade's not interested in me. We all have to be nice to him because of you and because of Grandma. She likes him best of all."

"Better than you?"

"Questions that shouldn't be asked shouldn't be answered. Are you coming down to say good night or are you not? For that matter, you didn't say good night to any of us." She leaned over and tousled his hair.

"Go away from me!" he shouted angrily.

"I'm sorry I came up. Good night."

He heard her cross the room and switch off the light. He opened his eyes and could distinguish the bare framework of the window against the night sky. Rain was falling, scrabbling on the pane like mice and tapping on the sill. He thought of his boat and wondered if the rain would blow in upon the warm bowl of oil and quench the light. He sat up and listened for sounds about the house, but he could hear nothing, not even the heavy tick from the grandfather clock on the landing outside his door. He was alone, and the meanness of his action crept coldly over him like guilt. He felt the sting of tears in his eyes and he lay back and bit his lip to ward them off, and tried to think of his boat swaying on the rain-disturbed pond.

"You couldn't guess where he is." Anne said, opening the drawing-room door. She stood with her hand on the door-knob and stared at her mother. "In bed, if you please."

"I'm glad he's getting a little wisdom," the old lady commented, searching for a plausible excuse to explain his behavior. "It's long past his bedtime and he has had a long, exciting day."

Without a word Mrs. Newman rose up and went out of the room with Anne.

"You'll not fail us about coming back," the old lady said to Andrew when they were alone.

"I hope not."

"Come here to me," she said, holding out her hand. "You're setting out on a long journey and you need an old woman's blessing."

He blushed as he went toward her. She raised her hands, placed them on his head, and drew them slowly down his cheeks. Her gesture dismayed him.

"My mind will not be at rest till you're back among us. Wherever you go you'll not mention my name. You'll be cautious in that respect."

"I'll be cautious in every respect," he said, and drew back from her.

"The house will not be the same when you're gone. I'm as sad at your parting as I will be at Anne's."

He stared at her in confusion. There was nothing he could say that would reveal the truth of his position. His relationship with her was false and words would only deepen the falsity.

Footsteps sounded outside the door and he was relieved to see Mrs. Newman and Anne come back.

"Philip asks me to say good-by for him," Mrs. Newman said. "You'll excuse him for going off to bed. He didn't wish to interrupt us when we were dancing. He'll be writing to you at Christmas."

"Tell him a card will be enough. Good-by now, and take care of yourself." He shook hands with the old lady and made her keep her seat.

In the hallway Mrs. Newman helped him on with his

overcoat and with firm pressure of her hands smoothed down the shoulders. She pushed an envelope into the pocket. "A little present for Christmas," she said.

"I don't deserve half your kindness."

"Your presence means much to . . ." she paused, "to Philip and to mother. To all of us, in fact," and she looked at Anne for corroboration.

"Yes, that's true, Mister Wade," Anne said. "He thinks the world of you, though he's a bit awkward at showing it."

"You're very kind—all of you. Good-by." He shook hands with them and hurried through the rain to his car.

Through the mirror he saw them standing in the lighted doorway, and as he moved off they waved their hands, and when he reached the turn in the avenue and looked back they were still waving to him.

He gave a long sigh. If they knew the truth about the court case he'd be happy. He should have told them long ago, and given them the choice to get rid of him or accept him. Now that he'd be away for a while they might hear about it from Doonan should any of them happen to visit the bank over Christmas. Doonan, he was sure, would tell all with appropriate relish. He shrugged his shoulders. He shouldn't give it another thought. He had done no wrong—he was sure of that. It was the newspaper reports that had given the affair an adulterous look.

At the gateway he slowed down before entering the main road, and in the beam from the headlamps he saw Father Lavelle pass, his head bowed against the rain, a walking stick in his hand.

Andrew caught up with him and offered him a lift.

"I'll be grateful for it. I was out for my usual walk before bedtime but the rain came on and spoiled it."

Andrew told him he was going home for Christmas and would be back again at the New Year.

"That's good news. Your parents will be glad to see you

and the Newmans will be glad if you'll be able to return to them for a while."

"To tell you the truth, Father, I feel a bit of an impostor in regard to them. For one thing the old lady feels I'm protecting her from Jewish persecution."

The priest laughed. "Let her feel it; it'll not do her any harm and it'll soothe her mind. I've long since discovered it's no use trying to convince her of her delusions."

"As soon as she mentions them I don't know where to look or turn. And then on top of it there's that other incident in my own life, stifling everything I do. I can't even accept a kindness without a sense of shame."

"I advised you to bury it."

Andrew told the priest about the arrival of the new bank clerk and sensed that in a short time he would noise it abroad.

"A man in his position isn't likely to do that."

"It was a man in his position who brought me into court and has paid dearly for it since. He was changed to the back of beyond."

"That's all the more reason why your friend will not be apt to speak of it. Would you like if I told them?"

Andrew paused for a few moments before answering. "No, Father, I'd rather tell them myself. I mean I would rather face up to it in my own way. If I could do that it would choke the cowardly part of my own nature."

"Usually when we have keyed ourselves up for a major crisis it turns out to be a very minor affair entirely. People always know more about us than we think."

"You mean that the Newmans know already!"

"No, no, I'm just speaking in general terms," the priest added quickly, for he had written to Andrew's parish priest and found what he had already surmised on his first meeting with him, that he was an honest and well-meaning young man who had somehow got involved in a nasty court case.

Andrew stopped the car at the priest's gate and before getting out Father Lavelle asked him how his thesis was getting on. Andrew told him about his visits to the library and how he had given a lift to Mrs. Quinn on a few occasions.

Father Lavelle laughed once more. "I heard of that. Indeed there's not much you can do in this small place without being seen. But take my advice and insist on her bringing one of her little boys."

Andrew reddened: "I see," and he shook his head despairingly. "To think that that has been talked about. Human nature is certainly warped."

"It is." The priest smiled and put a hand on Andrew's shoulder. "And there's a straight grain in it too. It's an act of charity to bring that woman in to see her husband, and I hope as long as you're here that you'll continue the good deed. But be more circumspect, if you know what I mean."

"Never, not once, did it occur to me that people would talk so twistedly about that. I'm an awkward man."

"People talk more than they should. It's just human nature; it's the same the wide world over. Unfortunately the good that people do is less interesting than the bad, and is not often talked about. But when our good deeds are turned by ill-natured gossip into bad it is hard to bear it in patience. But we must try. Take care of yourself." Squeezing Andrew's hand that rested on the steering wheel, he wished him Godspeed on his long journey tomorrow.

12

Early the next afternoon he arrived in Mullingar; after leaving his car in a garage for servicing, and having a couple of hours to wait for the train that would bring him home he went to a hotel for a meal and from there to the church where amid the noise of men hammering at the Christmas crib he prayed that his stay at home would be a quiet one and that his parents would not force him to abandon his present mode of life.

At the station, draftier than most Midland stations, only a few people waited for the train, and when it drew in with all compartments alight, there was no hurry or scramble as there would be if he had waited until Christmas Eve. He got a compartment to himself and having stowed his suitcase on the rack he waited until the train was stretching itself in the open country before he went off to the buffet for a drink. Passing along the corridor he glanced in at each compartment and in a corner of one of them saw a girl who looked like Marion. He passed on, but on his return from the buffet, jolted from side to side by the speeding train, he halted momentarily outside her compartment and she raised her eyes and looked at him. They recognized each other simultaneously, and he slid back the glass-paneled door and held out his hand to her.

"Marion, what on earth are you doing here?"

"And what may I ask are *you* doing here?" She rolled up her knitting and placed it inside a magazine on the seat beside her.

She was pale and tired and far gone in pregnancy, and he kept his eyes averted in order not to embarrass her.

"So we've met again, Marion."

"Yes, Andrew, we've met again. And what have you been doing with yourself ever since? You seemed to have disappeared off the map entirely."

He had had his fill of deception, and without any hint or halt of self-consciousness he told her where he was and what he was doing, and having freed himself in this manner he felt his soul flood with joy.

"There was a rumor that your father and mother didn't know where you were."

"I pledged them not to tell anyone."

"And you don't mind now?"

"Not much. The publicity of the court case sickened me for a long time, but it's wearing off now."

"It sickened us all. And to this day I'll never know why Henry did it. We never mention it to one another. If we did . . ." She shook her head and stifled the unworthy impulse to criticize her husband. "Henry's transfer to Dunvargan was no promotion, I may tell you. But I'll not speak of it. . . . Your new abode is agreeing with you."

"I should be saying the same about you, Marion."

"Why don't you say it? It would please me though I wouldn't be fool enough to believe it." She laughed and looked at the window where their reflections were visible in the dark glass. "You needn't ask why I'm going home. It's obvious to anyone with half an eye. Mother wants me to have the baby at her home. I was in Dublin on a little private business connected with the same event and all's going well. Still, it will be a laboring sort of holiday for me. About yourself? Are you going to stay at home for good?"

"No, Father's not too well. It's that that's bringing me back."

"But surely you wouldn't stay away from home at Christmas?"

"I didn't intend to set foot in the town again. It has no interest for me, and my presence will stir up a lot of talk."

"Let them talk to their hearts' content. It'll not do you any harm for you're unlikely to hear it."

He shook his head. "But you can feel it—feel it by the way people stare at you. You can sense condemnation even when no words are spoken."

"You need toughening up a bit. I don't care a hoot about what they say." She took up her knitting, and they talked of their college days and of friends they had both known and how all were scattered: some to England, some to America, and some to Nigeria.

The carriage got warm and the window misted over. Crossing the Shannon Andrew swept the pane clean and looked out at the gleam on the river and the lights from the houses reflected in the water. He asked her to come to the dining car for a cup of tea, but she declined as the jostling of the train would be a bit dangerous for one in her condition.

Near the end of their journey he fetched his suitcase from his own compartment and lifted hers from the rack and placed it on the seat beside her. As he struggled into his overcoat she guided his arm into a sleeve the lining of which was torn and told him he badly needed a wife to look after him. She touched up her face, folded away her knitting, and as the train stopped he held her arm against the forward jolt.

"Perhaps, Andrew, you'd rather go on ahead. Someone will be at the station to meet me and I know how you must feel and me the way I am."

"No matter how I feel I'll carry your case for you."

They were deliberately slow in getting out, and he laid the cases on the platform and helped her down the high step. They were at the end of the small line of passengers, and though he strove to convey an appearance of ease, his distracted voice, thick with nervousness and fatigue, betrayed him. Marion's father, waving a folded newspaper, came forward to meet them, and without a word took the case from Andrew, as he would from a porter, and linking his daughter's arm led her to a car outside the station. She turned around. "I hope Andrew, I'll see you over Christmas," she said and didn't wait for an answer.

"I don't think I'm very popular in this town," he said to himself with dry irony. He passed through the dark streets, not looking to right or left, feeling like one returning from a long imprisonment. However, it'd not see much of him; he'd take good care of that.

He reached the house and rapped on the door. Mark barked from inside and on the door being opened and his mother greeting him the dog pushed his way between them, licked Andrew's hand, jumped up on him, and ran along the hall where the mats slid under his paws.

"Somebody's glad to see you anyway. And Father's waited up for you. We thought you might have come on an earlier train."

His father, seated at the fire in a gray dressing gown, struggled to his feet and held out his hand: "I'm glad to see you, boy," he said in a voice heavy with a cold.

He had failed; he was thin and shrunken, and the white hairs on his unshaven chin revealed his years more than the loosening of the flesh on his throat.

The dog ran round them, whining with delight, and then crouching on its forepaws it barked, whirled from the room, and tore back again, bumping into Andrew's chair.

"We can't hear our ears with that dog. Put him out, Mary."

"Lie down, Mark. That'll do you now. Quiet, quiet!" Andrew patted the dog and held him forcibly against his knee.

His father wasn't smoking, a bad sign; and when Andrew took a bottle of whisky from his case and stripped off its tissue-paper his father shook his head and said he had lost all taste for it. It was over two weeks since he had enjoyed a smoke, and as for golf he hadn't had a game for the past two months. A bad cold he got had turned to flu.

"The aftereffects of flu—the depression, I mean—is worse than the flu itself. But it will pass," Andrew consoled.

"It has taken this one a damned long time to pass, I may tell you. I've lost interest in everything."

"Don't let it get you down. You have to fight against it!"

"Now, now, you should be the last one to offer advice like that!"

Andrew recoiled in silence from this unexpected retort, lowered his head, and put his arm around the dog's neck.

"Maybe you've been up long enough, Frank," the mother said. "If you go up to bed I'll bring you a nice meal on a tray."

He didn't look at her or answer her but stared at his hands on his lap, at their swollen veins, and then at the dog, its nose dry for want of exercise.

"I often think of you in that lonely spot by the sea," he said slowly, "and wonder to the good God how you put in your time. I hope you'll have the good sense to stay at home now that you are at home."

"We'll see," Andrew said, touching the dog's nose that was as dry as old rubber.

"There should be no seeing about it!"

The mother spread a cloth on the table and told Andrew he'd have time for a wash-up before the tea was ready. The dog followed him upstairs to the bathroom.

"Don't upbraid him at this stage, Frank. You're not well, and you'll be saying something hurtful without meaning to."

"My reason's unimpaired, thanks be to God. If my limbs were just as fit I wouldn't mind." He stared sourly at the two cups on the table. "You may put a cup down for me; it'll save you a jaunt up the stairs."

"I don't mind that part of it."

"But I do." He glanced at the whisky bottle she was stowing in the sideboard. "Hold on," he said. "I might try a dram of that after all."

"Do, Frank, it'll do you no harm. It'll please Andrew to see you sampling it."

She poured some into a glass, added a little water, and handed it to him. He wished her good health, took a few sips, and smacked his lips in an endeavor to taste its flavor. "Not bad, not bad," he said, and stared at the label on the bottle, holding it in his outstretched hand, too tired to fumble for his glasses.

The tea ready and the three of them seated at the table, she asked Andrew about his journey and the route he had taken. He told everything except the meeting with Marion Burns—to mention that in his father's presence would provoke another eruption.

Suddenly the father slapped the table with his hand. "I nearly forgot: that scamp Doonan has been shifted to your part of the country." He advised Andrew to avoid him: he was no fit company for him, he was a wastrel, a good-for-nothing, a soak, a gambler, a sponger. Andrew, in silence, reflected with inward humor on his father's summing-up of his friends, often condemning them before he had ever seen or heard of them.

"You needn't worry, Father," Andrew said quietly. "I've already met him—once. I care as little for his company as you do."

"You'd be safer at home than within hailing distance of the same boyo. But of course you'll stay."

"It would be a bit difficult at this stage." He explained in detail his correspondence courses and spoke of the Newman boy whom he was coaching for exams in the summer.

His excuse didn't satisfy them, and they pointed out that he could conduct his correspondence courses from here and that the Newman boy could obtain the services of some teacher near at hand.

"Having put my hand to the plow you wouldn't have me turn back. Let me do what I want to do for at least a year. That's all I ask. I've made promises and I don't wish to break them."

"The strangers are always first in your thoughts. You've a good home here and you're always welcome. You know that."

"I do, Father, I know that well."

"Then why don't you stay?"

"Listen to me," the mother interrupted, "let us give this vexing topic a rest. It'll lead nowhere. You're both tired, and this isn't the time for a cross-examination."

She refilled their cups, and as Andrew was sitting sideways to her she thought he looked thinner and she inquired if he had been laid up at anytime. Nothing of any consequence, he told them: a bit of a sore throat and a touch of housemaid's knee!

The father stirred uncomfortably on his chair. His face was flushed and his forehead red as a first sunburn. He tightened the cords of his dressing gown and turned around, aware of a draft from under the closed door.

"You feel all right, Frank?"

"A trifle hot, that's all."

"You should get back to bed. You've been up long enough."

"Take a good bowl of punch and sweat it out of you," Andrew urged. "That's the oldest and best cure."

"Have you been reading about the old Irish sweathouses in your visits to the library?" He struggled up from the table and at the door he turned round. "If you bring up the punch, Andrew, I'll give it a try. I'm tired of all the tablets and pills that are the whole go now. They never prescribe anything out of a bottle. I don't know what the world's turning to. A time is coming when we'll carry our breakfast, dinner, and tea wrapped up in an envelope!"

He moved up the stairs, and in a few minutes they heard

the pad of his feet in the room above them and the sound of his cough as he got into bed. Mother and son relaxed.

"Do you see much change in him?" she asked.

"He's failed a bit. But his impatience and temper haven't lost their edge."

"He eats his heart out over you."

"He should have more sense. The time has come when I must be allowed to stand on my own feet and make my own way in the world. I'm twenty-eight, remember."

"You don't understand, but someday you will. We can't cast you off, shrug our shoulders, and say that what happens to you is nothing to us. You are everything to us, Andrew; everything till the day we breathe our last!"

Her lip quivered. He lifted a scrap of bread from the table, held it poised above the dog's nose, and asked him to beg for it. The dog sat back, raised its front paws, eyeing the playful movement of the crust. Suddenly the crust flew into the air and the dog caught it before it reached the floor.

"I'll make that punch now."

"Do, Andrew. There's plenty of hot water in the kettle."

"I hope the stuff will make him more benevolent."

"I'd rather it would shift his cold and Christmas on our heels."

When the father was settled for the night, mother and son sat close to the fire, the dog stretched on the rug between them.

"Mark will break his heart if you leave us. But you won't do that. All the old talk of the court case has blown over."

"It'll blow up again as soon as I'm seen about the streets. But they'll see precious little of me. I'll only go out at dark."

"Do you know, you're still a child!" She shook her head in disapproval. The whole town, he must realize, was in sympathy with him. After the Burnses were transferred to Dunvargan it leaked out that they were in debt to half the town and that the court case was a trumped-up affair to extract money from an innocent lad and that Marion was the prime mover in the case.

"That's enough, Mother. I don't believe it. I met her on the train today."

"I hope you cold-shouldered her."

"There was no reason to. I warm-shouldered her if you'd like to know."

"She was up to her neck in the whole nasty business. They needed money badly."

"That's only malicious gossip."

"You only believe what you want to believe."

"I believe in decency, in good sense, in kindness, and in gratitude. And no matter what is said, Marion Burns possesses them all."

"You said that so earnestly it would give one to think you were in love with her."

"I respect her and always did, and always will, despite what is said about her by the spiteful people of this town. They rend their neighbors limb from limb and would never think of troubling the priest with it in the confessional. Some dreary bit of sensuality they'll confess, but not *that*! And what they say of the Burnses they'll say of me."

"Oh, Dunvargan will cool the same Burnses. It was no promotion, I may tell you. We were in it when you were only three. Do you not remember the little window in the gable of your room? You don't. I nursed you through the measles in that little room. Sometimes you could see the moon in the window, and when you didn't see it you cried for it. It was a miserable place and I prayed daily to get out of it."

Their stay in Dunvargan had lain deep down in her memory, and in her desire for the ease that talk would bring her he listened to her without interruption. The place hadn't changed, she believed, since the days of the Famine. There was no running water to the house, and each day, wet or dry, she had to make her way down to the foot of a field to fetch a bucket or two of water from a spring-well. The water was so cold it would have made your teeth chatter and it was so hard it made the soap curdle like sour milk. And there was scarce a soul to talk to—only the curate—and not enough friends to make a game of cards in the evening. The school-teacher was a dry old stick, as aloof and as cold as a crow's nest. He grew his own tobacco, and the few occasions he visited the house the smell of his pipe clung to the curtains as tenaciously as the pattern on them. And he was an odd creature into the bargain, boasting that he was not a day off school in his life, and thanked God that his old bedridden mother died during the summer vacation or he would have had to take a day off for the funeral.

"Yes," she sighed, "devotion to duty can make a man in-human. Is it any wonder your father's sojourn in Dunvargan turned him sour? So take heed in time and don't force your-self to live in loneliness if you can help it. It will change you and change you for the worse." She stretched out her hand and held his sleeve. "But you'll stay, Andrew. The whole town's in sympathy with you."

"You talk, Mother, as if I were a political leader unjustly spurned, and now return in triumph to receive the freedom of the place."

"Don't be so cynical; it only coarsens you. I only ask a human thing. And I ask for the sake of your father."

"I've made up my mind to stay for a year. I can't break my word."

"Even a year in a queer and lonely place can bring un-expected changes."

"The Newmans are not queer."

He paused, recalling the old lady, and spoke instead of Philip and his mother's ambition that he should go to a university like his sister.

"His sister! You never spoke of her before."

"Hard for me; I only met her a short time ago when she was home on holidays."

"And then?"

"Well, I met her. She's a pleasant girl, but beyond that I know little about her."

She waited, expecting to hear something more about the Newmans, more about these people who seemed to have such a hold on him, but the dog rose up from the rug, yawned, walked to the door, and stroked it with his paw.

"He wants out, Mother. I'll put on my coat and take him as far as the end of the prom."

"Don't be late. You're fagged out and you need your sleep."

They walked briskly along the deserted seafront where only a few lamps were lighted and a stiff wind blew in from the sea, wetting one side of his face and dripping noisily from the handrails along the promenade. The dog ran ahead of him and he could see it for a moment in the light from a lamp standard and then it would disappear into the darkness. When Andrew halted and looked out at the flashing lights that marked the entrance to the harbor the dog, no longer hearing his footsteps, would race back with a slap of wet paws, lick his hands, and scamper off again. The sleety rain turned to snow and when he reached the end of the prom he intended to shelter for a while in the summerhouse but a courting couple mumbled huskily from one corner to make him aware of their presence and he hastened out again, and with the wind at his back he turned up the collar of his coat and set off toward the cluster of lights around the harbor.

His mother had waited up for him and had his slippers warming on the rack above the stove.

"Did you go far?" she asked him.

"As far as the end of the prom."

"Did you meet any old friends?"

"Not a living soul, thank God."

"You're far too sensitive entirely, and you'll have to get over it. A few of my bridge friends are coming tomorrow night and I hope you'll be nice to them."

"I'm giving you due notice I'll not be available. I don't want to listen to old women's chatter."

She could do nothing with him. He avoided people and stayed indoors reading until darkness fell. On Christmas Eve his father was in better form; the new brand of whisky, he believed, had done the trick, and in the afternoon he got up, shaved, and put on his clothes. Although the day was dry and the winter sun shone, it was too cold for him to venture out and to Andrew's regret he sat in his armchair at the fire and harangued him in a voice that was rapidly regaining its strength. He lectured him on the virtuous values of courage and declared that since he had now reached man's estate he must behave like a man and not hide in a hole all day like a cornered rat.

"I know you're only waiting for darkness to fall before venturing out. Foxes, bats, badgers, owls, and hedgehogs do that, but not man. What are you afraid of! Up, like a man, and face them boldly!"

Andrew put away the book he was trying to read and got to his feet, aware that there'd be more comfort in the free air than listening in patience to these hortatory skirmishes.

The afternoon was dry, the sun skimming the rooftops as he set off for the promenade with the dog. At the sea's edge he hurled a tennis ball into the waves and Mark plunged in and retrieved it. A group of boys playing around one of the summerhouses halted when they saw him approach. They recognized him; they were pupils out of his old school, and too shy to speak to him they scurried around to the townward side of the summerhouse and hid under the seats till he had passed. Giggling to themselves, they peered through the windows at his tall striding figure and at the irregular line of wet paw marks on the dry boardwalk. When he was a safe distance ahead of them they shouted "How is Marion! How is Marion!" and then after a short silence: they chanted "Andy, Andy, how is Henry!"

He heard them but didn't turn round, and as he increased his pace they realized they had annoyed him and they came out from the summerhouse; and as their cries mounted in volume on the empty prom, he was sure they could be heard in the streets of the town.

"A parcel of bastards!" he muttered to himself, and on reaching the end of the prom and the last summerhouse he sat inside and filled his pipe, his hands shaking. Through the window he watched the boys, five of them, far down the prom, mounting the horizontal railings, turning somersaults, and dropping to the shore where he could no longer see them. They seemed to have forgotten about him and he called the dog, which shook itself and lay under the seat beside him.

The sun, a deep red, hung above the lid of the sea and frosty vapors spread up and over the far headland. Sand blown into the summerhouse clung to the wet hairs of the dog as it licked its paws and looked up at Andrew, waiting for the tennis ball to be thrown. "Quiet, Mark! Lie down now," he said soothingly, and on peering through the window again he saw sticks being thrown over the railings and onto the prom. The boys were gathering driftwood and they might glean the full length of the beach. He crouched in a corner, lowering his head below the level of the windows. One boy returned to the prom; stooping over the wet sticks he placed them in two neat piles and returned to the beach to do more foraging. Their voices came nearer. Wet sticks clattered over the railings and alighted on the concrete path in front of the summerhouse. Andrew sprang to his feet, heaved himself over the railing, and jumped to the shore.

The boys scattered except one who was absorbed in hurling stones at a fishbox floating in on the waves. Andrew gripped him by the jersey, clouted him about the head, and seeing another one had stumbled and fallen on the beach he ran and overtook him. The boy stopped. His forehead was cut and bleeding, and before Andrew reached him he was crying out: "I didn't shout, sir, it was them ones!" and he pointed to the boys who were fleeing along the prom.

"For two pins I'd throw you into the tide, you brat you!" Andrew twisted his arm, pushed him up a flight of stone steps to the prom and threatened to take him to the police.

"If you ever shout at me again I'll break your damned neck. Do you hear that?" He cuffed him and let him go and on his way back to the summerhouse he kicked one of their heaps of sticks and sent them flying onto the shore.

He lit his pipe and sat in the summerhouse and smiled when the dog appeared dragging a flat stick in its mouth and dropped it at his feet. It barked and wagged its tail. Andrew smiled and made him lie down under the seat. They stayed there till the buoy lights brightened in the shrinking daylight and the far-off lighthouse stretched a ruler of light across the sky.

At home he made no mention of the incident. But later that night his mother answered a knock at the door. A man had come to complain about an assault on his son whose forehead had to be stitched and whose jersey was torn to shreds.

"I'll deal with him," Andrew said, going to the door.

"You split my Pat's head open!" the man shouted at him.

"I did not. He fell on the stones when I chased him for shouting at me."

"You're too ready with your hands, young fella! Would you hit me?" He stood back from the lighted doorway and raised his fists.

"Don't make an ass of yourself," Andrew said quietly. "Let your son tell you the truth and you'll understand. It's too bad a decent man can't go for a walk without being insulted."

"And who's the decent man, may I ask!"

"Take yourself off out of this or I'll ring for the police!" Andrew said firmly, slammed the door, and came inside.

"What was all that about?" his father asked.

He told what had happened on the shore.

"Indeed, Andrew, you should have had more sense. You should have walked on and not heeded them. Boys are pleased when they know you'll give them a chase. It's not devilry on their part, it's sport only; and if you don't give them the sport they'll go elsewhere."

"I'll not be here to provide sport for them. I'm the one who'll be elsewhere."

"Don't let a group of children spoil your Christmas."

"There's more in it than the children. That man at the door insulted me. I hate the place, and when I leave it this time I don't want to set foot in it again. Time and time again you, Father, have said that your transfers from one town to another left you rootless and with no attachments. That feeling is in my own blood and when I leave, the only regrets I'll have will be my leaving you."

Listening to him his father realized that they could not hold him—that it would be wrong to hold him. A protective tenderness stifled all desire to oppose him.

"If that's how you feel, Andrew, we must be content. But you'll always be welcome here should you ever change your mind. And no matter what has been whispered about you—and whispered wrongly—we have great faith in you. Your mother, there, could be worse off. It isn't as if you were setting out for Australia where she wouldn't see you, God knows, for years on end. But this country of ours is small and you're not too far away when all is said and done."

"I'm sorry I'm such a worry to you. But you see now it's better for us all that I live away from here."

They remained silent and he knew that they agreed with him; and after he had gone to bed they sat talking about him until late into the night.

"We needn't try to hold him any longer. This incident has finished it. But he was foolish to have raised his hand to them. And, yet, I might have done the same myself if I had been in his place."

"He seems right and fond of these Newmans. I wonder what they'd do if they ever get a whimper about the court case."

"Do! What would you expect them to do! Sure there was nothing in it after all. It was these damned newspapers that made it out worse than it was. I declare to God that if two boys had a fight after school the newspapers would say there was a riot in the town. The Newmans will be sensible people. I'm sure Andrew's proving his worth."

"But, Frank, we should advise him to tell them."

"We'll do nothing of the kind. It's for him to decide without our prompting. That blackguard Doonan will tell them if he doesn't. And a lovely story he'd make of it, I'm sure! The same boyo will try to make himself important. I'd love to hear how he'd describe me to his cronies. I'm sure his words would be unprintable. When I was in the bank I made the same fella skip. I never saw him come in early in his life."

Mary wasn't listening to him, and when he paused for breath she shook her head and said: "To think that such a small affair can ruin a young man's peace of mind."

"Is it Doonan's peace of mind you're talking about!" he shouted angrily.

"No, no, Frank. It's Andrew I'm thinking of." Watching him take out his tobacco pouch, she stifled a yawn, said she was dropping off her feet, and hoped he wouldn't mind if she went to bed.

13

TWO DAYS after Christmas he rose at five in the morning while it was still dark to catch the six o'clock train. His mother was already up, moving quietly around in her dressing gown, preparing his breakfast and making a last effort to persuade him to prolong his stay. His packed bag lay under the hall table, and the dog was crouched beside it, sensing departure.

Before leaving, Andrew went up to the bedroom where his father lay awake, expecting him. The bedside lamp was lighted, its shade tilted to keep the glare from his eyes.

His father warned him to keep Doonan at arm's length and to readopt his original Christian name as soon as possible; there was no call for that inversion, he told him, it was a foolish stroke, for to live healthily was to face difficulties boldly: to do what was right no matter the cost. Lies were unmanly, and half-truths, no matter how slight, were reprehensible when employed to deceive.

"Thanks, Father. I'll act on your advice. Take care of yourself and don't be worrying about me. With my degree and my years of teaching I'll always be able to carve out for myself a means of livelihood. Maybe you'll drive up in the early spring and stay for a few days. I've mattresses to spare and you need only bring a few blankets. You'll come?"

"I'm afraid my long-driving days are over. There's too much traffic on the roads and driving is too much of a strain. We'll see. You'll write often. A letter gives your mother great comfort." He held out his hand, "Good-by now, and God-speed."

Andrew had seldom seen him so subdued, so warm-hearted, and as soon as he reached the door the bedside light was switched off and the room plunged in darkness.

In the lighted hallway his mother waited for him.

"Button up your coat now, and tighten your scarf. It's terribly cold." She gave a slight shiver and handed him his tweed cap. She kissed him and stooping low held back the dog by the collar. He pulled the door quietly behind him and stole down the deserted street to the station.

He had a compartment to himself, and as the train moved out he looked through the window at the lights in the harbor shining wetly on the tarred sheds. It might be the last time he'd be looking at it, he thought; sighing loudly, he leaned back against the leather headrest, experiencing no sense of joy or relief.

He opened his coat and fumbled in his breast pocket for a card that had arrived from Philip at Christmas. It was a hand-made card, a photograph of Rock Lodge in the snow, and on the inside folder were the signatures of Philip, Anne, and their mother.

"A fine substantial house," his mother had said the morning the card had arrived. "It would take a mint to keep that establishment. Someone has money somewhere."

There was a faint perfume from the card and he put it back in his pocket, closed his eyes, and dozed to the loose rattling of the train.

In the afternoon he arrived in his old car at the bungalow. The air was cold. The tide was full in and covered with frosty vapor, and in a nearby field a man was plowing with a tractor. Andrew took off his cap, felt with relief the free air on his forehead, and smiled. He was glad to be back.

He swung open the garage doors and halted. The inside appeared strange. His books were neatly laid out on a shelf; his blankets were wrapped neatly in brown paper, and on top of them a bundle of unopened letters which he lifted and stuffed into his pocket. He looked at the house. No smoke came from the chimney and all the windows were closed. He went around to the front door and saw that a new Yale lock was affixed to it. He tried his key in it, but it did not fit and he realized then that he had been politely evicted. But the house seemed untenanted. The curtains in the sitting room window were not drawn close and he peered in and saw the table freshly polished, the grate bare and swept of ashes.

He stood and pondered his position. The tractor chugged over the field, the farmer looking around at the spinning discs as they cut the soil in long brown strips that attracted the gulls. Should he hail him, he wondered, and inquire if any new tenant had come to the bungalow? No, better not, in case his predicament would be noised around the countryside. He'd tackle Miss Reid himself—that's what he'd do. He'd not let her off with this. She had no legal right to fling him out without so much as a word of warning. And hadn't he paid the rent till the end of the month? That was his trump card. He'd seek her out and demand the key. He'd sit on her doorstep till he got it!

He hastily looked through the letters in his pocket. They were nearly all Christmas cards except one which was a note from Doonan to say he'd call on him before the end of the year. He's the least of my worries at the moment, Andrew said to himself, and tearing the note into fragments scattered them like confetti at his feet.

He got into the car and drove back along the sea road. What he'd say to Miss Reid he did not know, nor would he allow his mind to rehearse a scene or a syllable beyond the asking for the key. He'd be a damn fool if he'd take this lying down.

He drove through the village, sped past the entrance to Rock Lodge, and on arriving at Miss Reid's found the hall door open. He rang the bell and waited. The wainscot of the vestibule was bright with white varnish and on the floor were flowerpots of chrysanthemums, the mold black and damp from a recent watering. There was no sound from within the house. Maybe they had seen him approach and had intended to avoid him, he thought. He rang again, pressing his finger firmly on the button of the bell, hearing it ring loudly at the back of the house. A light step approached. The inside door opened and Miss Dympna Reid stared at him in astonishment. Her neck reddened, then her face, but no word issued from her lips.

"Is your sister at home?" Andrew said quietly. "I'd like to see her if you don't mind."

"Stay here till I get her for you," she said nervously.

Affecting a misinterpretation of her request he followed her into the carpeted hallway, and seeing the drawing-room door open he went in and sat down on a chintz-covered chair. In the silence he could hear them talking: the loud masculine voice of Miss Isobel Reid followed by the thin, quavering voice of her sister. She seemed a long time in coming to him, and to present an appearance of ease and unconstraint he lit his pipe. The room was chilly, the grate covered with a beaded fire screen, the brass firedogs shining. The lace curtains were stiff with starch and tied at the waist with broad mauve ribbons. It was a room that wasn't lived in.

Presently there was the heavy tread of Miss Reid and as her huge bulk appeared in the doorway he stood up and with studied politeness asked for the key of the bungalow.

"You've come for it, but you're not getting it! All your goods and chattels are in the garage and you can take them to wherever you like. You can't have the bungalow any more. As a tenant—you're unsatisfactory."

"You can't do this without due notice. I am entitled to the usual three months' or even one month's notice."

"You did worse to my sister. Not one hour's notice did she get. She lost her little bit of teaching because of you. She was mortified and humiliated by the whole procedure, and her nerves are still unsettled."

He explained that he wasn't responsible in any way for that. All he had done was put an advertisement in the local paper and Mrs. Newman had sent for him and employed him, and as far as he could understand her sister was only too eager to have the boy off her hands.

"That may be your version of it but it is not ours." He was prepared, he told her, to step aside and allow her sister to take up the work again if Mrs. Newman would agree.

"I'd have you know that we are not grovelers. My sister would not return there under any circumstances."

"Since that matter is amicably settled perhaps you'll tell me why you withhold the key."

"You left without saying where you were going and I presumed you had left for good. You left no address and I had no opportunity of informing you of my intentions."

He pointed out that he had paid the rent till the end of the year and as there were still a few days left he was legally entitled to occupy the house for those days at least.

Recognizing her mistake she raised her voice: "You're not getting it, I tell you!"

"I'm not going until I do get it. You've no legal right to evict me."

"I've the right to ask you to leave this room. You stepped in here uninvited."

"It's not a case of breaking and entering. It's a friendly call, nothing else. Let's sit down and discuss it quietly."

"I'm not sitting down."

"Then I'll have to stand and wait. May I ask why you changed the lock on the door if you thought I wasn't coming back?"

"To keep you out, sir."

"Am I so obnoxious?"

"I find you both obnoxious and impertinent. And what with all the scandalous talk bandied about the countryside concerning you and Mrs. Quinn I'll be glad to keep you out."

"If there's talk of that nature, you know full well there's no truth in it." He looked steadily at her, and as she flinched under his stare he said with cool composure: "Perhaps you're the one that helps to spread these rumors."

"I'll not be insulted in my own house. Get out at once, sir, before I ring for the police! Don't dare to light that pipe! Get out, I say!"

Her loud, threatening tone brought her timid sister rushing to the room.

"Isobel, please, we mustn't have a scene. My nerves wouldn't stand it."

"Leave this to me, Dympna, I'll deal with this impostor in my own way."

"That's a dangerous word to use."

"I don't want any legal quibblings from you."

"Neither do I. All I want is the key."

"If you're not out of this in five minutes I'll ring for the police."

"I'm not going in five minutes, nor in fifty minutes till you hand over what is legally mine."

"Please, let him have it. We can't have the police coming in here. He's determined to hold out; you can see he's brazen."

The two sisters left the room and closed the door behind them. Andrew sat down. He put the pipe in his pocket and waited, his hands drooped between his knees. Over the privet hedge in the garden and above the thin telephone wires the sky was blue. A truck rumbled past, the floor throbbed under his feet, a tizzing sound came from the brass implements in the grate, and some soot stumbled behind the fire screen. Andrew looked at the clock on the mantelpiece and for the first time was aware of its delicate ticking. He listened to it and strove to remain calm.

The door opened rudely and Miss Reid marched in and handed him the key: "There it is and you have three months' notice along with it, remember. My solicitor will send you official notice in due course."

"That will not be necessary. I never stay where I'm not wanted. I shall vacate it as soon as alternative accommodation crops up."

"The sooner the better!" Before he had time to leave the room she crossed to the window and flung it open to drive out the disgusting smell of his pipe.

He got into the car and as he neared the entrance to Rock Lodge he caught a glimpse of Mrs. Newman on horseback and Philip on a pony turning into the driveway. He was glad they didn't see him and he drove past, intending to call on them tomorrow.

14

Mrs. Newman saw him arrive the following afternoon. She was standing at her bedroom window gazing anxiously along the drive, expecting Anne and Philip. They had gone to the city and had promised to be back by two. It had now struck three and there was still no sign of them. The avenue was empty, and white smoke from a fire of rotting straw whorled across it and tangled itself in the branches of the trees.

The preceding evening, as she led in her horse, she had spoken sharply to Thomas about the untidy state of the outbuildings, and in her anger had told him she'd not put up with him another day if he didn't bend his back and exert himself. She was tired of these periodic rows and yearned for the day when Rock Lodge would be sold and all were living in a smaller house on the fringe of the city. She had often pleaded with her mother to sell out, enumerating the advantages it would mean to them, and of what it would mean to Philip should he pass his matriculation. But the old lady was immovable. They were secure here and at peace, surrounded by friends and unspying trees, and as for Philip they could think about that when the day arrived. Father Lavelle had been inveigled into the conspiracy but she rebuffed his timid skirmishes with polite comedy, pointing out that their departure would leave his parish very poor and that the laws of charity forbade it.

But if Richard had been alive there would have been no thought of leaving, for when the war was over he had intended to retire to Rock Lodge and develop the land, the cattle, the sheep, and the piggery on modern lines. She remembered clearly their last talk concerning his retirement, and how he had planned to take her on a long motoring holiday round the coast of Ireland and renew the days of their honeymoon. "Though I suppose," he had added in his own wise way, "It's idle to try to bring back days we have both outgrown." They had been seated together at the side of the pond. It was a day in summer and the sun shone on the brown water of the pond and on the green weeds below the surface. He had pebbles in his hand and with a flick of his thumb was shooting them, one by one, into the pond, and watching the rings widen upon the water and fade into nothingness.

"If Philip were only reared," he had said, "I could return to this war with a lighter heart. It will be hard on you, Helena, should anything happen to me."

"Don't say that!" she had cried and put a hand to his mouth.

Even now she could recall his moist breath and the sweet pain in her own hand as he squeezed it tightly. "You'll be back," she had said. "Within a year the war will be at an end and you'll be away from the sea forever and we'll live close to one another as God intended."

He had smiled then, that sad smile of his, and nodded gravely: "Yes, I'll be back. And the day Philip leaves the university with his degree will be the greatest day of our lives."

"We'll live to see that happen, never fear. God compensates the maimed in His own mysterious way." Those words would remain forever in her mind.

She sighed loudly and straightened the curtain beside her on the window. The smoke from the fire had thinned across the drive and the trees were blurred. She dabbed her eyes with her handkerchief. She mustn't dwell on the past like this. It was wrong of her. But why, why, she thought, do the days around Christmas depress me so much? It was the season of joy, surely. Perhaps it'd be better to say it was the season for children. To have sorrow and to know how to live with it and how to transform it came with age. Children had their sorrows, but children were unthinking; they had to grow up and reach the maturing stage of Lent and with it an enhanced meaning of Easter. Oh, she must stifle her memoried complaints and this yearning to get away from this too-large house; she must learn to live each day as it came and rejoice like the canary in its cage.

A car emerged from the nave of trees and her heart eased, thinking it was Anne and Philip. But as the car drew nearer she saw it was Mr. Wade's and she watched him pull up below her window. The three dogs came racing from the buildings and as Andrew got out, tall and long-striding like Richard, he patted the dogs and they trotted after him, their tails wagging.

Mrs. Newman tapped her face with the powder puff, clipped on her earrings, smoothed her black hair into place, and descended the stairs as Mary was ushering him in in a loud voice of welcome. Mrs. Newman took his hand in both of hers; she was glad he had come back so soon, she said; and as they ascended the stairs together she told him that Anne and Philip were in Belfast but something must have delayed them. In the meantime she'd like to discuss the possibilities of extra coaching hours for Philip. They were all anxious for that, and her mother would have no peace of mind until each weekday was a full schoolday.

She opened the drawing room but did not enter. All was in readiness for Anne's party. The carpet had been unrolled, the Christmas tree gone from the window, the floorboards waxed and polished, and a brass wire guard in front of the fire. Chairs of various shapes were arranged along one wall, and the piano with its brass music rack was shining like new. The room was too bare to sit in, and she led him to a small room at the end of the corridor and bade him take a seat till she got her cigarettes.

The room was bright—a gray carpet on the floor, wicker armchairs, and green curtains on the window. The canary in its cage gave a few tentative chirps, glad of the company. From his chair Andrew could see the tops of the trees, and through the branches the sea flowing in like a river. He got up and crossed to the window and gazed down over the moldering wall of the garden to the round eye of the pond. His gaze ranged over its surface, trying to discern Philip's little boat. But he failed to find it and instead looked at Thomas who at that moment was slowly trundling a wheelbarrow, a fork stuck in a pile of wet leaves. Andrew watched him run it into the edge of a fire, lift the shafts, tumble the stuff out, and stick the fork in the ground; and as the white smoke rose up, thick as the trunk of a tree, he sat on the shaft and eyed the fire with the concentrated interest of a Gypsy.

The door opened and Mary pushed in a tea-trolley. Behind her came Mrs. Newman.

"Thanks, Mary. If Anne phones you'll call me."

"Yes, Ma'am. But don't be worrying any more. It's a fine day, thank God, and they're making the best of it."

"They promised to be back at two and it's now wearing on for four."

"Children don't measure time by the clock. They'll be all right. I needn't waken the mistress till they arrive?"

"No, Mary. Let her rest."

The trolley was placed near the fire between the armchairs, and as Mrs. Newman poured out the tea she asked Andrew how he had spent Christmas.

"Quietly and lazily," he said, adding that he was glad to be back here again.

"So you're still not tired of our company?" She smiled.

"No, but I'm afraid Miss Reid's tired of mine," he said, and went on to tell of his eviction from the bungalow and his dramatic reinstatement.

"If you lose your house there's always room in this one," she assured him. "Mother would love that."

"You've done too much for me already."

"The gratitude is all ours. You've done Mother real good."

"On false assurances, though."

"True or false, you can't alter them now or she'd break up completely. If you moved in here it would give her a new lease of life."

"But I'm not evicted yet. I'll wait until I'm thrown out."

"And then you'll throw yourself into our arms, I hope."

The tea finished and the trolley pushed to the side, she leaned forward with her long thin hands clasped about her knees and gazed into the fire. She wore a yellow woollen frock; a Tara brooch fastened near one shoulder caught the light. How young she looked, he thought, with her black hair cut short and her brown eyes enlarged by the firelight.

"How quickly the darkness drops down," she sighed, and smiled sadly across at him. "I wish they were home. Anne is always sharp on time."

"She may have met a few friends."

"Not a day passes but we read of some accident on the road," she said, following her own thoughts. "And Anne drives too fast and Philip often exasperates her."

She got up and crossed to the window. The lights in the village shone through the trees and Thomas' fire blazed redly, reflecting on the stonework of the outbuildings and on Thomas' red face and shirtsleeves as he sat on the shaft of his wheelbarrow at the edge of the fire.

She lit a cigarette, switched on the light in the room, and sat down again.

He had come to tell her about his court case but the time was not ripe, for she was too much absorbed in her own troubles, and to ease her mind from the anxiety of waiting he inquired about Philip's party and how the toy boat was faring.

The party had been a tragic one for Philip, she told him, and there wasn't a stick left of the little boat. He learned how two boys had stolen away from the party and had shot at the boat with an air pistol. They had tried to sink it but Thomas had come upon them and they had fled back to the house. But before darkness had fallen Philip, not knowing what had happened, had insisted on leading his friends down to see his boat. By that time it had drifted into the side. Its lamp had gone out; the glass bowl was cracked and the sticky oil had oozed into the hull. One side of the boat was peppered with pellets that shone like nailheads. Philip knew then what had happened, and in a rage he had flung down the boat and attacked the boy who had the air pistol. The little girls in the group had raced back to the house, screaming out that Philip was killing Tony Cooper.

"It wasn't as bad as that," she went on, "for when we reached them Philip had pinioned the boy to the ground. The boy's nose was bleeding and his suit plastered with soil. That ended the party, I needn't tell you. But later that night when I was in bed I heard the dogs barking and when I looked out I saw a flare of light on the pond. Philip had stolen out in the dark and set fire to the remains of his boat. No doubt he'll tell you about it and give you more of the details than I have done. But I do wish he hadn't struck his friend. Children play pranks that are often cruel, though they don't see it that way."

"We do things impulsively and live to regret them," he said, thinking of his own attack on Burns. Now is the time to tell her, he thought, but before he had time to frame his words she rose to her feet and crossed once more to the window.

"Oh, I do wish they were here! What on earth has delayed them! If you don't mind, we'll walk as far as the gate and meet them. I'll go and get my coat."

When she had gone from the room he reflected suddenly on his estrangement from his own parents and how his living away from them would cause them many an anxious hour.

He must write to them, and write often, and strengthen the thinning string that held them together.

Mrs. Newman came back in a fur coat, a scarf about her head. They walked slowly along the drive. Darkness had united the trees, the sky was splashed with stars, and the fire at the edge of the park smoldered redly and took the sting from the air.

"Anne should have phoned."

"You'll have the explanation soon and you'll be annoyed with yourself for worrying so much."

"It's well Mother's resting or she would have had me phoning up every hospital in the city."

She stumbled over an unseen pothole in the avenue and he caught her arm and held it firmly.

"That Thomas fella will break my heart someday."

"It looks more like he'll break your leg."

She smiled, and at that moment the headlights of the car lit up the trunks of the trees and swerved down the avenue.

"Thank God," she said, and disengaging her arm from his she stood out in the middle of the drive. The car halted in front of her.

"Well, what happened?" Then, before Anne or Philip could answer, she added, "Look whom I have with me."

"Hurrah!" they both exclaimed above the throb of the engine.

"I'm sorry for the delay, Mother," Anne said. "It couldn't be helped," and she explained how they had met Father Lavelle in the city and how he insisted on bringing them to the cinema and then for tea, and how she had tried several times to get through on the phone, but failed because of a breakdown on the line.

"But for Mister Wade arriving I don't know what I would have done with worrying."

"Get in, both of you."

"We'll walk; it's not worth our while."

"Oh, get in and don't stand there in the cold," Anne said with impatience.

"I've a headache and the night air will lift it."

"And I've one too with the wild driving," Philip said.

"You could have at least spared me that," Anne said, sending the car forward with a jerk.

"I could enjoy the air now," Mrs. Newman sighed, pushed back the scarf from her head, and shook her hair.

Slowly they walked after the car, and when they reached it Anne and Philip were taking parcels from the trunk. They helped them to carry them into the house and pile them on the hall table.

In the small room, alone with the canary, the old lady—who had heard from Mary that Mr. Wade had returned—waited for him, and as he entered the room with Philip she stood up and kissed them both.

The house was not the same without him, she told him; they all missed him, and she herself hadn't slept well since he went away.

Philip told him about the disaster to his boat, but didn't mention the fight; later in the dining room as they were finishing a meal Helena mentioned how Miss Reid had promised to give Mr. Wade three months' notice to quit the bungalow.

"Well, there are other places that will give you welcome, Mister Wade," the old lady said. "You can live with us and take your place as one of the family."

"That's what I propose too," Helena said.

"And I second it," Philip interjected.

"You should all allow Mister Wade to make up his own mind in the matter. He may not like what you all like," Anne said. "He has other work to do besides teaching Philip."

"He'd be free to do that here," Helena said. Turning to Andrew she added, "No one would interfere with your freedom, Mister Wade. You could have the little room we were in this evening all to yourself."

"But I'm not evicted yet," Andrew said. "It may be only a threat. But thank you all the same."

Anne, looking across the table at him, sensed that the conversation embarrassed him and said she expected him to sing at her party. He agreed promptly and Helena assured him that since the piano was tuned for the occasion the accompaniment wouldn't be as ragged as last time.

"And by the way," she added, "A Mister Doonan, a bank clerk from the other side has promised to come. He knows you, he told me."

Andrew felt his face reddening and hoped they didn't notice it.

"He knows my father better. I mean he worked under him for some years."

"He seems a pleasant young man and I'm glad for your sake he's coming. You'll feel more at home."

"I've always felt at home here," he said, pressing with his finger a few crumbs that were on the plate beside him.

He stayed late because the old lady asked for cards, and when he was taking his leave at the hall door Anne suddenly exclaimed that she had forgotten to put their car in the garage and walked out with him into the dark. They stood talking for a while and looked back at Philip and Mrs. Newman standing in the lighted doorway. Anne advised him to remain on in the bungalow as long as he could, for if he moved into Rock Lodge she felt he would lose control over Philip and not be able to get him to study.

"Hurry in out of the cold," her mother called from the doorway.

"In a minute, Mother," she called back. "Good night now, Mister Wade. I'll be looking forward to your help at the party. On Tuesday I'll be returning to Scotland, as you know. But it'll not be long until Easter."

As her mother moved out from the door Anne shook his hand hurriedly and got into the car. She switched on the lights and he stood and watched the car move slowly around to the garage at the side of the house.

15

ANDREW WAS putting into readable shape some of the notes he had accumulated on the Charter Schools when Doonan called to see him the following afternoon. He had got a lift in a ramshackle car near the village and arrived at the bungalow complaining of the cold and regretting he hadn't brought his heavy overcoat instead of a light waterproof.

Andrew pushed the armchair to the fire for him and tidied the notebooks and papers.

"The windows of the car didn't close properly," Doonan grumbled. "They were wedged with cardboard and a draft whirled round my neck like a boomerang. It would have been safer for the health, but bad for the feet, if I had walked." He held out his hands to the heat and rubbed them vigorously. He sneezed twice. "That's the beginnings of a right cold, I'm thinking. You wouldn't have an aspirin about the place, Andy."

"I could give you a drink if that would be any good to you."

"That should shift it. You're a real toff—and no mistake." He pulled the chair closer to the fire and jabbed the coals with the poker, and presently from the kitchen he heard the bright clink of a bottle and a whinge from a tight-fitting cork.

"Not too much, Andy, like a good fellow. During the festive season hands are usually unsteady and bottles unusually full."

"Mine's not in that category," Andrew shouted out to him.

"Hope you're not wandering from the straight and narrow, old boy. I've wandered so often I've lost my way on the tortuous climb to promotion. Many a lecture your father gave me on the same topic. Sorry I didn't heed him. Pleasure and promotion are bad mixers."

Andrew came up with the drinks on a tray and placed them on the table. They touched glasses and wished each other health and luck in the New Year.

Doonan took off his horn-rimmed glasses, wiped them with a handkerchief tucked in his sleeve, gazed round the room and out to sea where a coalboat was entering the lough.

"You need a stump of a woman to look after you properly in a place like this. You might as well be in a Trappist monastery."

"I'm getting used to it. I was at home for Christmas and was glad to get back here."

"You'll get odd if you stay here on your lone much longer. I wouldn't let the like of Burns drive me from my own hearthstone. I could tell you a thing or two about the same Burns."

"I'd rather not hear it. I met Marion when I was at home. She's expecting a new arrival."

Doonan took another sip from his glass, tapped Andrew's knee, and winked. "It's well you're out of earshot. You'd never know what they'd be siring on you next." He laughed loudly at his own joke.

"I don't like that remark."

"No offense meant. A good laugh is a tonic for the nerves. Wait now; I came on something yesterday of historical interest."

He opened his pocket case and with fumbling fingers extracted from it a folded piece of paper and handed it to Andrew. It was a newspaper clipping, cracked and frayed in the folds, and bearing the caption BANK CLERK AWARDED £100. Andrew read the heading, squeezed it into a ball, and tossed it into the fire: "There's the proper place for that!"

"You take life too seriously, man. If it had happened to me I'd have retold it with appropriate embellishments till I wouldn't have known what was fact and what fiction. I would indeed."

"It's easy to boast and swagger about hypothetical situations."

"Listen, Andy. Sure we all know there was nothing between you and Marion. I wish they had called on me to give evidence."

"Will you, for the love of God, stop talking about it then!"

"As you wish," Tim said, uncrossing his legs to preserve the sharp crease in his trousers. "But I'll say this: You're far too touchy about the whole matter."

Gulls flew over the house and dipped low over the sea to escape the strength of the wind. Andrew watched them moving in from the fields in twos and threes, heading for the headland before the fall of dark.

Doonan's efforts to make intimate contact had slithered away from him and he tried another line. He mentioned he was invited to a dance in Rock Lodge and intended to go if Andrew would give him a shakedown after it was over; it would be unfair, he pointed out, to ask the ferryman to run him across at two in the morning and maybe demand a couple of quid for such a short journey. By all accounts he was the only acceptor from the royal bank stables, the only novice who would endure the inconveniences of sea transport.

"I'll put you up all right," Andrew agreed, "but if you changed your mind the Newmans would understand."

"I wouldn't dream of letting them down at this stage. It would upset the male-and-female balance—if you know what I mean. I'm dying to see a bit of local talent. What's the daughter like? A younger edition of the mother would suit me."

"They don't resemble one another in any particular. The mother has dark eyes and the daughter's are green. The mother is much taller and is much the better dancer."

"You've rehearsed with both, I see."

"They played a record or two one evening and we had a flounce around the floor."

"And out through the door and into the moonlit night. You know, Andy, you're a positive danger to the married and the unmarried."

"Quit the damned codding! I teach the son, but beyond that I know little or nothing about them."

"Ach, you're far too tightened up! If I had the chance I'd try my luck with both. They have a fine place by all accounts," and he told how the man who had given him the lift furnished him with Rock Lodge history.

"The daughter was engaged to some playboy in the Navy. Did you know that?"

"I've told you I know very little about them."

"Are you not interested in them?"

"I'm interested in pushing the lad through his matric."

"There's an old grandmother in the establishment that's off the rails, I believe."

"There's very little wrong with her except old age." Andrew looked at the clock on the mantelpiece; he would make him something to eat and get rid of him. He got to his feet, took a tablecloth from a drawer, and spread it on the table.

"How about rashers and eggs for tea?"

"That'll fill the gap, Andy, though I've consumed so many eggs and bacon of late I'll soon be cackling or grunting."

Left alone in the sitting room, Doonan lifted up a bundle of penscript sheets on the shelf beside him and read: *It would excite indignation and disgust to see the descriptions of men to whom the education of children in these Charter Schools has been sometimes (almost necessarily) committed. Men of vulgar habits, coarse manners and coarse language, often ignorant in the extreme of everything, but the common rudiments of reading, writing, and arithmetic.*

Imagine an intelligent man bothering his head with stuff

like that, Doonan said to himself, and he put the bundle on the shelf and picked up a few loose sheets beside it.

Some scripts from his correspondence pupils, he thought. Doreen Denvir was written on top of the first sheet. A nice alliterated name, he mused. Wonder what she'd be like. Red ink comments were written along the margin. Space your work better, Doreen, a geometry problem is not a composition, remember.

He looked at another script that belonged to a Bridget Boylan. I don't like that name, he said to himself. I bet she's fat and dumpy. Hold up your chins, please, Bridget, all three of them. That's the girl—now you look better. Brace back the shoulders, Bridget. Now we have some straight line and projection. A little deportment is essential, ladies; it covers a multitude of defects. Please enclose photograph with your next script.

He was smiling at his own thoughts when Andrew came up with cups and saucers on a tray.

"You must be raking in a tidy pile from this harem of yours," Doonan said, tapping the sheets that rested on his knee.

"Enough to make ends meet."

"It's well you didn't follow in the paternal footsteps. We're overworked and underpaid, and to keep us from enjoying a weekend they make us toe the line on a Saturday morning. And I'm surrounded all day with shoals of cash and can't touch a halfpenny. That's one thing the bank does for one: it teaches us to resist temptation and it thick around us."

The noise of the frying bacon traveled up to the room and Andrew left abruptly to attend to it.

By the time they had finished the tea darkness had fallen on the headland and only the gray sea and the winking light of the buoy were visible in the window. Andrew didn't light his lamps and they sat in the firelight until Doonan stretched himself, yawned loudly, and said it was time he was hitting the road.

Andrew took out the car and drove him to the village. It was deserted; all doors were closed, lights shone in the blinded windows and as he walked with him to the slip a cold wind blew in from the sea. A light projecting from a Gents shone on the slipway and on the gray mooring ropes of the motor-boat.

Doonan coughed and the cough echoed hollowly among the boats that lay on trestles against the quay wall.

"I wouldn't like to be stranded here on a winter's night," he said. "Milton must have composed *Paradise Lost* in a place like this." And then as he buttoned up the collar of his raincoat he told Andrew that he had reached the bottom of the Christmas barrel and wondered if he could have the loan of a few quid.

"I could give you two."

"That'll do. It'll be paid back, never fear. . . . I'll meet you here tomorrow night at seven and you'll escort me to Rock Lodge."

"I'll be here."

The ferryman came along with his swinging lantern and Andrew stood on the quay until the boat had moved out into the darkness. The lamp, placed on the bow, shone on the varnished mast, on the trembling cords, and on Doonan's gray raincoat.

Andrew strode back to his car parked in the dark Square. A bleak dissatisfaction lay on his soul, and instead of turning home he went to Rock Lodge.

It was Mrs. Newman who opened the door for him, and he apologized for calling so late.

"Another eviction?" she smiled, ascending the stairs in front of him.

"No, not that. It's something else," he said solemnly.

"You're going to leave us—is that it?"

"It's not that either, I hope."

She led him into her own sitting room, which seemed smaller now with the green curtains drawn and two dogs spread out on the rug in front of the fire. She hooshed them from the room and ordered them to go down to Mary.

"I have guessed it. You're going to get married in the New Year."

"No, no," he said sadly, trying to quell her bright mood. "No, it's something that happened to me some months ago—something that made me leave home."

"The usual irrational misunderstanding with parents, I suppose? That wouldn't be anything new."

"Maybe I shouldn't tell you at all. It might startle you."

"It'll startle me if you don't." She leaned forward and put a log on the fire. "Now I'm all ready." She leaned back, relaxed, in the wicker armchair, and rested her head on her hands.

In silence he stared at her for a moment but did not return her smile.

"Last summer I was involved in a court case. I struck a man, a bank clerk."

"Not your friend across the lough?"

"No, a man he worked alongside. I struck him and he was awarded a hundred pounds damages. I told Father Lavelle about it long ago."

"I wouldn't have accused you of striking anyone, Mister Wade. I would not."

"His wife and I were always friendly, from our student days, and I used to visit the house after she married."

Mrs. Newman sat up, joined her long hands on her lap, and gazed at the flames wrapping round the log.

"I see," she said, and the expression of pained curiosity that spread across her face made him wince.

He stared at the green hearthrug at his feet; resting his elbow on his knee he shielded his face like a priest in the confessional and bit by bit wrung out every bitter drop of his predicament: the row with Burns, the court case, his coming here, and his inversion of his Christian names.

"And was she tall and good-looking, this Mrs. Burns?" she asked, amazed at herself for asking it.

"She certainly wasn't tall and I wouldn't say she was good-looking either," he answered—and realized by her question that she too was unconvinced about his innocence. "We were friendly all through our college days. We studied the same subjects and used to discuss them together. There was nothing but friendship between us, and nothing but friendship after she married. Nothing, nothing, nothing!"

"I'm sure there wasn't, Mister Wade," she said slowly and leaned back in her chair, her legs crossed.

He stared across at her; her face and eyes had lost their accustomed mobility and vivacity, and she seemed suddenly to have aged.

She recalled Miss Reid's alarming hints to her on the day of that lady's dismissal and she now found herself inquiring if he had known the Reids before he came here.

"No, I never heard of them till the day I rented their bungalow. Maybe you're thinking of asking her to come back again?"

"No, no, it's you we want for Philip, no one else."

"If you still want me I'll stay. And I'll see he passes in three subjects in June. A year later he can sit for two or three more."

"Of course we want you, Mister Wade."

"Thanks for saying that. You can depend on me."

"Wait a moment and I'll ring for Mary to bring us some tea."

"I'd rather not wait, Mrs. Newman, if you don't mind. It's late and I just had tea before coming out."

He stood up and she did not coax him. She yearned to be

alone for a while, to be alone before Anne came back from visiting her friends.

In the hall she held his coat for him, but when the usual friendly pressure of her hands upon his shoulders was withheld he knew that henceforth he would only be an employee at Rock Lodge, one who would be under suspicion. Her gestures and forced smile betrayed her.

"We'll be looking forward to seeing you on Sunday," she said, shaking his hand lightly. "How cold it has turned," and she twitched her shoulders and waited in the lighted vestibule till the car door had closed. He set off along the avenue; looking into the driving mirror he saw that the house was now in darkness.

From her unlighted bedroom window she watched the red taillights of the car appear and disappear among the trees in the avenue, and when they had gone from sight she switched on the electric heater in the room and sat down at the dressing table in the darkness. The moon slid past a single cloud and shone on a silver hairbrush on the table and on the Tara brooch pinned to her frock. In the mirror her eyes were large and frightened and her face cold as ivory.

Lies and deceit revolted her, and coming as they did from a man they had all trusted, her whole being stumbled and turned in a feeling of dread and unfriendliness. He was Philip's teacher, she mustn't forget that, or forget how quickly he was developing under his guidance. And he was Mother's protector—a bogus one no doubt, but one they could not wisely dispense with. They had all been too friendly with him, that was their main fault, and he on his part had made use of that weakness and by falsehood had eased his way into the very heart of her family. But things could have been worse, and would have been worse if he had been living in the house with them, a position that her mother would have welcomed. Already they had invited him to stay should Miss

Reid carry out her threat of eviction, but that invitation, she was glad to say, was not final and there was still time to edge it aside till it was forgotten and forsaken amid the trivial occurrences of each day. But she'd make no definite decision about anything till she had sought advice from Father Lavelle. He, at least, should have told her the truth about this stranger before now. Why he had withheld it she did not know. Father Lavelle was too old to be easily deceived.

She tried to smile at her reflection in the mirror, but the smile only produced lines of age at the corners of her mouth, lines that were slow to disappear. She sighed heavily. The moon hid itself in the tatters of the sky and the red glow from the electric heater dimly lighted the room.

She must have patience, she told herself, and not equal Miss Reid in her haste to condemn the young man. Miss Reid had already hinted about his attachment to Mrs. Quinn, but there was no truth in that—nothing beyond an unreasonable jealousy on Miss Reid's part.

She brushed her hair vigorously, plucked the loose hairs from the brush and, twining them round her finger, dropped them in the basket at the side of the dressing-table.

She must forget about him and think of Anne. Anne, she was sure, admired him, and during the holidays had been brighter than she had seen her for a long time—and it wasn't the advent of the party that was the cause. During the few days Mr. Wade had gone from them Anne had become moody and snappish with her and with Philip and it was only on Mr. Wade's return that she had brightened up again. Anne was fond of him; she was sure of that, though Anne had never outwardly expressed it to anyone. Having been wickedly deceived by one lover Anne would be wary of being deceived by another. But there was nothing that she herself had observed at any time that would convince her that Mr. Wade was attracted to Anne. From the day they had tobogganed in the snow they were at ease in each other's company, and on the evening they had all danced together in the drawing room they had moved as freely as a family.

She mustn't condemn him outright, she decided, and placing the brush on the table she smoothed her eyebrows with her fingertips and rose. She must strive to believe in him and not allow hardness to lodge in her heart. Father Lavelle would direct her and she hoped she'd have the wisdom to follow his directions. She must also remember that Mr. Wade was a bank manager's son and was not likely to be a rake, a trifler, or an exploiter.

She knelt on a *prie-dieu* in front of a crucifix on the wall and prayed for belief in what was good and prayed that, for her mother's and Philip's sake, she would not permit her mind to follow the easier path of suspicion.

The lights of Anne's car swept into the room like a shout. It startled her, and rising from her knees she hastened downstairs to meet her.

"You're late, Anne. They've all gone to bed long ago. You didn't meet anyone on the road?"

"No one, Mother. Whom did you expect me to meet?"

"Nobody. I just asked for the sake of asking."

"It's not like you to do that." As she took off her coat and hat Anne looked questioningly at her mother and waited for an explanation.

"The weather looks settled for the party," her mother said, stooping to brush the hearth. "It would be dreadful if it rained. I loathe people trooping through the house on wet shoes and squenching leaves into the carpets. However, it will only be for an evening."

"And a twenty-first birthday party is only once in a person's lifetime."

"That's true. Oh, I hope it will be a success, something you'll remember with joy."

"There were no cancellations over the phone when I was out?"

"No, why should there be?"

"I don't know. It's just that I feel you've had some disappointment. You seem sad."

"Me! Not in the least. I'm tired, that's all. I was reading that old Trollope to Mother and he bores me." She forced a yawn and looked at the clock.

"You'll waken me for morning Mass at the usual time, Mother?"

"Yes, I'll not forget. And you could ask Father Lavelle to call round tomorrow. Your grandmother would like to go to confession."

16

THE OLD lady's room was vacuumed, aired, and tidied for Father Lavelle's arrival, and the old lady herself was arrayed in her best bedjacket and her hair neatly set for the occasion. And Mrs. Newman, wishing to have Father Lavelle to herself when he had finished with her mother, had successfully persuaded Anne and Philip to exercise the horse and pony along the sheep paths that bordered the shore.

She was alone now in her small sitting room. The radio was turned low, but she wasn't listening to it, and a woman's magazine lay unopened on her lap. The morning sun shone whitely into the room, and the canary, sensing that winter was waning, was erect and active. Mrs. Newman watched him as he cracked his seeds noisily and with quick turns of his head cleaned his bill on the perch. He had a sleek coat of new feathers and his black eyes were glossy as elderberries. By his capers she could see he meant business, and lest he should disturb their conversation by rolling bursts of song she carried the cage into her bedroom and closed the door. She could hear the little swing ticking like a clock and knew that he was cross at being transported from the springlike brightness of one room to the cold blue of another.

She turned off the radio, plumped the cushions on the wicker armchairs, and stood on the hearthrug with her back to the fire. Certain that Father Lavelle would be exhausted listening to her mother, she rang for Mary and told her to tell him that coffee was ready for him.

In a few minutes he entered the room, smiling: "Your Mother, thank God, is in grand form this morning. She's glad, like the rest of us, to feel some heat in the sun. I saw some snowdrops in bloom the other day and in no time at all spring will be upon us." He crossed to the window and, leaning his hands on the warm sill, looked down into the walled garden where Thomas was scuffling the pebbled paths.

She poured coffee for him, and taking the cup and saucer in his hand he stood by the window and allowed his eyes to rest on the sheep that lumbered in their heavy fleece around the paddock.

"Your mother raised no objections to the party?"

"She'll do anything for Anne, Father."

"And why wouldn't she?"

"Still and all she'll be glad when it's over. She'll plug her ears and lock herself in her room till the party ends. Mister Wade has come back in time for it," she said, not wishing to be diverted from what perturbed her.

"A fine young man. I haven't seen him since he returned. From what I hear his correspondence courses are first-class."

"He was here last night." She stirred her cup gently. "He revealed things about himself I would much rather not have heard. They've upset me a great deal."

"What like, Helena?"

"Oh, I thought you knew!"

She glanced at him as he stood sideways at the edge of the curtain.

"Mister Wade was involved in a nasty court case. That was his reason for settling down here. It was a forced flight, you might say."

"Yes, now that I remember, he told me something about that," the priest said casually. He strode from the window, put his cup down on the tray, and lighting a cigarette sat down opposite her.

"I didn't sleep last night thinking of it, and thinking of Philip receiving tuition from a man I can no longer trust." She stared at the priest with a crushed expression he hadn't seen since Anne's broken engagement.

"But you must trust him, Helena," he said with quiet assurance. "You mustn't allow what he told you to disturb you unduly. I don't think the matter was all that serious. A bit of youthful indiscretion—that's all."

"It's Anne I fear most for. I must protect her."

"I would leave her alone. At twenty-one she must be allowed to stand on her own feet."

"I don't interfere with her. And anyway, she doesn't unlock her heart to me."

"Diffidence is a characteristic of young girls."

"But I feel she could grow fond of this Mister Wade and I'd like to stop it after hearing of this unseemly affair."

"There was nothing unseemly about it except we wish to read that into it. He may have had an infatuation for a married friend or he may not. We can't judge. If he had, there would be nothing inhuman about it and he has learned a hard lesson. He has suffered and it has left in its wake something lonely, generous, and appealing. I'm sure you've felt that?"

He raised his eyes. Mrs. Newman blushed. He noticed it, turned his eyes from her, and tapped the ash from his cigarette. Some of the ash fell on his sleeve and he brushed it with his hand and left white streaks behind.

She rose to get a clothes brush but he told her not to bother, and when she had sat down again he joined his hands on his lap and fixed his eyes on the white varnish of the windows.

"The young lady's husband was jealous of their friendship—that was evident from what Mister Wade has told us. And being her husband he had every right to be. Jealousy can come to all of us though we may be unaware of it. It can appear in strange guises and in unusual places. Brothers can be jealous of one another, though they'd never admit it and would be surprised if they were told it. And two sisters can be jealous of each other in a fiercer way."

"I'm glad I'm past the jealous stage." She smiled.

"No one is ever past it. Even old priests can be envious of one another."

"Mother is jealously fond of him. But I feel that that

relationship will break up and that the shadow will spread. I have suffered enough and don't wish to be waylaid into more heartbreaking disappointments."

"We can't avoid them. That's the problem in all our lives. But we must try to accept them and in that way transform them."

"Others have it easier."

"*Seem* to have it easier, Helena. The fiercest conflicts take place within the mind. Each has his own troubles, seen or unseen. You've had many and yet there has been some balance, some compensation." He pointed out that she enjoyed good health, that Philip was progressing with his studies, and that Anne was nearly finished with hers.

"And when Anne's finished, Father, I hope Mister Wade will be finished with us. Miss Reid, I may tell you, is ready to evict him. She has heard there's too much intimacy between him and Mrs. Quinn."

"Helena!" He turned to her and nodded his head hopelessly. He was surprised that she, an educated woman, would listen to such gossip or let it lie uncharitably uncovered in her mind. He had been in the little parish for over twenty years and had learned to dismiss his people's crude conjectures and to reduce their embellishments of gossip to the true diminutive size. Trivialities were always magnified. If a husband happened to have a row with his wife it would be told he had tried to murder her. If a child had the measles it would be rumored that its temperature was so high it could not be recorded on a thermometer; if a parishioner had a stone removed from his kidneys his relatives would tell it weighed two pounds and was now in a medical museum, and if a schoolteacher was seen taking a glass of stout of an evening it would be whispered about the countryside that he was hitting the bottle hard.

"And now our friend's kindness to Mrs. Quinn is twisted wickedly by some malignant gossips. People will never learn to control their tongues." He looked at his watch and stood up. "Listen, Helena, don't let your hospitality to our young man grow cold. Let him finish the good work he has begun. Miss Reid will not evict him! I'll speak to her about that."

"And if he flirts with Anne?"

"Better he should do that than flirt with her mother."

Again she blushed, looked quickly away from him, and laughed. "He's hardly like to do that and he ten years younger than I am."

"Upon my word I thought he was more. At least he looks very young to me."

"You, then, approve of him. You're sure he's fit company for Philip?"

A flush of anger appeared on his cheeks and spread over his brow and under the thin white hair.

"I do approve of him. And I can tell you in confidence that when Mister O'Brien retires from my school later in the year if our friend would be interested in it he'd have a very good chance of getting it. That's how much I approve of him!"

"I'm sorry I spoke as I did, Father. My heart feels lighter now."

From his pocket he drew out a small envelope. "That's for Anne. It's a little Celtic cross, one like your own. I'll offer up Mass for her tomorrow."

"You're far too kind to us. Maybe you'll drop in to see the revelers tomorrow night."

"They'll revel better in my absence. Good-by and be sensible. I hope the party will go off well and that the moon will shine on them. Mary showed me the cake with its twenty-one candles. Anne will need some help in blowing them out, I'm thinking."

17

ON THE NIGHT of the party nearly every upstairs window in the house was alight and their reflections, except when broken by someone moving about in a room, lay like flagstones on the lawn. In the brightly lit vestibule, heated by two electric fires for the occasion, Mrs. Newman with a black lace shawl around her bare shoulders and Anne, in a fur wrap, greeted the guests as they arrived. A young girl, halfway up the stairs, escorted the ladies to two bedrooms that served as cloakrooms, their partners being directed to the schoolroom where they laid out their coats on two tables placed end to end.

Of the thirty invited guests Andrew and Doonan were the last to arrive, for Doonan had torn the knees of his trousers slipping on the wet stones of the quay and they had to wait till the ferryman's wife had stitched the hanging pieces together. Being accustomed by his profession to neatness of dress he was discomfited by the grimacing stitches, and driving out from the village he complained bitterly of the insufficient lighting on the quay and wondered whom he could sue for damages.

"You shouldn't have jumped off the damned boat. The ferryman was ready to take your hand and let you step ashore like Prince Charley," Andrew laughed.

"It's no laughing matter. It'll spoil my whole evening."

"Cheer up. It's your face they'll be looking at and at the moment it's puckered up like the knees of your trousers."

Mrs. Newman and Anne welcomed them warmly, and to Andrew's surprise Doonan apologized for the state of his trousers and recounted in a querulous voice how it had happened.

Anne led them to the head of the stairs and introduced

them to a bunch of girls clustered around the open door of the drawing room. A piano and violin were playing, but no one had yet danced, and when Andrew came out of the schoolroom fingering his tie Anne touched him on the sleeve and whispered: "Do you mind if we take the first plunge? They're all too shy to begin."

He nodded, and with his arm round her waist they moved from the open door, and glided boldly and confidently into the center of the polished floor. They were soon joined by other couples. The dancing had begun. Mrs. Newman took off her shawl and danced with Doonan. Her frock of old gold and her bare shoulders made her hair look darker. She was much taller than Doonan and the grim expression on his face betrayed his ill-humor, and to his dismay she sat beside him at the end of the dance and strove to put him at his ease. They sat out the next dance. He was morose and unsociable, making no effort at conversation, and when a young girl had sung two songs he fingered the knees of his trousers instead of joining in the general applause.

"Perhaps, Mister Doonan, we'll have the pleasure of hearing you sing later in the evening?" Mrs. Newman asked.

"You wouldn't inflict that on me and me with torn trousers. It would be like facing a firing squad. Andy Wade will deputize for me."

"Don't be alarmed. We'll not take you by surprise." Andy Wade, she repeated in her own mind: it sounded strange to her and unfamiliar—she who had written John Wade on every check she had made out to him. Her partner, she was sure, could provide her with much desired information about Mr. Wade, but when she delicately and discreetly asked a few questions that would satisfy her curiosity Doonan affected not to hear or spoke instead of Andrew's father and how he had worked under him for a spell until the old man, to everybody's relief, announced his retirement.

"By all accounts Mister Wade doesn't take after his father," Mrs. Newman remarked.

"Thanks be to God he does not. If his old man glared at a vacant typewriter the keys would begin to hop of themselves."

She threw back her head and laughed, a silvery laugh that revealed gold filling in a side tooth.

From the opposite side of the room Andrew watched them and observing their laughter he believed that at that moment Doonan was mimicking Burns or rehearsing the court case with ridicule and scornful mockery. He decided to take her away from him and as soon as the pianist gave out the opening bars of an old-time waltz he strode across the room and asked her to dance.

The sound of the music was wafted through the corridors of the house and reached Philip as he sat on a chair in his bedroom trying to read *Wuthering Heights*. Earlier he had brought his telescope to the room and had viewed each car as it arrived, and when there was nothing left to look at except the stars above the trees, he endeavored to read instead of going to bed. But the excitement in the house scattered his interest and aroused an irritable agitation. He sighed, cast the book aside, and slipped down to the kitchen where Mary with the help of two other women was preparing the supper and carrying up laden trays to the dining room.

The dogs, filled to satisfaction with chicken bones, lay out of range of the women's feet and wagged their tails feebly when Philip sat among them on a stool. He yawned loudly and Mary asked him crossly why he didn't go to bed or take a seat in the drawing room.

"I don't want to," he answered gruffly, fingering one of the dog's ears and pulling it inside out.

The kitchen door was open because of the heat from the range and through it came the clapping of hands that signaled the end of a dance.

"There are some people can enjoy themselves," Mary said, more to Philip than to the two women who rested from their labors at the side of the range. He sat on, and presently they forgot about him as they spoke of dances that were held in Rock Lodge when the old lady was in her heyday and of the frocks that were worn and of what they had cost when bought in the great shops of London or Paris. Names of ladies were mentioned and Mary was able to supply her willing listeners with details of marriages, names of children, deaths of some, the success of others—but all recounted in a mournful, lamenting voice that at last drove Philip away from the kitchen. Unnoticed he stole upstairs and made his way cautiously along the corridor to the dining room where the white-clothed tables, shining with cutlery, were arranged in a T. He stood in the firelight, pushed back from the hearth a leather chair that smelled scorched, and looked at the tall windows covered evenly with unbroken mist. How easily, if he wished, he could draw on these windows sketches of yachts and boats, or scribble on the yielding moisture birthday greetings to Anne. He smiled at what he could write but refrained from doing so. His mother, he knew, would scold him for not being in bed or reproach him for being a vulgar busybody who couldn't keep his hands to himself. He had refused to allow a place to be set for him at the table, declaring that they were all too old for him. His mother had listened to him and let him have his way. Now as he walked round the table looking at the names of the guests that were printed in Gothic script on little cards he felt sorry that he would not be present when the candles would be lighted on the birthday cake, the lights in the room extinguished, and Anne's eyes shining as brightly as the ring that used to adorn her finger.

He moved around toward the cake and was straightening a tilted candle when the drawing-room door opened and voices flew out like a scatter of birds. Footsteps sped along the corridor and Philip crouched behind a chair in time to see Anne in her fur wrap and Andrew, holding her hand, pass the open door hurriedly. Philip didn't move and in a few minutes they passed again and he got up and peered after them. Andrew had a rope coiled over his shoulder and Anne had hedge-clippers which she placed outside the drawing-room door before pushing Andrew in ahead of her.

There was a long silence. Then there rose rapid bursts of laughter, harsh laughter from young men and the happy high-pitched laughter of young girls. The door opened. Andrew lifted the hedge shears, and withdrew quickly. Philip switched off the lights in the corridor and made his way quietly as far as the schoolroom. There he halted, ready to dart in at the first sound of an approaching step. Terrified screams came from the young girls, and impelled by uncontrollable curiosity he opened the drawing-room door slightly and looked in. The party was engaged in tug-of-war. Anne was shooting her arms forward, now to one group and now to the other, and shouting *"Heave! Heave!"* while Andrew, standing at the middle of the rope, pretended to cut it with the hedge shears.

Philip closed the door without being seen and made his way to the dining room. He switched on the lights and went to Anne's place at the head of the table. Andrew's card was on her right and he lifted it and exchanged it with one at his mother's place. His face burned, his hands shook, and as he backed away a young man appeared at the door. It was Doonan.

Philip pushed back the leather chair another inch from the fire and in a voice that trembled said that the leather was so hot you couldn't touch it with your hand.

"And I'm hot too," Doonan said and asked where he could get a drink.

"There's plenty of orange juice and wine in front of you," Philip said, pointing to the table.

"They don't agree with me."

"Do you mean whisky, then?"

"Yes, lad, that would do."

Philip opened the sideboard and told him to help himself, for he was going to bed.

"That's the right place for all of us," Doonan said, and as he lifted the decanter and poured out some whisky he asked Philip his age and inquired about the subjects he was studying under Mr. Wade's tutelage.

"Take my advice, lad, and keep to the books," Doonan commented, sitting down near the fire. "Good night again, lad. I'll rest here for a bit. I've a sore knee. I fell on the quay."

"Will I get you some Sloan's Liniment from the kitchen to rub on it?"

"Don't bother. It's not all that bad. Go on and get your night's sleep."

"Don't drink much of that or you'll fall again."

"A mouthful will satisfy me. Switch off that light on your way out, like a good boy."

With his two hands embracing his glass Doonan relaxed happily in front of the fire. It was very warm in the room and the firelight glittered on the glasses and cutlery and shone on the polished, opulent furniture. The sound of the dancing reached him and he wished it would soon be over. It was all too staid and too quiet for him and the way they shrieked at the tug-of-war was like a schoolgirls' party. And it was an expensive outing for him into the bargain. He'd have to buy a new suit for himself at the end of the month.

He stole back during a dance and maneuvered his way to the edge of the window where he could be half-concealed by the heavy folds of the curtains. He closed his eyes, dozed, and opened them in time to applaud Andrew's singing of two songs.

Andrew sought him out and asked why he wasn't dancing.

"The fall has stunned me—that's all."

"Your breath's poisonous. You've been drinking."

"Your young pupil treated me. I was on my way to make a necessary call when I met him."

"You shouldn't have taken it from him."

"I didn't like to insult his hospitality. It's a poor show where a man can't have a drink. There's as much orange juice on the table as would float a motorboat. I'm sorry I crossed the ocean to come to it."

"Take your hands out of your pockets and pretend you're enjoying it."

At that moment a young girl dancing too near the door caught her frock on the hedge shears that lay on the coil of rope and the clatter and commotion brought Andrew and Anne running simultaneously across the floor.

"We'll put them back in their proper place if you don't mind," she said, and together they hurried downstairs into the night.

The moonlight slanted into the open doorway of the store and by its light he hung the rope and shears on pegs projecting from the wall. She stood watching him, and seeing the sleigh and a rubber boot lying on its side she remembered the evening they had tobogganed in the snow. He too recalled it but said nothing.

They pushed the swinging doors together and as he shot home the bolt his hands touched hers. He pressed it firmly, held it, and she made no effort to withdraw it.

"You'll write to me about Philip?" she said, and pulling the fur wrap round her shoulders the Celtic cross dangled brightly at her neck. "I love to get letters, though I don't like answering them."

"I'll not mind writing them."

They moved slowly to the back steps of the house and halfway up they could see the oval pane of the pond cracked by the branches of the trees and in the stillness they could hear the sound of feeble waves breathing on the shore.

"Listen to it," she said, "that sound haunts me wherever I go."

Her hand in his was warm and he was conscious of her moist breathing and of a faint perfume from her wrap.

"I like Scotland," she went on, "and I like the Scots. I like their honesty, their ease, and their unaffectedness. Still, I'm always glad to get home."

"I'm sorry you have to go away so soon."

"And I'm sorry too." She shook her head and looked at him. "But it'll not be long till Easter. *Razorbill* will be launched then and with you with us we'll have a full crew for the races." She pressed his hand, ran up the remaining steps and pushed open the door.

The couples had ceased dancing and Mrs. Newman was clapping her hands for silence and asking the guests to please take their seats in the dining room. Doonan was the last to get to his feet. He was quite steady going along the corridor, and as he entered the dining room with Andrew Mrs. Newman tapped a hand on the back of a chair beside her and called out: "You're here, Mister Wade."

As Doonan took up his stand on Anne's right she lifted his card, looked at it, and put it back.

"Is this where I'm parked?" he said gallantly.

"Yes, it seems so," she said with enough grace to quell her surprise.

He pulled back his chair and sat down. He straightened his tie, teased out the tip of the handkerchief that decorated his breast pocket, and slipped the broad silver ring from his napkin. His eye ranged round the table to the bottles of white wine and glass jugs of bilious orange juice and he decided he was not going to enjoy himself.

At three o'clock the party came to an end. Mrs. Newman and Anne watched the last guests depart. Farewells were shouted from one group to another; car doors were slammed and the air was filled with the greasy smell of the exhausts.

Silence swelled out from the trees, crossed the dark avenue, and pressed soothingly around the house. The heavy outside door closed, the vestibule light was switched off, and wearily Mrs. Newman and Anne climbed the stairs to the little sitting room where the fire had sunk low and the canary slept in its hooded cage.

"We should go to bed, Mother. It's very late."

"I'll smoke one cigarette before I go. Sit down and relax for a few minutes. . . . You're happy it's all over and that it was such a success?"

"It may have been a success, but I don't feel it."

"You're tired, that's all. Too much excitement brings an aftermath of depression."

She put the long cigarette holder to her lips, inhaled slowly, and lay back in the armchair with her legs crossed. Anne watched her. Lines scored her forehead and shadows appeared below her eyes. And yet how youthful and elegant she looked when she danced with Mr. Wade. Everyone remarked them, they were so tall and slim.

"I didn't care much for Mister Wade's companion, Anne. He seemed soured and unsociable. And though it's vulgar to mention it, I must say he distinctly smelled of spirits throughout the evening."

"You shouldn't have placed him beside me at the table if you knew that. He didn't help me to enjoy my evening."

"I didn't place him beside you. It was you who arranged the places and no one was more surprised than I to find Mister Wade beside me."

"Nor more delighted, I suppose."

She detected a tone of asperity in the remark, but in her own mind attributed it to overwrought nerves and so took no further notice of it.

"Was your companion all that objectionable?"

"He was a complete stranger to me. I scarcely got one word out of him during the whole supper."

"I am sure he knows more about Mister Wade than we know and you should have seized the opportunity of gathering a little more information."

"Is that the reason you placed him beside me?" Anne said irritably.

" I told you I didn't do it! Mary must have done it, unintentionally of course."

"Mary would never do the like of that!"

"It's a mystery then. Don't think about it any more. It's done and it can't be undone. You need a long rest. You should take your breakfast in bed in the morning."

The offhand demeanor of her mother and her pleased and serene detachment disturbed Anne. She still believed it was her mother who had rearranged the two place cards, and tortured now by some repressed dissatisfaction she suddenly burst out: "There's no mystery about it. You did it! It was loathsome. You did it to nourish your vanity. Mister Wade attracts you. You had no smiles for anyone but him. And you were so engrossed with him at the table I don't believe you knew what you were eating."

She stared at her daughter, at her green eyes that were sharp with anger; stunned by the suddenness of the onslaught, she sat quite still and inwardly prayed for patience. And then some evil nudged her to disclose what she knew of Mr. Wade's private life, but she fought against it and beat into silence the few words that would destroy her own peace and that of her daughter.

She put away the cigarette, sat on the hearthrug beside her, and put her hand gently on her daughter's shoulder.

"Those words do not become you, Anne."

"Leave me alone, please," and she turned her head away and wept.

"Calm yourself, like a good girl. You're tired. We'll go to bed, in God's name, and forget about all this. This is not you at all. Tomorrow you'll be your own sweet self and we'll never refer to this again."

Anne's handkerchief fell on the rug and her mother lifted it and gave it to her. A door opened and closed, and presently there was the shuffle of feet outside in the corridor.

"Dry your eyes, Anne; I hear someone coming."

Philip, in his dressing gown, his braces strapped to his legs, was on his way to them. He hadn't slept. He had heard the last cars roar into the night, had heard the heavy hall door close, lights being switched off, the sound of his mother's voice, and then silence stretching into the darkness of a long night. By changing the cards he had done wrong and the guilt of it besieged him. Some wickedness had waylaid him and forced him to do it. He despised himself for what he had done. He had prayed God to forgive him and in his tearful penitence had hoped that sleep and peace would wrap him round. But his mind was too overcharged to sleep; it had throbbed and knocked like the engine of an old car. His grandmother had moved in the room above him; he had heard her, in her delusions, haranguing some people at a meeting, had heard her stumbling about, pulling out drawers, and closing the window. He had tried to keep his mind fastened on her movements, but when she had lapsed into silence his mind shied away like a fractious pony and thudded into a fearful wakefulness. He had closed his eyes tightly, and then there came silver asterisks bright as a firework and as they whirled around they changed to dancing frocks—greens, yellows, reds, and blacks—and they blended like the chalked colors he had put on a spinning top years ago when he was younger, and out of the whirlpool of colors Anne had risen up, tall as a tree, in her green frock, and her eyes flashed at him with the fierceness of a fox he had once seen in a trap. He had cried then, but the grandfather clock on the landing struck the half-hour and as he heard its weights stumble in its long mahogany coffin he rose from his bed and made his way along the corridor.

He heard Anne's voice and he rapped the door and entered. His mother and Anne stared at him. His fair hair was tousled, his face pale, and his eyes large and dark with fear.

"What's wrong, Philip?" his mother said.

He looked at her and then at Anne, who was tucking her handkerchief into her bangle.

"I did an awful thing. I don't know why I did it, but I did it and I'm sorry. I changed Mister Wade's card from beside Anne."

He shivered with the cold and his mother put Anne's wrap around his shoulders.

"But the partner I had beside me was interesting, Philip. There was really no great harm done," Anne said with a broken smile. "But you shouldn't play such tricks on us. They're not in the least bit funny."

"But it wasn't for fun I did it. It wasn't that. I was bad. I was wicked. It was just that I didn't wish him to sit beside you when I wasn't there to see."

"Oh, Mother, I wish I had another week to stay! Tomorrow I'll be away from you all. For some reason I dread going back this time."

"In another six months you'll be finished for good."

"That six months will be very long."

"Your work, please God, will shorten it. And, Philip will work as he has never done before. And then we'll all be together again and we'll be happier than at any time in our lives. We must help each other and not bruise each other any more. And you, Philip, will think of your future and work for that."

"I will, Mother. . . . And, Anne, I'm sorry."

He stretched out his hand and she took it and called her mother to join her hand with theirs.

"Now," the mother smiled, "We're all, thank God, joined together again."

"Wait," said Philip. "We'll play the game we used to play when I was small."

Six hands were piled one on top of the other, and the hand that found itself at the bottom of the pile had to withdraw quickly and smack itself down on the top again. For a few minutes they played at it and in that short time their eyes were bright with joy.

18

IT WAS near four when Andrew and Doonan got to bed. In a short while Andrew was asleep, but Doonan tossed and turned for a long time. The moon having reached its height was smothered in thick cloud and gave no light and a rising wind jiggled a loose slate on the roof and in the backwash on the shore pebbles and sand grated as harshly as in a sieve. The noise kept him awake. The bed too had not enough blankets on it and he was sure it was damp into the bargain. He'd be a fool to try to sleep in it and run the risk of pneumonia.

He threw aside the blankets, padded across to Andrew's room, and wakened him. He said his bed was damp and he'd rather dress and sit by the fire than go back to it.

"And how could it be damp, man? It's your imagination. I aired the mattress at the fire all morning. Go on back and give me peace."

"I'm not going back to it. It's damp, I tell you!"

"Take this one of mine and I'll take yours."

"You don't mind?"

"Not a bit. One bed's as good as another."

An hour later Doonan had wakened him again. His watch had stopped and he didn't know in hell what time it was. Andrew switched on his flash and saw by his own watch it was after five. It would be time enough if they rose at eight, he told him.

"And if your old car doesn't start—what then?"

"You can walk or swim."

"It's no laughing matter. I may be a bit of a rake in some ways, but I take pride in punctuality."

"Ah, go to hell," Andrew said. "The bank will soon have you as cantankerous as my own father."

"You're a nice friend. I came to the dance to oblige you and this is the thanks I get."

"You came because you wanted to come and it would have been better for all of us if you hadn't."

"You don't want me then—is that it?"

"I want you to let me sleep."

"That's easily done."

Doonan left the room and Andrew got up and gently turned the key in the door and for a long time afterward heard him blundering about the house and shoveling coal on the range.

At seven o'clock Doonan was thumping the door and rattling the knob and shouting at Andrew to get up. Did he not realize he would have to call at his digs and change his suit and shave; surely he didn't expect him to wait till broad daylight and have him walking through the town like a common navvy.

Andrew dressed hurriedly by the light of a candle and came down to the kitchen, where Doonan sat before the open door of the range. The kettle was boiling and an oil lamp was lighted on the table. Andrew made the breakfast and Doonan finished his hurriedly. But Andrew took his time. It was his own house and he wasn't going to be dragooned by anyone.

"Maybe you wouldn't mind leaving now?" Doonan said.

"There's bags of time. Smoke a cigarette and calm yourself."

"I'll smoke on the way in. The old car won't let us down?"

"It has never let me down."

"It's more than likely to do that now." His voice was husky from lack of sleep and when he saw Andrew pour out another cup of tea for himself he told him he was just doing it to annoy him.

"Whether you like it or not I'm going to finish my breakfast like a Christian."

"Perhaps I should walk on. I might get a lift if you don't overtake me in the meantime."

Andrew shot up from the table, pulled on his cap and heavy overcoat and got the car out of the garage. The morning was dark, a cold rain blew in from the sea, and the buoy flashed its light sharply.

Long strings of rain fell in front of the headlights on the black road. The village, when they reached it, was dark and deserted; a few lights appeared at upstairs windows, but there was no one on the quay and its one light shone drearily on the slippery stones and on the puddles of water left behind by the tide.

"What's the time now?" Doonan asked.

"It's a quarter to eight. I'll have time to go to eight o'clock Mass if you don't mind."

"And what am I to do?" Doonan said and moved out of the wind to the shelter of the quay wall.

"You can wait till the ferryman arrives or you can knock at his door."

"It'd be better if you knocked. I'm a complete stranger."

"I'll do nothing of the kind. You chivvied me out of the house and now you want to drag a tired man out of his bed. You can make up your own mind what to do."

Doonan, his hands in his pockets, stared glumly at the lights on the other side of the lough. Their twisted reflections revealed the heavy swell on the water. It would be a rough crossing, he thought.

A stiff door closed with a thud and feet hurried up the hill to the church.

"I'll have to leave you now."

"That's all right, John. Don't let me delay you," Doonan said with cold irony.

Andrew turned away, hesitated, and wheeled round quickly. "I heard the *John* all right. But there's no sting left in it any more—nothing left to feed your discontent or your power. My name is Andrew Wade."

"Is it that to everyone?"

"Yes, to everyone. To the Newmans too—since it's that that is in your mind. I told them the whole story."

"You don't think I'd have been nasty enough to do it for you and you hand-in-glove with the daughter."

"I'll leave you to guess what I thought."

He hurried into the car and stopped outside the church. He had five minutes to spare and he sat in the car and by listening to the rain beating on the roof he eased the beating in his mind.

As he opened the church door the wind rushed in behind him, banging a door somewhere in the sacristy and tossing the flames on the candelabrum. Five or six people were present and Father Lavelle was preparing the altar for Mass. Andrew knelt at the back, combed his hair with his fingers, and felt his unshaven chin. The door opened again and the wind blew cold on Andrew's neck and bumped against the windows. Mrs. Newman walked up the aisle, genuflected, and took her place in the full light from the sanctuary. Father Lavelle descended the altar steps and beckoned to Andrew from the communion rail. His usual Mass server hadn't arrived and he asked Andrew if he would do it for him.

A few minutes later Mrs. Newman watched them as they emerged from the sacristy and genuflected together at the foot of the altar. Andrew looked very tall and slim beside the priest and his movements were reverent and recollected. She felt an upsurge of pity for him and recalled the beaten look of his face the evening he had revealed to her his real reason for leaving home. She sighed and lowered her eyes to the missal in her hands.

"I will go unto the altar of God," she read, "unto God who giveth joy to my youth. Judge me, O God, and distinguish my cause from the nation that is not holy; deliver me from the unjust and deceitful man."

Her mind wandered from the words on the page. It was only natural, she thought, to be dismayed by what he had told her of his hidden life and she must be charitable and seek to forget it and not be waylaid by a vain satisfaction of spiritual superiority. Hadn't we all our secret lives and our hidden flaws and wouldn't wish they were publicly exposed. She, herself, in Anne's judgment had been guilty of some fault, but what that was she didn't really know. Still, it would be cowardly and unwomanly if she tried to evade the uncomfortable or to seek plausible excuses for a flirtatious folly—if it was that that was in Anne's accusation—a folly that would only end in remorseful misery. She liked Mr. Wade, she would admit that. And if she did admire him it was not for herself, but because he brought comfort to her mother and worked wonders with Philip. Beyond that, she believed, there was nothing, and she must continue to be hospitable and gracious in all her dealings with him. How could a person of her age attract a young man like that! It was absurd and she must never allow herself to succumb to such a pleasurable absurdity. Anne shouldn't have hinted at such a position. Still, she must forgive her; the child was overwrought and overexcited at the time.

The priest's voice raised at the *Kyrie* brought her mind back with a jolt and to keep distraction at bay she knelt erect and tried to pray with concentration. She had come out especially to pray for Anne and to pray for direction in all their dealings with Mr. Wade. She didn't expect to find him here this morning and she took it as a sign that her attitude toward him should undergo no unfriendly change. She should not belabor her mind any more with imaginings that would only encumber and diminish the peace of her own home.

She shook her head. Everything would solve itself. Meanwhile she must fill her thoughts and actions with all that is true and noble, lovable and gracious. And if problems do arrive she could always discuss them with Father Lavelle.

At the end of Mass she waited for Andrew and they went out together into the gray light of the morning. The rain had ceased but the path to the gate was soaked and the wind was laden with the noise of the sea and the dark flurry of the trees.

"I didn't expect to find you out so early, Mister Wade."

"It was forced upon me," he said and then explained why he was unwashed and unshaved.

"I made Anne lie in this morning and I took her place. I hope that wind will fall before her plane takes off in the afternoon."

"It's at its height now and it will die out soon. She'll have a smooth journey, no fear."

"I hope so. We'll expect you at the usual time tomorrow."

Her friendliness toward him underwent no perceptible change and each morning he arrived at nine at Rock Lodge, taught till three in the afternoon, and sometimes at the old lady's behest spent a half-hour reading to her Jane Austen's *Persuasion*.

Philip worked resolutely. They had made plans for his future and decided that he should concentrate on English, History, and Mathematics in the May examination and a year later sit for three more and enroll in the University in the Faculty of Law. . . . The legal profession would suit him best, they thought: a profession in which his physical disability would not be an encumbrance or an embarrassment. He could carry out his daily business from an office chair; he could be his own master, arrange his own timetable, and be completely independent.

Philip read quickly through the prescribed books in his English course, skirmished rapidly through the History course till he held it unified in his mind and then revised and expanded each section with material from books Andrew brought from the lending libraries in the city. His memory was sharp and what he read he retained because he willed to retain it. In the evenings he read aloud to himself the prescribed Shakespearean play, wrote appreciations of poems and later discussed these with Andrew. His mind ripened quickly, and when the days brightened and the sun grew warmer they abandoned the schoolroom for a while and, wearing overcoats, sat at the edge of the pond on the green seat and moved it with the movements of the sun. The air was fresh; snowdrops and crocuses that had bloomed under the trees had withered and dark green clumps of daffodil leaves pierced the short grass.

In an elm tree near the pond crows congregated on the supple branches that swayed under their weight. Their last year's nests had rotted during the winter and the wet broken sticks lay on the dark mold among the shrubbery. The crows kept up a continual cawing and often Andrew and Philip paused to watch them fight for nesting places and see their feathers floating down to rest on the surface of the pond.

One day a small yacht moved across the bay, disturbing the gulls and swans that fed and washed where the outlet of the pond met the sea. Philip saw it first and he stood up and exclaimed joyfully that it was high time their own yacht and punt were in the water. Andrew, who had been writing to Anne and was forewarned of Philip's desire, suggested that they wait until the weather was warmer. But Philip maintained that the weather couldn't be better for sailing and that if *Razorbill* were launched they could explore the lough on a Sunday and have a picnic on one of the islands and bring Mother with them.

"For one thing, Philip, it's not the time for picnics and for another, I'm not much of a sailor."

"It's time you learned to be one, then. You advised me to give the books a rest on one day of the week. Sailing could do that for both of us. You needn't be afraid. We could handle the sails ourselves. In fact I could handle the boat myself if she were in the water."

"We'd have to ask your mother first."

"She'll do what I ask. I know she will."

Not wishing to be inveigled into any stubborn agreement, Andrew stretched his arms and marking the place in his book with a laurel leaf he got up from the seat and sauntered along the edge of the pond and down through the trees to the sea. The little yacht heeled to the slight breeze, cut out to the fast-flowing current and was quickly carried out of sight behind the coal-quay wall. Small waves stumbled over the stones on the shore, and where the stream met the sea the water was darkly cobbled.

He jumped across the stream and wandered under the trees where the paths were dented by the hoofs of the cattle. As he sang to himself his breath turned white in the cold air. He was happy with himself and his work. The incident with Burns no longer troubled his mind or clamped his movements with predisposed fears. Mrs. Newman never once referred to the court case and the checks which he now cashed in his fortnightly visits to the city were made out in his full name: Andrew John Wade.

On reaching a small bay where the sea lay dark because of the pine trees that overshadowed it, a crane standing on its stiltlike legs at the edge of the water lifted its heavy wings and rose up with a scrake of rage. Andrew sat down on a flat rock at the edge of the shore and reread a happy letter from his mother and two letters Anne had sent him since her return to Scotland. The second letter, in answer to one from him, was long and free and in it she spoke of her experiments in the labs and how her fill of work was making the days fly toward Easter. In a postscript she warned him not to allow Philip to boss him—or, for that matter, her own mother: both unwittingly could make selfish inroads on his own time and he mustn't allow that to happen—he must assert himself and not bend to the whim of either.

Philip's shrill whistle reached him through the trees but he smiled at it and sat on, his hands clasped around his knees and his eyes on a tern that dipped into the water and left a nest of rings behind it like a rising trout. The whistle, urgent and angry, came again but he ignored it. Then a cold air passed through the trees behind him, the light darkened, and a few hailstones fell hard into the water. He struggled from the rock and sought shelter among the pine trees, the hailstones bouncing white and dry at his feet and stuttering madly in the water. Slowly the cloud passed, dangled long cords of hailstones above the sea, and in a few minutes left a wintry whiteness on the slopes at the other side of the lough. The sky cleared and the lough turned blue as Andrew hurried back to the pond. Philip was gone and on the green seat the melting hailstones lay like frog-spawn.

The whistle blew close at hand and he sought him out and discovered him in the boathouse sitting on a box surveying a rowboat that lay on its side.

"Did you not hear the whistle? I saw the cloud coming and I didn't want you to get soaked."

"I sheltered under a tree," Andrew said, looking at the dry timbers of the boat and the sand and dead leaves that had been blown in during the winter.

"I'll get Thomas to paint her and we could fish in the evenings. What do you say?" He pointed to two bamboo rods that rested on pegs along one wall.

Andrew lifted them down and examined them. The hooks were rusted and the rust had stained the white feathers of the flies. The lines snapped in frayed edges when Andrew gave them a sharp pluck.

"You'll not catch much with those. You're more likely to catch a cold or a headache."

"I can buy new lines in the village and I can make new

flies from gulls' feathers. You've no excuse for not fishing. And the oars—have a look at them!"

The oars stood upright in a corner, their blades swathed in cobweb. They were almost new and the varnish still held its gloss. Andrew lifted one; it was light to handle and as he examined the curve of the blade he recited:

> *"I dipped my oars into the silent lake,*
> *And, as I rose upon the stroke, my boat*
> *Went heaving through the water like a swan."*

"Old Wordsworth wrote that," Philip said, and added:

> *"with trembling oars I turned*
> *Back to the covert of the willow tree;*
> *There in her mooring-place I left my bark—*
> *And through the meadows went, in grave*
> *And serious mood. . . ."*

Their voices rumbling out through the open door attracted Mrs. Newman, who had come out to look for them.

"Oh, is this where you sheltered," she said and looked round at the warped sides of the boathouse and the knotholes in the timbers. "This place will tumble down some day if Thomas doesn't look smart."

"May I get him to paint the punt, Mother?"

"It would need it," she said and with her stick prodded the flaking paint and exposed its gray naked timbers.

Philip spoke of his plans for fishing and exploring.

His mother smiled. "You'll be gilly as well as tutor, Mister Wade, if all these plans come off."

"He doesn't want to sail in *Razorbill* till Anne comes home. He's afraid."

"It's the weather I'd be afraid of," Andrew interjected. "You need good warm weather for yachting."

"Mister Wade is right. It's too chilly yet to go on the water. I don't want an invalid on my hands."

"You'd enjoy the sailing as much as we would, Mother."

"Mister Wade knows I'm too old for such foolhardy expeditions. Wait until Anne comes home; she's more nimble in a boat than your mother."

"You'd love to come. You're only pretending you wouldn't."

"How you talk. Come in now. Mary has some tea ready for you."

They set off along the path round the pond, Philip between them, a few steps ahead, his strong arms propelling him forward. It pained her to watch his shoulder blades so prominent even in his heavy overcoat. He had grown a lot in the last few months and the movements of his feet seemed more controlled and more definite. The boy needed Mr. Wade: she was convinced about that and would do everything in her power to hold him.

Each Friday as he left Rock Lodge Mary handed him a basket of wheaten bread covered with a napkin; the bread was still warm when he got back to his bungalow and fixed up his fires and attended to his thesis and correspondence scripts. On Saturdays, once a fortnight, he drove to the city and brought Mrs. Quinn and one of her sons with him. Her husband was not being allowed home for the spring. He had lost weight recently and as he pulled back the sleeves of his pyjamas to show Andrew how pale and thin his arms were he said that if he could get home and get the sea air his appetite would surely come back.

"I miss the sea and the sound of it," he fretted, "and I miss the fields and the lambs in them at this time of the year and the skylarks going crazy over their songs."

"The doctors know best, Pat," his wife said. "They'll not keep you a day longer than is necessary. What do you think, Mister Wade?"

"I would abide by the doctors. They know their job much better than we do."

"It's hard, but I'll try and content myself for another while," he said and shook Andrew's hand. "You're a good friend to us and we'll always be grateful to you. You've made my life a bit easier, I needn't tell you. I'll say a prayer or two for you for I have nothing else to give you."

"I'll need them all, Mister Quinn. Content yourself now and in a short while you'll get your marching orders."

They arrived back while it was still bright. The people working in the fields saw them and spoke in whispers among themselves about this unusual friendship. They saw no good in it and were certain that no good would come out of it. And when Miss Reid collected her rent from them on her periodic visits she, too, was surprised that a complete stranger should be so friendly with a woman whom he hardly knew and whose sick husband lingered so long in the hospital. Indeed, someone should warn him in good time not to meddle too much in other people's affairs.

19

A WEEK later Andrew received a short letter from his father. They were coming to see him and, as on their previous visit, they would follow the same course and arrive on Saturday morning should the fine weather hold out till then.

The letter surprised and puzzled him, for his mother hadn't even hinted at a visit in any of her letters. Whether they were coming to persuade him to go home with them he just did not know. In any case they were bound to notice a change in him for the better, he thought, and would be less inclined to harangue him to return home. For another thing he was more relaxed and moved around with the easeful energy of one pleased with his way of life and his surroundings.

The windows of the bungalow he left open all day to the sea air, air that was tempered by a sun that grew in strength as it rose above the sea and spread its beams inland. At his breakfast he could see the knee-high mists dissolve and the laborers arrive in the fields while the grass was still wet and drops of moisture hung like glass beads on the hedges. Tractors opened drills, and men and women planted the seed potatoes on manure forked freshly into the furrows. The hedges were slashed to allow the fields their fill of sun and when the loppings were burned the smoke drifted through the windows of the bungalow, leaving a pleasant smell that lingered until Andrew returned in the afternoons from Rock Lodge.

On Saturday morning, the day of his parents' visit, he arose earlier than usual and had his breakfast finished and the fires reddened before the first tractor lumbered past on its way to the potato fields. The sun shone, but the air still held a touch of the night's frost, and his empty milk bottles that lay on the grass at the inside of the gate were misted over with dew.

At ten the car drew up and Andrew went out to welcome them and they stood on the road together looking at the calm open sea and the damp sand of the bay steaming in the sun.

"It looks less bleak than when we were here last," his mother said, standing close beside him.

"Yes," the father added grudgingly, "it doesn't look too bad."

Andrew held the little gate open for them, and his mother, seeing his shirt and two collars hanging in the shade at the side of the house, moved toward them. Andrew followed her. He sensed that she desired to speak to him alone but his father, determined to prevent it, stuck close to them.

The mother unpinned the shirt and collars from the line; they were slightly stiff from the night's frost and smelt clean and fresh as the surrounding air.

"I'll iron these for you while we're here," she said and stood for a moment looking through the hedge of the adjacent field at the workers crouched with their boxes of seed over the furrows. "There are more women out there than men," she said, noticing the red or yellow head scarves against the brown soil.

"I suppose they're cheaper," the father said.

She dropped a clothespin deliberately and as Andrew stooped to lift it she whispered quickly: "He has a nasty letter with him."

They moved into the house together. The fire was red and the sitting room warm. The father took out his pipe and as he filled it he asked Andrew with experienced casualness how he managed to put in each day. Andrew told him of his full-time teaching in Rock Lodge, of his correspondence scripts, and of his fortnightly visits to the libraries in the city.

"And is that all?"

"I think it's more than enough for any man. It takes me all my time to cope with it—that's if I'm to get my night's sleep or cook a decent meal for myself."

"But surely you talk to someone besides your friends in Rock Lodge."

"I'm friendly with all the people I meet if that's what you mean. I chat with anyone I see along the roads."

"Do you invite anyone into the house?"

"No one calls except the postman, the baker, the milkman, the butcher, and the grocer. Miss Reid, my landlady, used to call for her rent, but now I post it by agreement to her agent."

"And what's she like?"

"Oh, I never liked her, but the dislike is mutual, I think."

"And does no one else call?"

"No one."

"Now, Andrew, I want the truth," his father said quietly. He was determined not to lose his temper, but at any moment he felt he would lose it.

"I don't know what you're getting at, Father. Honestly, I don't."

"Tell him, Frank, what you know and have done with it," the mother said impatiently.

"Hold your tongue for a minute, Mary. It will all come out in good time."

"I'll not hold my tongue. A judge in the witness box couldn't be any colder than you are. You'd think you were conducting a state inquiry. Show him what you have in your pocket and stop playing this cat-and-mouse business. Don't you see the boy is puzzled."

Andrew looked from one to the other. "What is it all about? Tell me, please."

"Would it surprise you if I told you you were being talked about?" the father said and eyed him sharply.

"Do you mean talked about at home?"

"No, here, in this very place."

"It would surprise me very much," Andrew said, his mind leaping to Rock Lodge, to Anne in Edinburgh, and to Doonan whom he hadn't seen for over two months.

"Read that—and then answer truthfully," his father said, handing him a letter. "It's the Burns business all over again, only worse."

Andrew studied the letter. It accused him of carrying on scandalously with a woman whose husband was in hospital. The handwriting was lopsided and some of the words, he thought, deliberately misspelled.

"I know now what that's about," he said, and tossing the letter on the table he told them about Mrs. Quinn and the lifts he gave her to the city.

"And why didn't you tell us about her from the very first? Did you conceal it because you knew there was something unwholesome in it?"

"It should have occurred to me but it didn't. It was told to Father Lavelle but he made light of it. And to stop any further talk he advised me to take one of her children with us when going to the hospital."

"It's hard for me to swallow that," and he pointed out that if this scandalous rumor was bandied about the countryside the neighbors might throw him into the tide some night. If that happened his name would surely reach the headlines again. The matter was serious; it concerned them all, and the least he could do would be to spare them another scene like the last.

"But there's not a grain of truth in that document, Father. It's all lies I tell you."

"There's no smoke without fire, Andrew."

"Listen, Frank, I'd believe Andrew before I'd believe the contents of that wretched letter. No reasonable man would be swayed by it. There's no name to it and you should have burnt it when I told you."

"Before I leave this day I'll get to the bottom of it. I didn't make the journey for a change of scenery I may tell you. Where could I find this Mrs. Quinn?"

"She's out working in the potato field if you want to see her. . . . No, it would be much better not to alarm her. She'd avoid taking a lift in the car, a lift that means much to her at the moment."

"But you can't continue with this misplaced and misjudged charity. Your whole life could be ruined by it. You'll come home with us and give us peace in our old age."

"I can't do that. I have promised to see the lad through his exams and I must and will do that. And when I'm finished with him I'll go somewhere else—to England or Scotland but not home. I'll not forget how the boys shouted after me the last time I was at home."

"Can you do nothing with him, Mary? You leave everything to me."

"We can no longer treat him like a child. He must order his life in his own way. He has been through all this before and he's not likely to go through it again."

"Well, Andrew, I'm going to call to see this priest you think so much of. You wouldn't want me to do that?"

"Do, if it would ease your mind."

"It doesn't seem to upset you."

"A little, perhaps. But there are other things of greater importance that I must and will do." He looked at the clock on the mantelpiece. "If you hurry now you'll catch Father Lavelle before he takes Confessions at twelve."

"I'm not likely to run in to Doonan, am I?"

"No, Father. There's a wide stretch of water between him and you."

He directed them where to go and leaned on the little gate and waved them off. The tide was full out and gulls rested on the dry sand in the sun. High above the house larks reeled and unreeled their long lines of song and he shaded his eyes and picked out three of them, tiny as asterisks against the blue sky.

As he turned into the house a man looked over the hedge of the nearby field and asked him for a drink of water. Andrew brought it out to him in a jug, a cup balanced on the mouth of it, and handed it through the hedge. Presently the man was joined by three more of the workers, Mrs. Quinn among them. She wore Wellingtons and a man's burberry knotted with a belt that had lost its buckle. Her face was smeared with clay and the red headscarf tied under her chin was stained with oil. As she waited her turn for the cup she plucked grass from the butt of the hedge and wiped the clay from her hands. She smiled at Andrew, aware of him only as a friend, a friend of her husband's, a man who was always kind enough to offer her a lift when he was going to the city.

She held the cup by the handle, threw the dregs into the hedge, and tightened her headscarf as she went back to her work. He knew by her look, by her gestures, that she was completely unaware of any scurrilous talk that was being stirred up about them.

"That was a fine car I seen outside your door a short while ago," the laborer commented, handing the jug through the hedge.

"That was my father's," Andrew explained with a directness that freed the conversation from overdrawn subtlety. "And my mother's with him," he added for good measure.

"They've brought the fine weather with them."

"They're going away again in the afternoon."

"He has to get back to work like the rest of us?"

"No, he has retired. He was in the bank all his days."

"A good clean job. God grant him health to enjoy his rest. Thanks for the water. I must get back now and do another spell of work," and he walked off, pleased that his curiosity about the car was satisfied and that he had some information to dispense to the other workers in the field.

Within an hour his parents returned. They had seen Father Lavelle and he had made light of their anxieties. They were to pay no heed to the anonymous letter. The place was small, and because a few outrageous things happened in it the frivolous was magnified and made heinous. He assured them not to worry: the people of his parish were slow to take to strangers, but in a short while that would change, would ebb away, and they would accept their son as one of themselves. In the meantime he would do all in his power to put an end to these ill-natured rumors.

Andrew told them that he himself could stop it within a week if he wished. He could travel to the city without Mrs. Quinn. But then if he did that, he pointed out, what could he say to her husband when he'd call to see him or what would her husband say if he didn't call at all. Whatever way he turned there would be difficulties and it would be better not to change. His mother agreed with him: she could see no harm in offering a decent person a lift and if Mrs. Quinn wished to travel with him he shouldn't go out of his way to avoid her—if there's talk Mrs. Quinn would surely hear of it and take steps to stop it.

The following morning at Sunday Mass Father Lavelle delivered a sermon that, Andrew thought, may have been the outcome of his parents' visit.

The priest usually spoke a few words on the epistle or gospel that was read in the Mass and always concluded by urging the people to be people of prayer and to help one another in the spirit of St. Paul's great epistle on Charity.

But this morning he stood in the middle of the altar and with his hands folded under his purple chasuble he nodded his head and began in a conversational tone:

Do you know what I am going to tell you, my dear people,

Christianity hasn't failed for the simple reason it has never been tried. A famous man said that—and I am wondering is there any truth in it. We, in this little place, can't speak for the world at large, but at least we can speak for one another and ask ourselves have we really tried to live the Faith that we believe in.

On most Sundays throughout the year we have read in this church many of St. Paul's epistles. These epistles or letters he had sent to various peoples in the early days of Christianity to tell them how to lead a Christian life. Occasionally we, ourselves, grasp a few of St. Paul's thoughts, intend to make our own of them and to bring them to bear on our daily lives. We try, perhaps, for a while and then give up the struggle. But these truths of his—if they are to take root in us—must be renewed daily. We must dwell on them and put them into practice.

To transform and renew the face of the earth we must first of all transform ourselves and give Christianity a trial. The worth of a country lies in the goodness of each of its members, and our worth as a people will be judged by the things each of us considers worthy. If we admire worthless things and worthless living we shall never be a Christian people. Let each begin with himself, with his own heart and mind—it's there that the first cleanings and sweepings have to be done.

In one of St. Paul's epistles he tells us not to lie to one another. Do we carry that out or do we only tell the truth when it would be unprofitable to tell a lie? In another letter he advises us not to let the sun go down upon our anger. What does that mean? It means much. Anger, if prolonged, can lead to the breakup of a home. Brother quarrels with brother, husband with wife, son against father—all common complaints. But St. Paul in his wisdom advises us not to stoke up the anger, not to let a single day pass until the quarrel is settled. Do we heed that—as good Christians should—or do we let sinful pride possess us and force us to shout out:

"Never, never, will I forgive him or speak to him!" And with prolonged anger goes hand-in-hand hardness of heart, a living hell: a hell that can spread through a village, a countryside, and even into a seminary. Hardness of heart! If that possesses us we are living in sin and grave sin at that. Where true and loving kindness exists God is. But where we have hatred and spite and malice and anger you have evil in its full flowering. But where we have joy, peace, laughter, and tranquility, we have the flowering of real Christianity. Kindness nourishes this kind of life, but hate withers it.

And St. Paul also tells us that Christians shouldn't steal. Many of us wouldn't steal a penny from a neighbor or circumvent him in business, and if a child stole a shilling, say, his parents would be greatly upset; yet the same parents may do a far worse stealth and, alas, remain unruffled. I mean they could steal from a man his greatest possession: his character. At school we learned in our catechism: "Never to injure our neighbor by word or deed, in his person, property or character; to wish well to him, to pray for him, and always to assist him as far as we are able in his spiritual and corporal necessities." Perhaps we find that hard to do. But if we intend to lead a Christian life—and this life is of our own choosing—we must try. And if we do we are beginning to give Christianity a trial.

All these things are summed up in the Book of Proverbs: There we are told the things that God hates: lies, pride, anger, swearing that lies are the truth, running off to a neighbor with the latest scandal and helping to spread it—and lastly what God detests above all is the person who sows strife wherever he goes. Avoid these troublemakers, my dear friends, they are usually people who talk too much, but never in the spirit of charity; there are also people who sin by silence or with a few sharp words keep strife on a keen edge. Both these kind of people judge rashly and read dark motives into every kind action that they see.

Think over these things as you kneel down to examine your conscience, and don't make the mistake that, because you have avoided the lying, the anger, the hatred, and the rest that all is well. Faith without good works is dead. We must do good while we can. Good works are the life of our Faith: the seed, the growth, the harvest.

When we were at school we rhymed off the opposites to the deadly sins: humility, liberality, chastity, meekness, temperance, brotherly love, and diligence. Perhaps, if we concentrated on these we would be better Christians. Let these be our standards and try to live up to them.

And lastly I must say a word about sickness and suffering. How does that fit into the Christian life, you may ask. It doesn't fit in at all—it is at the very center of it. He who founded our Faith got it hard in this life, and we, if we are to be His disciples, must be prepared to follow the same rough road. No one escapes from suffering. It comes to us all in some shape or form. Sometimes it's not seen: it's borne within the mind, and suffering of that kind is often the hardest to bear.

Without suffering and the releasing into the world of all the kindness and sympathy that go with it and out to it our lives would be hard and bitter and cruel. But suffering must be and should be shared with those who wish to share it with us. We can be even sinful in our suffering filled with false pride and false courage.

Our Savior on the road to Calvary did not chase away Simon who put a helping hand to the cross, nor did He refuse the towel Veronica offered to wipe the blood from His face. In these humble acceptances he defeated pride and the proud man: the man who desires to go it alone and who refuses all help. We should accept help when it is offered to us and be grateful for it. We should not always be a giver only—that can be admirable but it's not enough. We must also be good and grateful receivers. Both together can defeat pride and envy and selfishness.

We have two weeks left now of Lent and we should all try, even for a fortnight, to think over these things and to put them into practice. In that way we can begin to give Christianity a trial.

He turned to the altar, lifted a small notebook, and read out the announcements for the week. Then he asked for prayers for the recently deceased of the parish and for those whose anniversaries occurred about this time.

On coming out from the church the men lit up their cigarettes and congregated in groups on the road, discussing fairs and the prices of cattle and sheep. Philip moved past them and sat in the car, and while waiting for his mother he reflected on the sermon, striving to unify the pieces into a few brief statements that would satisfy his grandmother. He knew she would have already studied the day's epistle and gospel and would have composed a sermon of her own. But her sermon today, he thought, would be completely different from the priest's and as she would be unable to anticipate what he was going to tell her he smiled with secret satisfaction.

20

Shortly before Anne arrived home for Easter Mrs. Newman got the boatbuilder to launch *Razorbill* and moor it in its usual place in the harbor. It was to be a surprise for Philip, and at breakfast next morning—his usual time for entreating her to have the boat launched—she said she was sure she saw *Razorbill* at anchor when she was getting up.

"But James wouldn't launch it without your permission!"

"He may have got that already," she smiled across the table.

"I'll go and have a peep at it through the telescope."

"Finish your breakfast first. You have plenty of time to look at it later. And remember: no sailing in it until Anne arrives."

"But, surely, I may row Mister Wade out just to see it. There'd be no harm in that."

"I suppose not. And when Anne does come home I hope you won't be selfish and quarrelsome with her in front of strangers."

"Mister Wade is no longer a stranger, if that's what's in your mind. His pockets are bulging with her letters and he's always happy the day he gets a new one. I have shown him her letters to me but never has he shown me any of his. I suppose they're full of love-sonnets and all that kind of palaver."

"No matter what they're full of—and I'm sure they contain nothing foolish—they're his own private property and you shouldn't pry into them."

"I never asked to see them."

"You're curious about them and I'd rather you weren't. A homesick person is glad of letters from any source. Indeed, it's very kind of Mister Wade to give her so much of his time."

"If I were away I bet he wouldn't write to me."

"I don't answer hypothetical questions."

Breakfast finished, he made his way to the telescope and focused it on *Razorbill* and on a gull standing on its flat feet on the deck. Other boats were moored close to it, all facing the incoming tide, their masts tilting with the movement of the water. She would do well in the races this year, he thought, and last year would have won most of her races if she hadn't been holed. That was Anne's fault: she wouldn't give way going round a mark and the other boat rammed us. It wouldn't have happened if he had been at the tiller.

He pointed the telescope at the trees and watched young crows perched on the branches and others quarreling in the overcrowded nests. From early morning until sunset they kept up a continual cawing and the ground underneath was spattered with droppings that looked from a distance like a shower of cherry blossoms. He smiled at his incongruous comparison and on hearing the landing-clock strike nine he moved down to the storeroom, pulled the sailbag from a corner, and spread the sails on the lawn before Andrew arrived for the day's work.

In the afternoon when lessons were finished they rowed round to the harbor and on reaching *Razorbill* Andrew held the dinghy steady while Philip rested his arms on the stern of the yacht, levered his body forward, and wriggled over the deck.

"That's how it's done," he said triumphantly as Andrew watched him with a sense of physical pain.

Philip maneuvered his feet into two sockets specially made for him and gazed with pride at the fresh varnish on the deck and mast.

"This is where the skipper sits and issues his orders," he said.

"She looks a bit small when she's in the water," Andrew commented.

"She couldn't sink, if that's what you're thinking. Listen," he knocked with his knuckles on the stern seats and drumbeats echoed back. "There are airtight containers all round her and under the deck at the bow. She's as light as a cork but as safe as a boathouse!"

"And have you to race against that big one over there?" Andrew asked, pointing to one that was longer and thinner than *Razorbill*.

Philip laughed: "That one is stiff as a church," he said, repeating one of the boatbuilder's phrases. "She'll be last, and we'll be first if I'm at the tiller."

On Easter Monday eight boats, *Razorbill* among them, got ready in the harbor for the first race. Three of a crew were in each boat: men wore colored woolen caps and jerseys and two or three boys wore red rubber lifejackets. Philip threw his under the seat when Anne pleaded with him to wear it. He had worn it on the day it was bought but, conscious of criticism, he had sensed that every laugh he had heard was directed at him.

Anne, in slacks, hopped about the deck and helped Andrew fit the runners of the sail into the brass track on the mast. Jibs flapped in the wind and cords, hard as rods, thrashed against the masts.

Philip sat at the stern, gripping the tiller, determined to steer for the whole race. After breakfast he and Anne had tossed a coin for who would steer and he had won. He now gave orders that annoyed her. She knew what was to be done without being told and she yearned to tell him that he was just showing off in front of Andrew.

A red pennant, showing the direction of the wind, streamed out from the tip of the mast. The sail was hoisted and as it flapped vigorously Anne released the mooring rope and Philip hauled at the main sheet. The sail filled evenly in the breeze; the boat slewed past the buoy and headed toward the motor cruiser that marked the starting point.

Eight boats turned around like racehorses and moved forward in a ragged line, the air filled with the purling of water from their bows. A shot rang out and the yachts moved quickly past the starting point. *Razorbill* was third. They sped past the coal-quay where a knot of people watched them. Then the lough opened out in front of them, the wind gusty, and far ahead the first mark with a red flag fluttering from it. Philip steered to the leeward side.

Anne watched the heavy squalls puckering and darkening the water far out from the port side.

"Loosen the sheet, Philip. Another squall's coming," she shouted. But Philip ignored the warning and held grimly to the cord that screeched around the pulley block. The sail took the full force of the squall, the boat crunched the water white, and when the squall eased he noticed he had left one boat behind and was now in second place.

A rough patch in the water where tides collided lay ahead, and as Philip tried to pilot the boat round the edge of the patch an unseen current forced them into it. The boat bucked and swayed like a rocking horse, the main sail staggered, the jib swung loose, and two boats passed them in the windward side.

"May I steer for a while, Philip?" Anne said.

He didn't answer her but swung the tiller full to starboard till the sail once more snatched its fill of wind.

"Go on, Philip. Let Anne take over for a while," Andrew coaxed.

"I won the toss and I'm not going to throw away my luck."

Andrew and Anne sat together amidships, and as Anne stooped to tie her shoe Philip could see a bare part of her back and three vertebrae like knuckles.

"Anne, I can see your bare skin," he said.

She pulled down her jersey, turned, and looked at him scornfully. Then she pointed out to Andrew the landmarks on the shore: their boathouse, gray and peaked like the gable of an old chapel, and beyond it through the thin greenery of the trees the upstairs windows of Rock Lodge. She waved her hand a few times in case her mother should be following the race through the telescope.

A few black figures stood on top of the quay wall. The houses above it looked like toys and the red doors of the stores with their white letters were too far away to read.

As they approached the first mark they were again lying third, but Philip skimmed dangerously close to the mark and edged into second place.

"Well done, Philip," Anne said. Resting her arm on Andrew's shoulder she called out the names of the little islands scattered around them. They were islands with no history, she told him, and no character except the neutral character of rocks and rough ground and ruins of a Herdsman's hut. There to the left was Jackdaw Island with no trees, Sheep Island with no sheep, Calf Island, and Bull Island—all commonplace names that had made their way, when she did not know, into the ordnance survey maps. Castle Island, with its trees and shrubbery and old ruins was the only one worth visiting and someday before she returned to Scotland they would all sail up to it and have a picnic.

She took out a cigarette and Andrew lit a match and cradled his hands around it until the cigarette was well lighted. She lit one for him and as she handed it to him a squall struck the sail; she fell against Andrew and he put his arm around her waist and held her close to him.

"Be careful, Philip, or you'll capsize us," she said, and shook her fist at him.

"Keep your eye on the jib and the boom. I'm going to tack now."

He veered with surprising suddenness and they had just

time to lower their heads as the boom swung to leeward. Philip stumbled and fell as he changed his position, but by holding onto the tiller he was able to pull himself up before Andrew had laid a hand on him.

As they edged out from the shelter of two islands they felt the full force of the wind. Some of the other boats had hove to, and men were standing up to reef the sails.

"Straighten up, Philip," Anne said. "The other boats are reefing."

"There's nothing to fear," he shouted. "We're in the lead and we'll stay there!"

The boat heeled over, a wave brushed the tip of the boom, and the boat sprung suddenly upright, tumbling a bailing bucket and an oar.

Anne threw away her cigarette. She was frightened and she called out to him to allow her to steer and that it didn't matter if they were beaten.

"It's too rough here to change places," he shouted, and looked back at the other boats straggling after him with shortened sails.

Razorbill crashed into the waves and drew farther ahead. Water streaked blue under the boom and curled white over the foredeck. The sail once more tipped the water; Anne closed her eyes, held on to a stay-rope to keep from falling and with the other hand gripped Andrew's arm. Locked together they edged along the seat and pressed all their weight to windward. Both were afraid and did not speak.

Philip's eyes were on them. Their closeness and silence disturbed him. His brown eyes were hard-set as pebbles and his fair hair was darkened by splashes of water. He cried out to Anne to separate and give the boat more balance. They didn't answer him; they were too frightened to move.

With each squall that hurled itself at the boat the tiller throbbed and knocked under his hand, but he squeezed it with all his strength, forcing it to oppose every movement that would throw the wind from the sail. Jealousy had flung aside his fear. Nothing would defeat him and when the shot rang out over the bow to proclaim his victory they would be proud of him.

In a few minutes they would be round the last mark and then they would have the long easy reach for home. He looked at the wet patch on the sail spreading above the reef cords that trembled like fish in a net; it was a cream color, he thought, or, maybe, the color of fear or the color of seasickness. He smiled at his thought but his smile had no sweetness, and as *Razorbill* cleared the last island and sat erect with the wind behind her Philip knew that nothing could overhaul her.

"We're out of danger now," Anne said to Andrew as they moved into the center of the seat.

"We were never in danger," Philip corrected. "I was in control all the time."

"You mean your foolishness was in control. You should have reefed like the other boats. It was a race without pleasure and we're both soaked to the skin."

Andrew rolled back his sleeve; his arm was swollen where she had gripped it. "The marks of victory," he laughed as she took his arm and massaged it gently with her fingers.

"Would you like to steer now, Anne?" Philip asked.

"No thanks. It was your race and you can take the full pleasure of winning."

His hand rested lightly on the tiller. Behind them the boat gouged out a trough of calm water and the helm scored a wrinkled line upon it like a relief map.

They passed the coal-quay, then the harbor with its cluster of houses and people standing at the doors. They reached the motor cruiser, and as a shot rang out to signal victory Andrew patted Philip on the shoulder and said: "Well done! You deserve it."

Philip didn't raise his eyes. He felt miserable, isolated,

and unclean. He had no pleasure in his victory and no joy. It was better to say nothing and in that way conceal the sadness that bruised his heart.

Their car was at the quay where they had parked it. He climbed into the back seat and without a word allowed Andrew to sit in front with Anne. He withdrew into himself. His right hand was numb from the throbbing of the tiller and his eyes moist from the sting of the salt water.

His mother, who had seen the finish through the telescope, was at the door to greet them. "Congratulations!" she exclaimed. "You won at your ease. But, oh, there were times when I was frightened for your safety and I had to come away."

"It was Philip who steered all the time, Mother."

"You mustn't take risks, Philip; it's not worth it. There was one time when I could see the whole underside of the boat but no sail."

He frowned and chewed his underlip. He was annoyed with himself and annoyed, too, with their criticisms. There were boats around that could have saved us, he said to himself, but in his heart of hearts he knew he hadn't thought of that at the time.

"Get changed at once, Anne, you're soaking," she said, feeling the shoulders of Anne's jersey. "And, Philip, tell your grandmother about the race. She's expecting you."

He moved away from them and went up to the large drawing room where his grandmother was seated on an ottoman at the window.

"*Razorbill* won," he said sulkily.

"So your mother told me. Had you a good race?"

"No, it was horrible. Anne and Mister Wade are both soaked."

"Salt water will do them no harm. And who was the captain for the day?"

"I was."

"You're like your father, a worthy captain."

"I'm not worthy. I won out of spite."

"What nonsense to say, child. You won because you're a good seaman like your father. The sea's in your blood. What spite could you have against anyone except the wicked Jews who have tortured me for years?"

He swayed politely away from her and gazed at the bright wires of the canary cage and at the tiny pulse in the bird's throat as it sipped water and held its beak erect. In a few minutes it would be singing and save him from talk.

His mother came in and rested her hand on his damp head.

"He told you the great news."

"He did, but you told me more yourself and you weren't in the race at all."

"I don't want to talk about it. I want to be left alone. I'll go and change my clothes."

After a few minutes his mother followed him along the corridor to his room.

"What's wrong, Philip?" she said, sitting on the low bed beside him. "You seem unhappy at having won. That's not like you."

How could he tell her that there was something ugly in him, something that he despised but couldn't understand?

"There's something on your mind. Tell me what it is."

"I tried to capsize the boat!"

"No, no, you didn't. Don't say a thing like that!"

"I did! I did!"

"What nonsense! Why should you want to do anything so devilish!"

"When I saw Anne and . . . and . . . Andrew happy together and their backs to me something urged me to pitch them into the water."

She was eager for him to tell her all that burdened his mind, and twisting her hands on her lap she listened with impatient silence as he described the race and how the other boats had reefed and they had not, and how he had held the main sheet tight to every squall.

"You only imagined that you tried to capsize it. Don't think about it again. Put it from your mind," she said with hurried fright.

"Oh, Mother, I did," and he shook his head and put a hand to his brow. "But I didn't tell them. Like you, they wouldn't believe me if I did."

She put her arm round him and drew him close.

"I don't accuse you, though you may accuse yourself. You'll go to confession soon and you'll confess all that's troubling your mind and your sorrow for those things."

"Yes, Mother," he said penitently. "Something forces me to destroy what I don't want destroyed. Something rises up in me to wrench Anne away from him."

"You'll have to forget about yourself and do all in your power—as restitution, say—to help them to know one another. You have your own life to live and Anne has hers. She has had one great disappointment in life and you wouldn't want her to have another."

"No, Mother, I wouldn't."

"If this friendship were broken all our selfish desires would turn sour." She thought for a moment of her own foolish infatuation for the young man, an infatuation that Anne had noticed and exposed. Since then she had fought against it and conquered it. "Each Christmas," she went on, "You build a little boat with your own hands. You would like to keep it but you sacrifice it and that gives you happiness. You've made this friendship with Andrew—we'll not call him Mister Wade any more—and by sacrificing it for Anne's sake it will bring you joy. You'll try to do that."

"I'll try."

"On Sunday if the day is fine Anne wants to go to Castle Island. We'll all go with her. It will be her day. You'll let her take command. Will you do that?"

"I will," he said, and as he smiled she stood up and fetched a towel for him from the rail at the washbasin in the room.

21

THE AFTERNOON was fine for Castle Island and all four went in the car to the village and rowed out to the yacht, and in a short time were out on the blue water where the air was cold in spite of the sun and where other boats, white and definite as swans, sailed apart, each selfishly intent on its own journey, on its own remote island.

The wind was light, and the dinghy in tow slapped the water from under her heels and rose light and crisp on the tips of the waves, and Philip, wedged in its bow, held the rope taut and called out orders that reached the bigger boat unheeded. Off Castle Island the sail was lowered and Philip pulled the towrope and drew alongside *Razorbill* as the anchor was lowered. They piled the rugs and picnic baskets into the dinghy and rowed until the keel shooshed on the sand. Andrew took off his shoes, tied the rope to a flat stone, and carried first Philip, then his mother, and then Anne across the thinning water to the shore.

They spread the rugs in the shelter of a grassy bank where the sun lay warm and from where they could see the long finger of blue water and the sloping fields and the white villages in the scoops of the hills. They had the island to themselves. Mrs. Newman sat down on a rug, took up her knitting, and suggested to Anne that she take Andrew round to the old castle.

"I could go with them, Mother," Philip said, slinging the strap of his camera around his shoulder.

"The ground's too rough and too steep. We'll get the primus going."

"If it's ruins they came to see we could have anchored at the other side."

"We have more shelter here," she said, looking around at two thorn trees whose roots were exposed like antlers.

"We'll not be long, Philip," Anne said cheerily.

"All right, go on without me, but when you hear three blasts on the whistle you'll know the kettle's boiled."

Anne and Andrew hopped up the bank between the storm-bent trees and strolled over the golf-green grass that sloped up to the bleached walls of the castle.

Below on the shore the tide was ebbing fast; the dinghy now lay on its side and its rope hung limp from the bow and turned gray as it dried in the sun. Philip wandered down to the boat and baled out the water in the stern. Looking up he could see the whole island and Anne, in her yellow jersey and navy slacks, holding Andrew's hand as they climbed the hill. They reached the top, sat down, and waved to him. He waved back, and in a few minutes they had risen to their feet and had disappeared over the brow. They would approach the castle from the other side, and if he would wait they might climb to the square tower by the stone steps and stand in triumph above him.

He glanced at his mother, her knitting needles flashing, a magazine open on her lap. She raised her head to look at a speedboat that tore past, obscured in its own spray. Waves spread out from it and scrambled over the shore and filled up the keel-rut made by the dinghy. The speedboat turned back and as Philip tried to snap it on his camera it sped quickly out of sight.

Behind him he heard a faint call from Anne and then a deeper bass-call from Andrew and he knew they were at the top of the castle. He shaded his eyes and looked seaward. But when his mother called him sharply he turned his head and saw she was standing up and pointing to the castle. He was forced to look and see the two figures moving at the top of the square tower, their handkerchiefs fluttering. They halloed to him and their joyous voices rang unimpeded over the island and out to sea. He put the whistle to his mouth and blew till there was a sting in his ears and his head was light. And when the sounds had ceased and the air was still he moved along the sand that was drying under his feet and knotted with whorls that reminded him of chewed string.

Up in the castle they would now be scraping their initials on the gray stone: *A N* and *A J W*. But they wouldn't think of him—he was sure of that. He moved farther along the beach and picked up two corks that were stuck to dry seaweed. The corks were large and circular with rope-holes in them. He held them in his hand and searched around till he found two feathers. He stuck one in each cork and placed the corks in a pool of water and watched them swivel round in the light wind. He tried to make them race, but they spun round and clung together, and in disgust he lifted them and flung them into the sea.

He glanced sideways at the castle but there was no sign of life about it. He put the whistle to his mouth to call them, changed his mind, and continued his journey along the lanes of sand between the rocks. Clumps of damp seaweed hissed like crabs in the sun and limpet shells crunched under his feet. The shore grew rough and he stumbled and fell on a mass of salt-stiffened straw. As he pulled himself up he saw, entangled in the straw, a thin piece of wood spattered with shining pellets. He tore the straw from it, turned the wood over and examined it. It was charred at one side. It was a piece of his little Christmas boat. He brushed it on his sleeve, rubbed the pellets till they shone like nailheads, and put it carefully in his breast pocket. His eye ranged over the lough as he pondered on the long journey the stick had made; he pictured it struggling through the grille of the pond, stumbling over the wet-polished stones of the stream till it reached the sea and was carried on the swift current and washed ashore on Castle Island. How long it would have taken to drift up he did not know.

He would keep it; he would store it away in a box, and years later he would draw it forth and he would talk about it—to whom, he wondered. He paused and flexed his arms; they were strong and his hands were large and strong too. He was growing tall and the sleeves of his coat were now too short for him. His mother was to buy him a new suit before his exams. Andrew said he'd pass in all three subjects. Yes, with God's help he could do that. He'd not be like this bit of riddled stick that has drifted aimlessly on the tide. "Andrew has steered me and I'll obey," he said aloud to himself and turned back along the shore.

His eyes shone happily and his ungainly shadow swayed on the sand behind him. He saw his mother resting on the rugs, her hands under her head. He approached cautiously; her eyes were closed and there was a sweet smile about her lips. What she was thinking about he did not know, but whatever it was it was something pleasant, something to do, perhaps, with the future, with his success and with Anne's.

High above her the skylarks stitched the air with twirling threads of song. The light wind lifted a leaf of the magazine on her lap and the leaf wavered for a moment before settling back again.

Quietly Philip got ready his camera, but the stones under his feet knocked together and his mother stirred, opened her eyes, and stared around.

"Oh, it's you, Philip." She glanced at her watch and then at the camera. "You didn't snap me, I hope?"

"I wanted to, but you wakened."

"No sign of the others? Come and we'll get the things ready."

He joined her, lit the primus, and when the kettle was near the boil he blew his whistle three times and listened to the sound breaking against the hills and the trees on the mainland.

For half an hour they waited and then Philip spied them

coming round by the shore, Andrew carrying driftwood under his arm and Anne holding his hand.

"Good old Philip, you've the kettle boiling," Anne said, slumping down on the rugs and breathing heavily.

The boiling water poured out from the spout over the primus; Philip attempted to grip the handle but it burnt him and as Andrew pulled out his handkerchief to put around the handle the handkerchief fell on the rug beside Mrs. Newman. She saw stains of lipstick on it and averted her eyes quickly. Andrew's face reddened, but as Mrs. Newman pointed to a small black speck far out from the boat and asked innocently if it were a cormorant he felt she hadn't seen the telltale spots on his handkerchief.

"That's not a cormorant," Philip answered. "It's the corks of a lobster creel."

"My sight is not as good as it used to be. I thought it was a bird."

Anne handed around tea and sandwiches. Clouds, high up, were reflected in the blue lough, and along the margins of its shores sunlight flashed on the windshields of cars that moved on the unseen roads. The tide was far out now and would soon be on the turn.

Philip brushed the crumbs from his lap, and getting his camera ready he ordered them to tuck in their feet while he took a few photographs.

"And now I want one of Anne and Andrew together," he said and directed them to stand between the two thorn trees from where he would have the castle in the background. "Stand closer, if you please. That's better. Now, Andrew, if you'd put your arm round the young lady you'd be closer still."

As they laughed, real unforced laughter, the camera clicked.

"I have one more left. If you sat down on the rocks this time we could get *Razorbill* and the lough for background."

"No, Philip, no," Anne said. "Let me take one of you and Andrew for a change," and as she ran down to him he unslung the camera from his shoulder, handed it to her, and stood with Andrew near the dinghy. Andrew put his arm on Philip's shoulder and stood with him like father and son. The camera clicked. Anne raised her head, brushed back the hair that had fallen over her brow, and said: "That will be a good one, I think. You'll develop them soon, Philip, and send them out to me."

"Not till after my exams. I'm going to work like billy-o!"

"You'll crack up if you study all the time."

"I don't mean to. We'll go fishing in the long evenings."

"I wish I could be with you. Tomorrow morning, before either of you are up, I'll be on my way to catch the plane for Edinburgh."

"And in two months you'll be back again with your degree," Philip said. "And you'll not be going away any more."

"I don't know about that," she said and stooped to shake a pebble out of her sandal.

Her mother clapped her hands and called to them. "Time we were leaving," and they walked across the sand to her and helped to shake and fold the rugs.

And in the long evenings after Anne had gone back to Edinburgh Andrew and Philip put new lines and flies on the small rods and rowed out in the dinghy before sunset and fished along the tree-lined shore where the water lay dark and oily as the back of a fish. Other small boats would be out with them and as they passed and repassed each other the rhythmic rock of the oars would travel far and wide over the still waters. And then suddenly the fish would strike and the surface of the water would be torn as the caught fish flapped and panicked like disturbed sea birds. And long after they were caught they would thump the bottom boards of the boat and flitter the bilge water that scarcely covered them.

Philip would take his turn at the oars and Andrew would

sit in the stern, take out his pipe, and as he lighted it his cupped hand would glow pink and the match that he flicked overboard would hiss, once only, in the water.

Then as darkness rose thick among the trees and the lights from Rock Lodge struggled through the leaves they would roll up their lines and row, slowly and reluctantly, for the slipway below their own boathouse, and after they had maneuvered the boat on the trolley and wheeled it above tide mark Andrew would gut and clean the fish by the water's edge, and Philip, waving his arms to and fro to warm them, would stare at the opposite shore where the headlights of a car stretching behind the hedges would look like a train moving into the night with all its carriages alight.

And after stowing the rods in a corner of the boathouse they would walk, silent and at peace, round the dark pond where they would hear the *churruck-churruck* call of the water-hen or the scuffle of a hedgehog or a fox in the thick shrubbery.

They would enter the house at the back where Mary waited for them, her table neatly laid. And while they were away in the bathroom to wash the blood from their hands and change their clothes she would roll some fish in flour and butter and get ready the pan. She loved this time of the night when she had the two of them to herself, the dogs lying on the raffia mat at the range and the old clock on the wall loudly ticking out the seconds.

But as the date of the exams drew near the dinghy was wheeled into the boathouse and Philip was sent early to bed where he continued to work in secret, pausing to hear the woodpigeons *coo-cooing* from the cool depths of the trees or a thrush singing its final song in the seclusion of the walled garden.

And then on the first morning of the exams the yardman polished the car, and before setting out for the city with Andrew, Philip had to go to his grandmother's room to receive her blessing and down to Mary in the kitchen to ask her to say a special prayer while the exams were in progress.

Andrew left him at the examination hall and spent the time during the morning and afternoon sessions in the university library, leafing through old books and pamphlets that would give him a page or two for his thesis on the Charter Schools.

Returning each evening he would let Philip relate how he had answered each question, and though Andrew realized he had omitted some important points he withheld all comments that might dishearten him. And when Philip would press him as to how he had thought he had done Andrew would answer: "I feel you've done well and I think you'll pass."

And one afternoon, the day the results were expected, they were out riding on the pony and horse when Mrs. Newman rang up the secretary's office at the university; there was a long pause and she could hear the soft sound of paper being turned, and then a polite clearing of a throat and a man's voice speaking clearly: "Newman, Philip: Passed in English, Mathematics, and History."

"Thank you," Mrs. Newman answered with studied control.

She put down the receiver, rushed into the drawing room, and looked across the paddock to the outbuildings. There was no sign of them and she raced along the corridor to her mother's room. "Mother, I've great news for you. Philip has passed! He has passed in all three subjects."

"Splendid, Helena. Great news, indeed, for our poor boy!" and as a tear glistened in the old withered eyes Helena flew downstairs and into Mary's kitchen where the old servant was seated upon the table grating carrots on a newspaper.

"Mary, he has done it! Philip has passed!"

"I knew he would, Ma'am. Day and night I have prayed for that. They'll be a happy pair this day."

"They're out riding. They don't know yet." And opening the back door she ran up the steps and down by the pond and sat on the green seat and waited for them. A breeze rippled the face of the pond and she thought of Richard and how happy he would be if he had been here to share her joy.

She heard the drumming of hoofs and she stood up and saw the pony in front trotting under the trees and the dappled sunlight flowing from its flanks. She waved her arm, and when pony and horse reached the path she ran forward shouting out the good news. Philip blew his whistle that was round his neck and sent the pony forward at a gallop. Its tail stretched out as it raced across the paddock, and Andrew followed, holding in the horse while the sheep bunched together and ran off in fright.

Mrs. Newman returned to the house, phoned Father Lavelle, and put a call through to Anne in Edinburgh.

22

AFTER SHE had rung up Father Lavelle he drove out in the early evening to see Andrew and found him reading in a deck chair at the back of the house. Andrew jumped to his feet, fetched another deck chair from the house and placed it in the sun. The untrodden grass in front of them was soft and cool and darned with spiders' webs. Heat lay thick around the walls of the house, and cattle rested on their own shadows in the flat fields.

"Congratulations on Philip's great success. You must feel proud."

"I feel pleased, Father. The lad worked hard and if some of my correspondence pupils do well my year here will not have been wasted."

"And are you going to pack up now and leave us?"

"I've still some work to complete."

"And then?"

"I don't know really. I'm unsettled as to the future."

"Would you care to settle down here?"

"That I don't know. I like the countryside and the sea and I like the Newmans, all of them."

"If you were married it would soon settle you. Anne Newman, for instance. You'd travel far before you'd meet her like."

"Indeed, that's true. And I must say we get on well together and write friendly letters to one another—still she'd probably aim at something higher."

The priest advised him to think better of himself: with Philip he had made a success out of an apparent stubborn failure and he had helped to bring joy to a house that had known much sorrow. Did he not realize what his coming had meant to them? He spoke of Philip's father and how he had been lost at sea and told of Anne's broken engagement, an engagement that was all the better for being broken.

Andrew listened in silence, recalling to himself the snowy day that Philip, in a fit of temper, had revealed Anne's secret to him.

The priest lit a cigarette, leaned back on the deck chair and rested his eyes on a far hill where a rope of fire-smoke curved over the top.

"I have been wondering for a long while if you'd be interested in what I'm going to put to you. Mister O'Brien, the principal in the village school, is retiring soon and I'd be glad if you took over. It isn't a big school but it's a pleasant one. There are two young lady assistants in it; unfortunately they don't stay long; they get married or they hop off to a school in the city at the first opportunity. Two elderly ladies would be a better proposition, but one can't very well advertise in the press for two elderly, unattractive women." He laughed and tapped the ash of his cigarette onto the grass. "Maybe you'll think it over like a good man. You could call in at the school and have a look at it first. I could tell Mister O'Brien to expect you. Of course you needn't commit yourself in any way."

"It's very kind of you to offer it to me."

"I'd be happier if you accepted it."

"There wouldn't be any teacher to oppose me if I did?"

"There's always local competition in these matters, but there's not much in this case," and he inquired if he had ever met Phil Meighan, a teacher who lived in the village and taught in Ballynasaggart.

Andrew hadn't met him, although Mrs. Newman had mentioned his name and that of Mr. O'Brien when he had accepted the job of teaching Philip.

"But you needn't worry about him," the priest added.

"He'll growl and scowl a few times at me but that will be the height of his protest."

"I wouldn't wish to accept it if I thought you'd have trouble over it."

"I have to do my duty to the children even if it brings me some discomfort. Trouble is part of life and we have to learn to live with it and to manage it. You've had your own share already."

"I'm afraid, Father, I've tried to flee from it."

"You've struggled with it fairly well. One grows in wisdom by learning how to endure. Endurance ripens us all." The priest got to his feet and dusted the ash from his jacket. "You'll think over what I've said. And you'll have a look in at the school?"

"I'll call in tomorrow."

They strode down the triangular patch of grass to its very tip and peeped through the hedge at the potato field where the rising stalks gave out a warm sweet smell in the evening sun.

"You could make a fine sheltered garden if you decided to stay. And Miss Reid would raise no objections once she was sure of a permanent tenant."

The following morning Andrew called at the school and Mr. O'Brien showed him around and introduced him to the lady assistants. The school was bright: bright with the colored frocks of the little girls and bright with children's paintings that covered the walls; and framed in each window, like a picture, was the lough outside, a yacht upon it, and the blue-slated houses shaking their reflections in the water's edge. The sound of trees filtered through the open windows into the rooms and mingled with the mischievous whisperings of the children—the Quinn children among them—as they eyed Andrew and Mr. O'Brien moving up the aisle that separated the boys' desks from the girls'.

Whether he had come as a visitor or as the prospective principal Mr. O'Brien did not know and did not ask; and aware that Phil Meighan would rail for months against such an appointment, he showed Andrew around with slow caution and without friendly enthusiasm. If Father Lavelle had decided to give the school to this stranger Mr. O'Brien was sure that the decision was no hasty one. It was a good school, he refrained from telling Andrew, a school rated highly by the inspectors, a school he would like to see pass into capable hands. The easygoing Phil would let it rot under him—still, he wasn't going to make an enemy of him by condemning him or a friend of him by recommending him.

"Thanks for showing me round," Andrew said on leaving.

"Visitors are always welcome," Mr. O'Brien said, and closing the door looked through the window at the tall figure striding happily across the clean playground to the gate.

Andrew accepted the job, and within a week word flew through the village that the man in Miss Reid's bungalow was to be the new principal. And when Phil Meighan heard it he called on Father Lavelle one wet evening just as the priest had finished tea. The priest saw him passing the window, and on hearing the doorbell he told the housekeeper to bring the visitor into the parlor and he'd attend to him presently.

Phil sat in an armchair indicated by the housekeeper and balanced his damp hat on his knees. He was stout and middle-aged, red-faced, and his hair was rough and two-toned like a shaving brush. He bit his fingernails and watched the drizzling rain darken the limestone of the church and hang like cobwebs on the leafy trees behind it.

The priest knocked the door and entered. Phil stood up, and in a voice husky from an immoderate shouting at his pupils, asked why he was not being appointed to the school.

"Is an explanation necessary, Phil?" the priest said quietly. "I made the appointment in what I believe to be the best interests of the children. There's nothing more I can add to that."

"But there's something I can add and multiply to it."

"If you'd speak in a lower key you might make your points more reasonable."

"I'll speak in the voice God gave me."

"He gives us many gifts, but we sometimes warp or mutilate them."

"I'm not here to listen to a sermon or to polite insults. I'm here to state my just claims to this job in my native village," and raising one hand with the fingers outspread, as if teaching a first lesson in notation, he enumerated each item that enforced his rightful claims to the job. The sole opposition to him, he explained, was a complete and total stranger, a stranger who had come from God knows where and had ferreted his way into the monied class in the parish. What brought the stranger here, everybody would like to know. He was supposed to have a university degree in his favor. Well and good. But sure every teacher in the land was capable of getting a degree if he wished to keep his nose to the books for a few extra years. Indeed, he could teach the heads off most of them if it came to the bit. And this stranger was so much of a stranger in the village that few had ever exchanged a word with him.

The priest listened in silence, impatient with chagrin at the splutterings of this foolish man.

"And where do you come in in all this?" he asked quietly.

"Where do I come in!" Phil shouted, and his hat fell off his knee and he lifted it and squashed it under his thigh. "Where do I come in! I'm just warming up to that."

For one thing, he told the priest, he was in the village long before the priest had come to it. He was baptized in that church out there. His father and mother had always paid their stipends to the Church, their weekly rent to Miss Reid, and their yearly rates to the County Council. He had been trained as a teacher in the capital city of Ireland. He had been teaching for nearly thirty years in Ballynasaggart and had to cycle to his school in hail, rain, or snow. The children he had to teach, he would assert categorically, were of poor intellectual quality. The inspectors' reports on his work, he would admit, weren't of Grade-A standard, but for that matter they weren't good in any department of the school, and for the simple reason the yearly crop of children was always a feeble crop.

"The children in Ballynasaggart are of the same root, stalk, and branch as the children here," the priest said. "When a teacher complains of the general dullness of his pupils he is really condemning himself. Bright and alert children are the products of bright and conscientious teachers."

"I don't agree. The children in Ballynasaggart are all problem children."

In the hands of problem teachers, thought the priest.

"It's high time I was getting something out of it."

High time he was putting something into it, echoed in the priest's mind.

Philip paused, swept out a handkerchief, and blew his nose loudly.

The priest lowered his eyes. How could he tell him that he wasn't suitable and that Father Naylor in Ballynasaggart would be glad to get rid of him from his school? A teacher's ability or lack of it runs ahead of him, the priest reflected; and it was well known that Phil went on the spree when he got his check at the first of the month and it was also known that, in strict accordance with the dictates of a medical dictionary, he took two days per month in bed to ease his blood pressure and at the first newspaper scare of an imminent epidemic of influenza he didn't venture out of the house for a week.

"Well, Father, have you finally settled the appointment?"

"I'm afraid my mind's made up and I see no reason to

alter it. You know, Phil, Father Naylor asked you some time ago to resign. Isn't that so?"

"It is, but the Teachers' Union briefed me to stand up for my rights and not resign."

"But surely a union of professional men would investigate why a teacher is asked to resign. And if they learned he was slothful—and I am not saying you are that—unpunctual, irregular in attendance, uninterested in his work, they would reprimand him or request him to leave the union. Children have also their rights—rights are only relative—and in this matter theirs are prior to yours. They have the right to be taught by those who are paid to teach. A teachers' union is surely interested in the best education, and if it wishes to retain respect it must remain unimpeachably respectable."

"After long years of constant struggle our Union has grown powerful," Phil said defiantly.

"Power grows corrupt if it nourishes corruption."

"I'll hand this case over to them, I can tell you."

"I wouldn't if I were you," the priest said with slow gravity.

"You're afraid of exposure in the public press."

"No, Phil. It's neither honest nor honorable to ask your union to defend what's indefensible. In all these disputes your union can voice its claims in the press but we, as managers of schools, can't very well reveal ours, no matter how legitimate."

"Your predecessor promised he'd give me the job should Mister O'Brien leave at any time."

"It was a slight indiscretion on his part to make decisions for me."

"Well, he did."

"I don't doubt your word. I only say he shouldn't have done it."

Phil lifted the hat from under his thigh, reshaped it, and stood up. "You're making little of me in front of my own people. But you haven't heard the last word about it, I may tell you."

He hurried from the room, made his way down the hill in the rain, entered a pub, and took a drink to settle his nerves. A few men leaning against the counter and standing in pools of water from their dripping clothes were also drinking. Phil stood them drinks apiece and recounted what he had said to the priest.

They all agreed with him that it was a crying-out shame that one of their very own wasn't considered good enough to teach the children how to read and write or add and subtract the few shillings they would ever handle in this life. Phil would be a damned fool if he wouldn't raise Cain. They would all be behind him to a man. All they had to do was to keep their children at home—and if you've no children you've no school.

Within a few days it was whispered around the village that Mr. Wade was not a suitable person to let loose among innocent school children. Surely Father Lavelle, they circulated, was being deceived. He was getting too old and was too easily swayed. Did no one tell him how this stranger was driving round the countryside with a woman whose husband was lying sick in hospital? They wouldn't stand for such conduct and if Father Lavelle wouldn't listen to them they would refuse to send their children to the school.

The Newmans were unaware of the threatened strike until Mary heard of it one day in the grocer's shop in the village. Miss Reid was there and a few other women with her, all in no hurry to be served. They mentioned Mrs. Quinn's name to Mary and linked it unseemly to Mr. Wade's and in a rage Mary rounded on them and flashed out: "It's all lies, lies, rotten lies I tell you! You should be ashamed of yourselves! That young man, if you'd like to know, is to be engaged to Miss Newman when she comes back from Edinburgh. You're all out to ruin their happiness! But you'll not do it! You'll not, I tell you!" and she darted out of the shop and left them.

On reaching Rock Lodge, before taking time to take off her hat and coat, she knocked at Mrs. Newman's sitting room and entered. Mrs. Newman was knitting and her mother sat in an armchair with a hot-water bottle on her knee. The canary was singing loudly and as Mary launched forth with news of the threatened strike in the school Mrs. Newman lifted the cage, put it in her bedroom, and closed the door.

"But they couldn't do the like of that, Mary. It's unheard of."

"It's that Phil Meighan, I'd say, who's the backbone and middle of it. And he'll hide in his bed till it's all over."

"I know who's directing these perfidious operations," the old lady said, raising a hand from the hot-water bottle. "It's the Jews! The Jews! Mister Wade was in danger from the day he decided to take me under his protection."

"It's no Jews! It's that Phil Meighan. And who, in Heaven's name, would want him in charge of the school! I'd school him if I'd the chance."

"It's the Jews! They have an insidious way of creating trouble. They come and go in their motorcars and distribute their pamphlets. They come in disguise, in their yachting caps and navy-blue jackets."

"There isn't a Jew in the whole village and there isn't a good Christian in it at the moment either, if I'm any judge. The place is littered with rotten talk, it's hissing and boiling over with scandalous gossip about Mister Wade and Mrs. Quinn. If her husband hears of it it'll kill him stone-dead and if Mister Wade hears it he'll quit the country and we'll all lose him." With her underlip drooped she stared penitently at Mrs. Newman. "Forgive me, Mistress, for what I'm going to tell you. In my anger I told them lies. To stop their wagging tongues about Mrs. Quinn I told them . . . I said—" Her voice broke and she began to cry.

"There would be no harm, Mary, in whatever you told them, I'm sure of that," Mrs. Newman said kindly.

Mary wiped her eyes with her handkerchief. "You'll forgive me. I told them they'd be hearing soon about Miss Anne's engagement to Mister Wade."

"That will come despite the age-old persecutors. We will defeat them in that," said the old lady.

"Anne will make her own choice in matters of that kind," Mrs. Newman said without reproach and lifted her knitting. "You may go now, Mary, and don't distress yourself any more. You spoke out of time and out of the goodness of your heart. Don't say a word of what you've heard to Mister Wade. He may not hear of it. The people who call with him—the postman, the grocer, and the rest—are unlikely to tell him anything that would upset him."

But Andrew did hear of it the following afternoon. He was driving home from Rock Lodge and overtook the Quinn children, who had their satchels over their heads to shield them from the rain that was falling heavily on roads, on hedges, and on the hay lying soaked in the fields. He opened the car door and they bundled into the back seat and giggled as the car hissed and sloshed through the puddles.

"You tell him, go on. . . . No, I'll not. . . . You tell him," they kept saying to one another.

"What have you to tell me?" Andrew said over his shoulder.

They began whispering among themselves and he coaxed them to tell him their secret.

"The boys and girls are not coming to school on Monday," the eldest said.

"Is that so?" Andrew said, slowing the car to a halt. "And why would they do that?"

They giggled and pushed one another to tell. "Their mothers said you were a bad man and they don't want you.

And they said you were in love with my mother." They giggled and hid their faces behind their wet sleeves.

"Don't repeat that nonsense to your mother or she'll beat the life out of you," Andrew warned and set off again, striving to keep his mind on the steering.

All that evening he was unsettled and time and again he stood at the door in his raincoat hoping to see someone he could chat with and overhear, perhaps, what was astir in the village. But no one passed on the road and no one was about in the rain-drenched fields.

He made a meal for himself and while sitting down to it he heard a tractor rumbling up from the shore, but when he rushed for his coat and had gone out on the road the tractor was moving away from him, the blades of the shovels shining on top of the soaked sand. Two youths upright on the load and empty sacks over their heads waved to him cheerily and one shouted: "The rain will keep her at home." Andrew winced, wondering whether they meant Miss Reid or Mrs. Quinn. No, he mustn't read irony into the simplest of salutations, he advised himself. They had never shown him any unfriendliness, and he recalled the day he had helped them to load the tractor with gravel after Miss Reid had warned him to help her to prosecute them.

After tea he tried to loosen his mind amid his chapters on the remote Charter Schools, but couldn't concentrate. His thoughts leaped ahead to Monday morning, the day he was due to take command of the school. He saw the parents marching with placards printed with slogans: AWAY WITH THE SCANDALMONGER: WE DEMAND PROTECTION FOR THE INNOCENT. He saw the newsmen and photographers arrive in the village. . . .

He shook his head and dispelled the wild whorl of images. He walked to the window and stared out at the sea that was smooth and gray as steel under the fall of rain. He'd call on

Father Lavelle—that's what he'd do. If they didn't want him in the school he could go away. He cleared away the tea things from the table and backed the car out of the garage.

Father Lavelle received him warmly. He had hoped he wouldn't hear of the threatened strike, but when he saw Andrew's grief-ridden face he knew he had heard of it.

"Is it true," Andrew asked, "that the parents are up in revolt against me?"

"Parents don't always know what will benefit their children," the priest said, standing at the window and gazing down the steps that led to the school playground. "Taken individually they have sense, but when they gang together they have no sense." The rain had ceased; the playground was bare and a wire wastepaper basket containing crumpled paper and orange peel hung forlornly in one corner. "It's disturbing news, I know. But we mustn't get alarmed about it. Excitement doesn't last long in these parts."

"I could go away, Father, if it would get you out of a difficulty."

"You mean you'd leave me in the lurch. If you did that it would give some truth to their foolish rumors. You need fortitude. You mustn't waver. Promise me you won't."

"I'll try not to."

The priest pressed a hand firmly on his shoulder. "On Monday morning you'll take over. I can't do it for you. You'll not let me down."

"No, Father, I'll not let you down."

"Tomorrow's Sunday. I may call a meeting of the parents. I'll think over it. I haven't yet decided what I'll do."

"And do you want me to appear at the meeting?"

"I do not. I want you to appear on Monday morning at the school. Don't discuss it with anyone. Now sit down and take a glass of sherry. It'll cheer you up."

"I'd rather get back, if you don't mind."

"Back to brood. . . . Sit down and relax. The more

you think about it, the more it will grow, and the more you'll weaken. I wish you hadn't heard about it at all. Be manly; be strong. Pray for fortitude. Within a week, less than a week, we'll be out of the storm."

He filled a glass for him. "Here's to your success, to Philip's and to Anne's," he said, and as they sipped the sherry a coalboat hooted below at the quay and shortly afterward there rose the harsh rattle of an anchor chain.

That night, to keep his mind from wandering into the vexing problem of the school, he walked along the shore and watched the moon rise yellow above the rim of the sea and turn to silver as it strode up the sky. The night was still, the earth breathed out its wetness, and a ship's engine seemed to shake the ground as the ship, twinkling its lights, passed close to the headland.

After midnight he went to bed; fagged out he fell asleep. But at two he wakened, his heart thumping loudly and his courage gone. He could never go through with it, he said to himself. If he only had someone with him to talk to. It was easy for Father Lavelle to tell him to come in on Monday and take over. But why should he force himself into a school where he wasn't wanted? And if there happened to be a scene on Monday it would be in the newspapers and it would bring his father and mother hurrying across the country to see him. If he had any filial feeling left in him he should spare them that, spare them another Burns affair. It would be better for all if he stole away quietly. He could write Father Lavelle and tell him why he did it—to relieve the priest of all trouble.

He paused and let that solution simmer in his mind. It eased him to think that way, the way of comfort. His car was in the garage. He could pack up all his belongings quickly and move off without being seen by a living soul.

The moon shone in the window, and the curtain moving in the night air brushed against the sill. He was wide awake now and he pondered on some of the things that had happened during the year: the row he had with Miss Reid over the key, the Quinns and his visits to the hospital and to the city. And he thought of the kindness of the people in Rock Lodge and their concern about him when he was laid up with a sore throat. And he thought with pleasure of Philip's success and how Anne, perhaps, could remain at home for a year and help him with the rest of his exams.

And what about Father Lavelle and the promise you made to him? You told him you wouldn't let him down. He warned you not to brood upon it. And here you are doing the very thing he didn't want you to do.

He gave a long sigh, clenched his fist, and said aloud to himself: "I'll not go away! I'll stay! For the sake of those who believe in me I'll stay. I'll see this out to whatever end God has ordained for me. If I have to crawl in Monday I'll do it. I'll not let it defeat me. I'll not go under. I promised I wouldn't waver and I won't!"

He turned on his side and dozed over. The alarm clock wakened him for Sunday Mass. The sun shone brightly into the room and the gulls on the shore were noisy. He felt dazed and still fagged out. He wasn't fit to get up, and in the stuffy air of the Church he'd probably faint and cause a stir among the congregation. It would be better for him to lie on. There was no guilt in staying away when he was unwell. He must be prudent and not injure his health.

He gathered the blankets round his shoulders and decided not to go. He could hear the gulls washing themselves in the water and the swallows streeling past the sunny window. The day was already warm and in the afternoon the cars would be parked on the road and children bathing on the shallow shore.

He threw aside the blankets and stood up. He was unsteady on his feet and the air in the room seemed stale and nauseating. He put the kettle on the stove and got ready for Mass. He would take his breakfast on his return.

In the church he sat near the open door at the back. If he felt faint he could slip out without being seen or at the end of Mass he could get away quickly without having to speak to anyone.

After standing for the gospel the people sat down and waited for the usual sermon, and were surprised when Father Lavelle announced that on account of the lovely day he wouldn't keep them long. Although it was Sunday he would urge those who had hay lying in the fields to try and save it and give it a turn or two in the warm sun. They must be sensible in these matters. The usual Sunday observances could be shelved when work that was absolutely necessary cried out for immediate attention. He could assure them that if they spent the afternoon at the hay they could do so without embarrassment to their souls or to his.

"I must also take this opportunity," he continued in a carefree, happy voice, "to convey our thanks and good wishes to Mister O'Brien who, as you all know, has now retired from the principalship of the school. He has given us long and faithful service and we all hope he shall have a long and happy retirement. He was devoted to the children of the school and he did not spare himself at any time in advancing their educational welfare. Over the years he has established admirable traditions, traditions that have won the respect of all visiting inspectors. I can also assure you that the man I have appointed to succeed him will continue to build and foster, what I may call, the O'Brien traditions. I have given this new appointment deep consideration and I am convinced that I have made an excellent choice, one which will not disappoint you. Mister Wade is a highly qualified and upstanding young man, a man with much teaching experience, one who has had much success in the short time he has settled among us. For the sake of the children I am really glad to obtain his services and I hope he will remain with us for many a long year. The best way, my dear people, of demonstrating your appreciation of the appointment and the greatest compliment you can pay to Mister O'Brien's successor is to see that the children are sent out in good time tomorrow morning. Nothing pleases a new teacher so much as punctuality . . . we shall now say a prayer for all our deceased relatives and friends whose anniversaries occur about this time."

With subdued coughs and a shuffling of feet the congregation knelt and answered the prayers in a loud and unified tone.

Andrew, kneeling in the back seat, felt an ease and peace spread over the congregation. Sunlight at the windows increased in brightness and the cool air coming through the open door pressed forward with welcome freshness.

After the Communion bell had rung out, people moved in twos and threes from their seats to the aisle and walked slowly to the Communion rail. Andrew joined them. Mrs. Newman was ahead of him and Philip, awkwardly swaying from side to side, was in front of her.

On his return to his seat Andrew bowed his head and opened his heart in full and earnest prayer: *Christ be with me, within me; Christ behind me, before me; Christ beside me, to win me; Christ to comfort and restore me; Christ beneath me, above me; Christ in quiet and in danger; Christ in hearts of all that love me; Christ in mouth of friend and stranger.*

With slow concentration he said the *Anima Christi: Soul of Christ sanctify me; body of Christ save me. . . .* and with his eyes raised to the tall plaster crucifix that hung above the altar he repeated the *En Ego*. He prayed then for his parents, for the priest, for his friends and for the unfriendly, and after saying the Divine Praises he slipped unnoticed from the church as soon as the priest and acolytes had genuflected and were moving to the sacristy.

In the afternoon with the sun tracing heat scrolls above

the road and children bathing with delight in the shallow water below the bungalow Andrew took a towel and bathing togs and walked round the headland to a sandy inlet of deep water.

He took a leisurely swim and on coming out lay in the tall bent grass above the sand. He tried to read a few scripts he had with him, but his eyes closed with weariness, and covering his brow with the towel he fell asleep.

Bathers plunging into the inlet from the rocks wakened him and he sat up, filled his pipe, and read for a while. On returning home he saw farmers in their shirtsleeves tossing the hay in the fields, and from a long distance across the bay saw the sun shining on the tops of cars and an orange rubber dinghy floating near the shore.

As he pushed open his door an envelope shuffled under the threshold. On the back of it written in pencil he read: *Some photographs enclosed. Sorry we missed you. H. N.*

Somehow he had sensed all afternoon that Philip and his mother would have come looking for him, but for some reason unknown he had no desire to see anyone until Monday had passed.

That night, his body limp from the sun's heat and his mind stilled, he slept. In the morning he rose early and drove into the village before the shops had opened for the day.

Father Lavelle, seated on a chair at the edge of his bedroom window, looked down upon the sunny playground and the roof of the school. With a smile of pride he saw Andrew push back the green gates of the playground and a few minutes later heard the thud of windows being opened to the morning air. Smoke from the chimneys of the houses rose up straight and untroubled. Three trucks drew up alongside the collier at the coal-quay; the crane bucket dipped into the hold of the ship and as it swung up and out coal was tumbled into the trucks and the heavy sound of its fall reached the priest at the window.

Children in twos and threes moved into the playground; their satchels were unhitched and placed along one wall, and presently four little girls in colored frocks were skipping in a secluded corner while boys played with a rubber ball.

The ferryboat moved out from the slipway with a few passengers. An acetylene welder in the dark open doorway of a garage hissed and flashed green light. It was an ordinary day, a day the priest had seen often but had never felt.

The school bell was ringing. Father Lavelle stood up, and pulling aside the edge of the curtain he saw the children line up in rows and the lady assistants clap their hands for order. The rows marched into the school. There was a long silence. A crow swooped down, snatched up a broken cracker, and flew up to the trees.

The priest went downstairs, lifted the receiver and phoned Rock Lodge.

"All went off well. I'd say there was a full attendance."

"Oh, thank God!" Helena answered in a breath of deep relief.